the
Lives
Between
Us

a novel

LEAH OMAR

RONZEWOOD *books*

EDEN PRAIRIE, MN

The Lives Between Us

© 2023 Leah Omar

Published by:

Bronzewood Books

14920 Ironwood Ct.

Eden Prairie, MN 55346

Cover Design: Bronzewood Books

Interior Design: Bronzewood Books

Edited by: Enchanted Quill Press

Paperback ISBN-13: 978-1-949357-74-5

eBook ISBN-13: 978-1-949357-73-8

To Khalil and Scarlett
I love you more

Chapter One

Carrie

THE SUN BEATS DOWN ON my face, and I grab my chair and drag it through the grass until I'm in the shade of the closest tree. Malik does the same. The relentless heat draws out every ounce of energy left in me. I fan myself with my purse, which doesn't provide a ton of relief.

"Mmm, much better." I look across the lawn at everyone celebrating tomorrow's nuptials of my friends Jake and Camilla. They said they wanted the entire weekend to be a party, and so far, it has been. Last night, we had a bachelorette party for Camilla. Today is the cookout at their lake home, and tomorrow, the wedding that all of Wheaton will attend.

My eyes cut to Dax. He stands not far away, engrossed in a conversation with two of Camilla's cousins. His skin is bronzed from the summer sun, and I'm happy he's back in town after spending much of the summer in Atlanta with his daughter. He pulls at his white button-up shirt and then rolls the sleeves to his elbows, exposing his muscular forearms . He yanks on a tie until it hangs loosely on his neck. He looks as uncomfortable as I feel.

"The shade or the view?" Malik leans back in his chair and grins at me.

"Obviously, I meant the shade." I grab my purse and sling it toward Malik, and his smile widens.

"Oh, Dax is ever so dreamy." Malik shimmies his shoulders, taking pleasure in my embarrassment.

"I was only staring at him because I hadn't seen him since the spring. He looks—"

"Gorg? Hot? Spicy?" Malik throws words out into the air.

"Healthy. I was thinking healthy."

"Makes me think of our list." Malik turns to me and rests his face in his hands.

Malik and I became fast friends when he moved to Wheaton two years ago to work for Jake's construction business. They knew each other from their college football days, and Malik wasn't set on moving back to his hometown of Guthrie, Oklahoma, so he moved here. Last year, he took pity on me and asked me to move into the guestroom of his house rent-free, and he's the closest person in the world to me.

I could say so much about Malik, but mostly, he's my rock. A year and a half ago, I started losing weight suddenly. I didn't think much of it at the time, but then I would almost fall asleep at my bank job, and something didn't feel right. It was the chest pain that finally made me go to the doctor. I was sure I had mono, so when Dr. Abram recommended that I get a biopsy of a swollen lymph node, I was understandably nervous. A week later, I sat across the desk from an oncologist in Fargo, listening to her tell me that I had cancer called non-Hodgkin's lymphoma.

Then, Malik insisted I move into one of his spare bedrooms and be his roommate. I refused at first, but who was I kidding? I couldn't wait to move out of the one-bedroom apartment over the Main Street Café. I needed help, and my mom couldn't give it to me. It's amazing what a person will agree to when it's a matter of life and death.

Malik and I lay on my bed one night. Both of us had our hands folded behind our heads. The room was filled with nervousness because the next day, I would have scans to tell me if the treatment worked or if we needed to change course.

"If my treatment is successful, I'll do anything. I'll pray to all the gods. I'll be a better human. I'll live a fuller life," I said into the empty night. I wasn't ready to go out like this. Not at my age. I hadn't even lived yet. Instead, I used my shyness as an excuse to say no to almost everything that had ever been presented to me.

Malik propped himself up on his elbow and turned to me. "If you get good results tomorrow, and if, sorry, when, you go into remission, we need a plan to help you emerge out of your shell and be the beautiful woman you are."

"Anything," I answered. "I'll do anything."

Malik wiped a tear that fell from my eye. "You need to start living, Carrie."

He then shot up, tucked his legs beneath him, and clapped his hands. I knew the look well. When Malik had an idea, excitement penetrated his entire being. "Fuck it list!" He continued to clap his hands.

"Wha—"

But Malik had covered my mouth with his hand before I could finish the question. "Yes. A fuck it list. We both need one. I get to add things to yours, and you get to add things to mine."

"Slow down. I don't even know what a fuck it list is."

"It's a, fuck it, you're alive list. A why not list. What could you lose? Start trying shit list."

"Okay," I said, but honestly, I didn't need to think about it. If agreeing to this list somehow helped my survival rates, I'd do it. I'd do anything.

Over six months ago, my cancer went into remission, and Malik and I huddled around his fireplace and started our lists for ourselves and each other. Only Malik wrote mine in code. I don't even know what half the things mean. One of the lines said Dax, and the next line said threesome. When I slugged Malik, he assured me it wasn't what I thought it meant. But I still haven't learned the meaning.

Fast forward a few months; I'm feeling healthy, cancer is in my rearview mirror, and I regret giving Malik so much control over my life.

I avert my eyes from Dax and look at Malik. "What does the line called Dax even mean?"

"Girl." Malik flicks his wrist and dangles his long fingers. "I think you should get out of your head and jump his bones."

"Gawd, Malik." I cover my face to hide how red I feel it getting.

"It's a great day to be alive, Carrie." Malik looks up at the sun and smiles.

"Do I need to tell you about eighth grade again?"

Malik plops his feet down on the grass and whines. "If I have to hear that story one more time, I may have to kick you out of my house and find myself a new and less annoying roommate."

It's true. I've subjected Malik to high school stories about Dax a few too many times, and it usually involves me having a glass of wine when I tell him. I was infatuated with Dax when we were in school. Everyone was. His older brother, Jake, had already moved to California and was a star quarterback on Stanford's football team, and all eyes stayed on Dax. He was the point guard on

Wheaton's basketball team.

His sandy blond hair swept to the side, his blue eyes captivating, and his tall and muscular build years ahead of everyone else's in the high school. He had his choice of women, as everyone wanted a piece of Dax. He always dated the most obvious choices. The girls everyone wanted to date. Spoiler alert; I wasn't one of them.

But Malik is wrong. I didn't pine after him. That can only be done when you have a chance with someone. Dax barely knew I was alive. He did, however, become the man that I've forever put on a pedestal, thinking no one else would compare to the man that Dax must be.

Well, he knew I was alive, but barely. When I was an eighth-grader, he was a senior, and I got brought up to the varsity women's basketball team to be their starting point guard. I was tallish for a guard and, according to my coach, had the tenacity of a bull. I could shoot the three, handle the ball, and create opportunities for my teammates. Basketball always came easy to me, even when the rest of my life felt like a big jumbled-up mess.

That eighth-grade year, my team won the high school basketball state tournament. Although I was still a middle schooler, I was brought up to play on the varsity team. After the game in Minneapolis, it felt like the entire town of Wheaton waited for us as we made our way outside to the bus. We walked out of the auditorium, and people cheered, held up signs, and hugged us. As I was about to get on the bus, Dax stood there with his black letterman jacket and a smile that only solidified his coolness. With the palm of his hand, he reached forward and squeezed my shoulder. "Great game, kid."

I was so stunned that Dax spoke to me that, instead of responding, I stared at him, mouth wide open, until he laughed and walked away. It turns out eighteen-year-old high school seniors aren't interested in fourteen year olds who are tall, gangly, and still waiting for their boobs to come in. And that is the story I can't help but tell Malik every chance I get. Especially after some wine.

"Whatever," I finally respond. "That was more than ten years ago, anyway. Yes, I was one of many who thought Dax was the bee's knees, but now I've grown up." I sit taller in my chair to prove a point.

Malik turns to me and wipes at the side of my mouth. "Then, let's get rid of this drool, thirsty girl."

Because life is cruel, and a greater force is trying to punish me, Dax approaches us at the very moment Malik wipes my mouth.

"Am I interrupting something?" Dax asks, and I use my hand to shield myself from the sun as he stands over us.

Malik gets up and pulls Dax into a hug. "You're finally back, bro. How was Atlanta? We missed you around here, didn't we, Carrie?"

"Umm, welcome back." I'm sure my face turns a shade pinker.

"Thanks, man. Yeah, it's good to be back. But Atlanta was needed. It was great for Kylie and me to spend the summer with Zari's family."

Dax hasn't had it easy the past few years. His wife died of cancer a couple of years ago, and he's been raising Kylie alone ever since. If anyone understands the frailty of life, it's Dax. He turns away from Malik, and my heart feels like it will jump out of my chest as he focuses his attention on me. He's the sun in every space he occupies. I'm the grass that shrivels from too much sun exposure.

"You look so great, Carrie." His gaze lingers on my hair, which has grown considerably over the summer. "Your hair's grown so much. And it's auburn now."

"Yeah." I smooth out my hair, self-conscious that he's still staring at me. I always had mousy brown hair, but when it grew back after the chemo, it came back auburn and with a wave that never existed before. I'm still unsure if the gods are looking out for me or punishing me, but I may start keeping score.

"I haven't seen you in months." Dax's mouth falls open, and he studies me.

"Yeah, I visited my mom for a month in the spring, and I guess you had already left by the time I was back."

I decide to leave out the part of my mom living with her fourth husband in a trailer in Apache Junction, just off the westernmost peak of the Superstition Mountains in Arizona. My family felt like the town joke when I was growing up, and my mom still hasn't turned her life into something that would be considered reputable.

Dax smiles his toothy grin and then squeezes my shoulder. "Well, it's really great to see you, Carrie." My heart pretty much stops when he winks over his shoulder as he walks away. "Don't be a stranger."

"Phone," Malik says when it's only the two of us again. He takes it out of my hand and navigates to my notes, where my list lives. He points to Dax's name.

"He was checking you out, girl. Like, he was legit looking at you in that way. You know *that* way." Malik smiles and hands my phone back to me. I see that he's highlighted Dax's name on my list.

"Malik, no!" I shout and then cover my mouth with my hands. "You are asking me to commit social suicide. What am I supposed to say? Oh, Dax, do you want to make out with me a little bit? Go on a date? Hook up? Umm, no."

But he doesn't look like he'll cave at all. He leans back on his hands, smiling at the sky, as I sit and think of a way to get out of this.

"Does Dax just knowing you're alive feel like enough for you?"

"Well, no," I admit because it isn't enough. I can't be

the only person who has ever wanted to chase the sun.

"Girl. You're beautiful. You're young, and most importantly, you're alive. What do you have to lose by telling Dax Abram that you find him oh so dreamy?"

"I mean, you're not blind, Malik. He is pretty dreamy." I watch the backside of Dax entering Jake and Camilla's lake house.

Malik leans forward and takes my hand. "I'm not asking you to throw yourself at him, but go inside, run into him. Start a conversation. Maybe share that you used to crush on him hard."

Before I have time to overthink what following Dax into Jake and Camilla's home means, I gulp down my remaining prosecco and get up. Malik's laugh gets quieter as I reach the door. I don't know my plan, but gravity pulls me toward Dax. Or maybe it's his tan forearms that keep me moving in his direction.

The house is quiet as everyone melts outside in the heat. I peek into the bathroom closest to me, but it's empty. I then walk to the other side of the house, and the bathroom door is open, and Dax stands, looking at his reflection. He turns his head when he hears me approach.

"Sorry, Dax," I say. "I didn't realize someone was in here."

He looks at me, and I know I'm caught in a lie.

"No worries," he says, looking in the mirror. "I needed a minute from the heat. And the people."

Dax fusses over his tie, trying to pull it over his head, but I can see the knot is tightly wound.

"Can I?" I motion toward the tie, and he nods.

I press my back against the counter and use my nails to loosen Dax's tie. Once I do, he pulls it over his head and throws it on the floor.

"Stupid tie," he groans. Dax looks in the mirror

through me, and I realize that he's practically standing between my legs and that my hands are still on the collar of his shirt. He looks lost.

"Were you looking for someone?" His gaze once again comes into focus as our eyes meet.

"I wanted to get out of the heat too." I take a deep breath, remembering how it felt to think I may not survive cancer. How, at times, I'm still scared it will come back. All the things I've missed out on, said no to, or didn't take part in flash before my eyes. Cancer has stolen so much from me. I'm tired of walking on eggshells as if doing so will keep the cancer away.

A choice lies in front of me. I can do what I always do and wait for something to happen to make my life more exciting, which rarely actually happens. Or I can initiate some excitement.

"Don't laugh at me." I meet his icy blue eyes. "But I had the biggest crush on you when I was younger."

My tan skin gets a shade darker, and heat comes out of every pore. My voice and body language are not things I recognize in myself. I hope Dax doesn't hear the shakiness in my voice.

Dax grins, and his cheek dimple pops out, and I'm sure I will faint. "Yeah, I knew."

"What?" I push Dax on his shoulder but look down because I am nothing, if not an awkward seducer. What am I doing here? I don't know how I have the strength to continue speaking. "How'd you know?"

He laughs, and I suddenly have the desire to escape. "You were never subtle, Carrie."

"Huh," I add. "And here I thought I was super discreet."

"Not super discreet at all." Dax laughs. When I look at him, his eyes are kind. He's not judging me.

His smile is toothy and boyish, and unless I imagine things, he takes a step closer to me. I may have been the one that came into the bathroom, but Dax is doing the heavy lifting.

"Why do you smell so sweet?" Dax leans forward, and we're breathing the same air.

Panic sets in. I almost have no words until I do. "I just had a starburst." Okay, I do have words, even if they are the wrong ones.

"A starburst?" He wrinkles his forehead like it's the strangest thing he's ever heard.

"A red one. 'Cause they're the superior starburst color."

Dax chuckles. "You're odd."

He's not the first person to tell me that, but I cannot be hurt because then Dax brushes my hair off my shoulder. It's finally long enough that there is actual hair to brush. His foot extends, and with a flick of his ankle, the door slams shut. Now we're alone, isolated from the world on the other side of the bathroom door. All I did was tell Dax I had a crush on him when we were younger. He's doing the rest. Dax licks his lips, and my mind goes to Malik. He'd be so proud. I shake my head to get my best friend out of it.

There isn't much time to think about Malik because Dax drops my hair and lifts me onto the countertop. Then, it happens. Dax Abram leans forward and kisses me. I'm so stunned that I forget to close my eyes. His lips are sweet with a hint of salt, and I slide my hands in his hair, which I've always wanted to do. Full waves of blond tresses between my fingers. His lips explore my mouth, and our tongues touch, causing my entire body to feel like it's melting inside, and then he moves his mouth to my neck.

"Red starbursts are now my favorite too." His hands

move from my hips and settle right below my bra line.

Where I'm all awkward, Dax is the experienced seducer. I've spent many years admiring him from afar and wondered what it would feel like if this moment ever came. That's what's hard about building someone up in our minds so much. The reality never lives up to the dream of it all. Until now. My skin burns where his lips touch my neck.

Dax's kisses are sweet and innocent, and maybe it should feel weird kissing a boy I've known forever in his brother's bathroom, but instead, everything feels good and natural. Like the two of us were meant to be here in this moment.

He pulls the wide strap of my dress off my shoulder and kisses the place that was just covered by the fabric. The strap comes down a little further, and then Dax's eyes widen, and he takes a step back, and my body feels empty.

Dax's entire face changes. His ice-blue eyes turn grey, and his dimple disappears. Dax puts my dress strap back in place.

"What is it?" I go to kiss him, but he backs up even further.

He closes his eyes and shakes his head. "We can't."

"Why?" I try to mask my disappointment and rejection. I feel alive, in ways I never have before. Screw the fuck it list. I liked being kissed by Dax.

"We're in a bathroom," Dax says, looking everywhere but at me. "I respect you."

I jump off the counter and look at my flushed self in the mirror. The feeling of rejection bursts through me. "You've slept with half the town," I say as I turn to him. "But kissing me in a bathroom feels wrong?"

Dax's mouth hangs open, his eyes doused with disappointment, and he reaches for the door. "Wow,

Carrie. I didn't have you pegged as a mean girl." He walks out, and the door slams behind him, leaving me alone to recover.

I catch my breath in front of the mirror. I adjust the strap of my dress—the place where Dax sweetly kissed me mere moments ago. My port scar peers out from underneath it, and I run my hand across the uneven skin.

The scar is one of my many badges of honor, but I wear clothes that purposely hide it, which is why I love a dress with wider straps. Then, it hits me. Dax was into me until he became disgusted by my scar.

Chapter Two

Dax

"DADDY, WHAT IF I FALL?" Kylie's brown eyes look up at me as she speaks.

I bend over and swoop her up. Her arms wrap around my neck, and she takes my breath away. Her hair is piled on top of her head in tight curls. Kylie's eyelashes go on forever, and I press my lips to her forehead. Damn, she looks like her mom.

"I won't let you fall," I say. "I'll walk alongside you the entire way and make sure you stay upright."

Kylie smiles and seems pleased with my response. "You promise?"

I put her down, and she smooths out her white flower girl dress. When she looks up at me, I am breathless again. My sister, Jenna, let Kylie wear lip gloss, and her lips shimmer with pink.

"You look just like your mommy," I say, unable to hide what I've been thinking from the moment Kylie put on the dress and got done up by my mom and sister.

Kylie lets a giggle out, and her anxious expression changes. "I bet mommy wouldn't be nervous. Nothing scared her."

Zari had a confidence I'd never seen in anyone. I don't know if she was born with it or learned it growing up, but she was the most self-assured person I'd ever met. I was intimated when I first met her at a collegiate athlete banquet we attended during my first year of university.

I glance at my watch. We still have a few minutes until Jake and Camilla's wedding starts. I get down on one knee to look Kylie directly in the eyes.

"Did I ever tell you about the day mommy and I got married?"

"Tell me, Daddy!" Kylie shrieks, putting her hands on my shoulder.

"Well, Mommy didn't want us to see each other until she walked down the aisle. But as I was getting ready, there was a knock at the door, and I opened it, and it was your mommy. And let me tell you, she was nervous."

"Mommy was?" Kylie asks, leaning into me even further.

"Yep." I poke Kylie's nose. "Mommy. And I had to help calm her down. She was scared she'd fall, or say the wrong thing, or have broccoli stuck in her teeth."

Kylie's hands fly up to her mouth, and she giggles. "Broccoli in her teeth. That's funny, Daddy."

"Even brave people get scared, Kylie. But I promise I'm not going to let you fall today."

Kylie seems satisfied with that answer, so I stand back up and grab her basket full of petals from the counter, and we walk outside to join the bridal party in the tent. It's almost go time.

Rows of chairs line the yard, and when the music starts, all eyes look to the back of the aisle. Jake and Camilla wanted only family to stand up for them, so Camilla's brother, Robby, and my younger sister, Jenna, walk down the aisle first. The guests smile at them as they saunter to the front of the aisle toward the lake, where white flowers decorate a canopy. Robby moves to the bride's side, as he's Camilla's witness, and Jenna moves to the groom's side.

Next, Kylie and I are up, and when I look down at her blowing out a nervous breath, just like her mom used to, the grief sneaks up on me, and my eyes pool. If I've learned anything in the last two years since Zari's death, it's that grief's a bitch, and shows up when I least expect it. And then, when I think I'm on the other side of it, it smacks me upside the head.

I wipe both eyes with the back of my hand, look down at the most beautiful girl, Kylie, and squeeze her hand. We walk down the aisle, and she throws aromatic flowers on the ground—clumps here and there. No one would know she was nervous as she works the room with her smile. Once we make it down the aisle, I place her in the front row with my parents, and I stand next to Jenna on the groom's side, where Jake already stands.

My eyes scan the crowd, and familiar faces stare back at me. Some I'm happy to lock eyes with, and others I wish I could unsee. Like the blond woman from the Pool Hall, who I hooked up with earlier in the summer, and then never called back. Or the hairdresser I made out with at a party once, months after she and Jake were sort of an item. My stomach twists and turns, looking at too many regrets, all here at once.

But then, my biggest regret comes into focus as my eyes lock with Carrie's, who turns away before I have a chance to. My biggest misstep to date, and I've had a few. I've known her my entire life. All of it. She's always been the awkward, quiet girl. I can't say who she was at all, except she's probably the best female hoopster I've ever seen play in person.

She got teased a lot in school. That much I remember.

Her mom was a hippie type, and for six months out of the year, they lived at the county park on the lake in their RV. During the day, Carrie's mom would drive the RV to town, give massages and sell hemp and essential oils. During the colder months, they moved to town and lived in one of the apartments over the Main Street Café.

Carrie always wore clothes five times her size. Big, baggy shirts hung halfway to her knees, with jeans always a few inches too short for her tall frame. No one really even knew who Carrie was until she put girls' basketball and Wheaton on the map.

Fast forward to yesterday, and the urge not to feel pain outweighed every logical bone in my body. Carrie wore a dress and one in her size. For the first time, her figure showed, and it looked nice. When she walked into the bathroom, she looked thirsty—for me. And I liked kissing her. The way her body felt and mouth tasted— like sweet candy—and how she ran her fingers through my hair. I was so turned on until—

When Camilla appears, I'm taken out of my thoughts as she walks down the aisle, accompanied by her dad and mom. Her delicate, white, silk gown hugs her, and everyone laughs when Kylie starts clapping. Zari is the only bride I've ever watched walk down the aisle. At weddings I've attended, I always watch the groom. Jake wipes away a tear and can't quit smiling. Damn. I remember being that in love. I want to be happy, but I also want to warn Jake that it won't last. It never lasts.

After the ceremony, everyone munches on appetizers, and I catch up with family I haven't seen in years. I take Kylie around to meet people, and when it gets darker, the band starts up. Jake and Camilla have their first dance as a married couple, and when they're done, I pull Kylie onto the dance floor. My desire to make Kylie's life wonderful outweighs my urge to sit in the corner and be a cynic. She is my hope and joy and the sole reason I put one foot in front of the other everyday.

"You're the most beautiful person here today," I whisper into her ear as her little arms wrap around my neck and her legs squeeze around my waist.

"Oh, Daddy. Camilla is. She looked like a princess." Kylie's eyes search for Camilla, and she relaxes into me when she finds her.

"You look like a princess," I tell her, and Kylie places her finger over my lips to silence me.

After my dance with Kylie, I grab a drink from the bar. I lean against the counter, cold beer in hand, and look at everyone who came here to celebrate love. My eyes find Carrie, who appears to be in a lively conversation with Malik. She once again wears clothes her size, and I barely recognize her.

Her shoulder-length hair hangs in loose waves, and her black dress stops above her knees. I don't know why I didn't notice before yesterday, but Carrie has a nice rack. Not too big, not too small, and my body warms when I remember my greedy hands all over her body yesterday. Carrie's high heels put her at almost six feet, and her dress cinches at her small waist. Blood reaches everywhere in my body, and I want to make things right with her.

When the song slows again, I slam the rest of my beer, put my glass down, and work my way toward her. Malik sees me first and gives me a fist bump, and Carrie looks in my direction.

"I was hoping you'd dance with me?" I ask and hold my hand out to her.

Carrie shakes her head. "I'm good."

Malik nudges her on the shoulder, and she looks at him, annoyed.

"One dance?" I ask again.

Carrie rolls her eyes but puts her hand in mine, and I lead her to the dance floor. I bring her to the middle, surrounded by other people dancing, so we can properly disappear. I've had enough wandering eyes on me tonight, and I don't need to be the talk of the town at morning coffee tomorrow. She stands there and looks at me, and I guide her free hand to my shoulder.

Her green eyes stare up at me, and I can tell she'd rather be anywhere else. I nearly chuckle at her inability to hide it.

"I'm sorry about yesterday," I say, and Carrie freezes. I grip her hand tighter to keep it in mine.

"Not necessary," she says, eyes going into a long blink before they pop open again.

"I know, but I want to apologize."

Carrie shrugs her shoulders. "I read the situation wrong."

"When you told me about the crush you used to have on me—"

I want to say so much more. That when she told me, it felt good. Even though I don't know Carrie well, my familiarity with her is comforting. Especially in my grief. But she doesn't give me time to say any of this.

"As an eighth-grader," Carrie interrupts.

"Right," I say. "The mood shifted. I shouldn't have let it happen."

The song stops, and Carrie drops her hand from my shoulder and crosses them over her chest. "Again, I read the situation wrong."

I laugh, which is the wrong thing to do. But it's my go-to when I'm nervous. I can almost see the steam coming out of her ears and the color on her face. She's furious with me. When I realize I'm still holding her waist, I let go.

"I mean, we were in a bathroom. Did you really want to hook up for the first time in a bathroom?" I ask her.

Carrie wrinkles her nose and swats me across the

arm. "I've hooked up—"

"I meant with me," I say. Carrie says what's on her mind. A lot of times, it's the wrong thing. Words always stumble out of her mouth.

She walks away from me and trips on the dance floor, and I sling my arm around to catch her. When she's upright again, she turns to me. "This is getting awkward." She huffs and puts her hands on her hips. "Everyone else in this town is good enough for Dax Abram."

I lean in to speak into her ear. "What is that supposed to mean?"

Carrie pulls away from me. "It means that you have a reputation. Word is, you've christened the bathroom at the Pool Hall. The Main Street salon. The water tower. Let's see, Dax. I know I'm leaving a few places out." She holds her fingers up as she silently counts.

"Is that what you thought was going to happen?"

She pauses. "Well, no."

Her green eyes are massive. They cover her entire face. Carrie isn't my usual type, but the more I look at her, the more I realize it's not because she isn't pretty. It turns out, if you look at her long enough, she's quite stunning. But she's awkward, usually dressed like a teenage boy, and now I learn she can be kind of a jerk.

"Is that who I am to you? Someone who sleeps around?" I ask. "Is that why you came into the bathroom? Trying to fill some childhood fantasy of yours?"

"I dodged a bullet." Carrie turns her back to me.

"You have no idea," I call after her.

She manages to trip again, and this time, I let her. Carrie turns, and her mouth opens and then closes. And she pushes me on the shoulder.

"I've never regretted anything more," she says as she walks off the dance floor, and I'm left standing alone.

I turn and walk in the opposite direction, unable to catch my breath. Who does Carrie think she is? I've never been anything but nice to her. She followed me into the bathroom. She came on to me. I'm a guy. We kissed a little. Things happen. Why is she mad?

I'm not proud of everything I've done since moving back to Wheaton. I've tried to fill the void of Zari in a few unhealthy ways, and yes, one of them is women. Since when is consensual hooking up a bad thing? I've been safe and stuck to my rules—never do it more than once. So much of what's being said about me is an over-exaggeration and has been nothing more than a little making out. But I learned a long time ago that it's not productive to go around trying to fix anyone's perceptions of you.

Kissing Carrie was nice. I loved how she felt pressed up against me. I'm happy I've never looked at her like that before. If I had, I'd be in big trouble. Correction, she'd be in big trouble. But if I tell her why I stopped, she'd never talk to me again. If anyone knew how much I'm still in love with Zari and will always be in love with her, everyone would stay away from me. Maybe that'd be for the best.

Chapter Three

Carrie

"OH, MEADOW, YOU HAVE MAIL," Malik sings through my bedroom door.

"Call me Carrie or I won't come out of my room all day," I fire back, and Malik laughs.

The name creates an identity crisis and reminds me of a life that no longer feels like mine. No one except my mom calls me that, even though it is my given name, and the name still resides on my birth certificate. My mom says she named me that because, when I was born in late spring, she passed a beautiful meadow of flowers on her way to the Wheaton hospital. My mom said that I reminded her of the beauty and promise seen between all the bland things in life. So, naturally, she named me Meadow.

In a small town where I craved nothing more than fitting in and being forgettable, the name always bothered me. On my first day of school, I shyly approached the teacher and asked her to call me Carrie. That was my grandma's name, a woman I'd never met but seemed like the kind of name of a girl who could fit in or fade into the background, whatever was preferred. Lucky for me, the name Carrie stuck. I'm unsure how many people know or remember that Meadow's my name, because everyone in town calls me Carrie.

"Why don't you change your name legally? Then this wouldn't be a problem anymore," Malik says.

I throw the arts section of the paper at him. "And offend my mother? Never."

Malik and I sit at the table. I eat cereal, Malik drinks black coffee and reads the newspaper. In so many ways, we act like an old married couple. I can't imagine any life where we don't live together and are not best friends. I love him because he inhibits all the characteristics I wish I had. He's brave. He goes after what he wants. And his tongue is sharp and witty. Malik sometimes jokes that if he ever liked women, I'd be his first choice. We fill in each other's gaps—he's the Ying to my Yang.

"We have two big things on our agenda today," Malik tells me. "And one involves us driving to the lake to see that listing again."

My soggy cereal no longer looks appealing as I push it around with my spoon. "What else do we have planned?"

"Well." Malik looks at me with his big brown eyes and pouty face, the one he knows I can't say no to. "I want to sign us up for something. If we win, you could use the proceeds on a charity of your choice."

He's piqued my interest. I set down my spoon and give Malik my full attention. "What is this thing you speak of?"

"Well . . ." Malik glances at me above the paper. "Think about how the extra cash could really help."

"Keep going," I say. His hesitancy to come out with it scares me.

"There is going to be a three-on-three basketball tournament in October. All proceeds will go to some charitable purpose."

"No," I say without hesitation.

"But Carrie," Malik whines. "I may have already signed us up. And paid the entrance fee."

"Are you being serious?" I ask, this time with a mouthful of soggy cereal.

"Carrie. The list. It explicitly says threesome."

"Umm," I look at Malik, confused. "I don't see the correlation."

"Threesome, Carrie. Three-on-three basketball tournament. That's the threesome."

Malik grabs my spoon and points it at me, and I shake my head. I pretend to resist Malik's persistence and dominance in my life, yet so many of the things I'm working toward are thanks to him. Putting myself out there is the most uncomfortable thing I can imagine, and Malik brings me to a level of discomfort.

"We wouldn't win," I protest. "The young kids who sign up would. And who'd even be on our team?"

"Me, obviously," Malik says. "And I may have mentioned it to Dax."

"No." I shake my head.

"Look, Carrie. The fuck it list. We need to do this. You need to quit saying no to everything. And Dax seemed super interested. You should have seen how excited he was."

"But I'll be busy for the rest of my life avoiding Dax. Plus, I already tried with him. Rejected. Big time, in case you'd forgotten."

"You tried hooking up with him. Going for someone takes more time. Think about it, but I think this would be perfect."

If there is one thing I know, it's how out of shape I am. I'd need to do so much conditioning to run up and down the court. Let alone the skills involved in playing the game. Skills I haven't worked on in ages.

After breakfast, Malik drags me out to see a property on the lake. It's our third time seeing it. I'm indecisive, and it would be the biggest purchase of my life. It's a little past the Abram and Bergland places but not as far as the county park. Malik turns down the gravel driveway; the tall corn sprouts out on both sides of the road, and the lake appears.

The bed and breakfast idea is all mine, although Malik did add it to my list to keep it on my radar. It's been my dream since I was little. My upbringing was unconventional at best, and the thought of running a business and showing people the love and charm of Lake Traverse is everything I want. I remember sitting in a freshman seminar, and the professor made us all say what we wanted to do after graduating from college, and I didn't hesitate when I said run a bed and breakfast. I was always going to end up back at the lake. I've known it my entire life.

There it is—The beautiful home with an A-frame second story on one end. It looks like an extra-long rambler home, and although the lawn is overgrown, the building is the perfect floor plan. We get out of Malik's car, and a vehicle pulls up behind us.

"I called Flo and asked her to show us the place again," Malik says, and I nod. "It's the one, Carrie. And you know it."

Flo lets us into the cottage. She points things out to me. "I think this would be a perfect bed and breakfast spot because of the layout. I know I've told you this all before, but Carrie, this is a gem." Flo points down the hallway. "Very little structurally would need to change. There are four bedrooms on the main floor, two with lake views, but the other two are lovely as well."

I look around the house. One of my favorite things about the layout is that the further inside I walk, the more the house reveals itself, like a present emerging from the wrapping. The long hallway has two bedrooms on each side, and then the kitchen and living room are one large room with beautiful views of the lake. Off of the kitchen is a three-season porch.

There's an odor throughout, but with new floors and fresh paint, the house could be as good as new. The only thing breaking up the open concept of the great room is the stairs leading to the loft.

Flo is a saint of a realtor. I have managed to find something wrong with every place she's shown us, but she never lets on that I'm frustrating her. A couple of places I've seen have been close contenders, but the energy never felt right.

We open the door, and the entire house is bright and airy. "The kitchen is quite large, and look at the large dining space. And then there is this lovely living room with a four-season sitting room off of it." "My favorite part of this place," Flo continues, "is the upstairs. There is a primary bedroom overlooking the lake, with a separate bathroom. You could live up here and have guests downstairs. You'd have your own private space."

We walk upstairs, and the owner's space is lovely. With a bit of updating, this could be my oasis. The large room overlooks the lake and has an attached bathroom. There is also space in a landing, with a counter to put a fridge and a coffee maker.

I turn to say something to Malik, but he and Flo have already headed downstairs. I can picture where I would put my bed, anchored between two windows that look at the expansive backyard. There's room for a dresser and a bookshelf. From the bed, I imagine I could look out at the lake. My body fills with goosebumps. Of all the places I've seen, this is the first place I can see myself in.

I've never owned land or real estate, nor has my mom. I love the thought of saying this is my forever home. I also once mentioned that it's a shame that unless a person has enough money to build a house or cottage on Lake Traverse, no one else gets to enjoy it. There aren't any cottage rentals or anything. I could be partly responsible for showing people the greatest secret on earth—the beauty and peace that Lake Traverse encompasses.

Our way back to town is mostly silent, but my internal thoughts overflow outward. "Malik, I appreciate what you're doing for me. I do. Every time I see that place, I fall more in love. But it's more than I was planning to spend."

"It's only a little outside your budget." Malik stares at the road. "You've been saving money living with me, right?"

I nod.

"You've also been working like crazy at the bank and picking up two weekly shifts helping with Sunny and Sis Bergland. You have the money. You have good credit, and—" Malik pauses.

I turn to him. "And what?"

"And I want to help financially."

"I could never take your money." I glance out the window.

"Consider it a loan. You're going to make money here, Carrie. It's perfect. I'll help modernize the space and see if some guys from Jake's Construction can help." Malik continues. "And you will make money. Even if you only rent out the rooms from May until after the hunting season ends in November, think about it, Carrie. If all four rooms were occupied for several months at a time, you'd make enough money to pay the mortgage and live."

It's at least the tenth property on the lake I've considered. I do want something that is mine. I can't rent a room from Malik forever.

"The outside is perfect," I say. "The dock and the

small, sandy beach. I know. I keep saying it. Perfect."

"I know." Malik winks at me, acting like he already has this in the bag.

So much has changed since I went into remission. Besides the obvious, like having hair again, but I'm also taking chances on things I would never have before. I've never pursued the things that I wanted in life. It's never been who I am. My entire life has been trying to blend in and disappear, which I always hoped would offset how eccentric and loud my mom chose to live.

Today's property is perfect. I knew it the first time I saw it, and I know it now. I couldn't have dreamed of a better layout, and most of the work is cosmetic and not structural. The bedrooms were large too. Many families could stay here at once. I have enough money to put in as a down payment and enough for renovations. It's not like I wouldn't have other money coming in. I could still work at the bank, and I have no intention of quitting my job with Sunny and Sis.

"I want to sleep on it, Malik," I say as we pull into his driveway.

Malik turns the ignition off and looks at me. "Carrie, I know you think I'm bossy, and if you ever want me to back off, say the word, and it's done."

"You're bossy." I raise an eyebrow.

"I've known you for years, and this is all you talk about. This is what you dream about. I know it's scary, and you'll sleep on it and think of a hundred reasons why you shouldn't do it. But you can do it. And you're not alone. I'll be here every step of the way."

Malik is always right. I'll lie in bed tonight, hyperventilating and talking myself out of it. Stability is what I want, but adulting scares me. It's only a pipe dream if I keep it that way. I've been talking for years about how my goal is to own my own bed and breakfast, a place I could also live in and call home. Malik and I have looked at many options on the lake for fun, but this is different. It feels different, and I can visualize it happening.

Malik lies down for a nap, and I decide to strap on my running shoes and get outside. Since being diagnosed with cancer, I've been so focused on staying alive and beating it that I haven't focused on other things, like my physical health. Lately, I've been trying hard to get back to fitness. I'm tired of feeling exhausted from simply walking up the stairs.

Malik's house is on the edge of town, so I turn onto the road that leads to the country. The pavement turns to gravel, and the houses disappear and makes way for green fields of corn and beans. As I run further, golden wheat fields, almost ready to be harvested stretch out across the landscape. I run for a couple of minutes and walk before jogging again.

When I reach the mouth of the river that flows into the lake, I jump when I see Dax standing there, hands on his hips. "Oh, hey," he says as our eyes meet.

I glance behind me and contemplate turning on my heels and heading back toward town, but instead, I stop next to him and breathe heavily.

"I didn't know you ran, Carrie." I'm envious of how quickly he stands up and catches his breath.

"I don't know if what got me here can be considered running," I say, nearly breathless. "But I need to get back in shape somehow. You run?"

"I try." He shrugs. "This is my favorite path. I thought maybe you came out this way searching for me. You know, wanting to talk about the three-on-three basketball tournament we're going to enter."

I nearly trip as I glance at him. "Umm, no. I didn't come looking for you."

"Malik called me this morning," Dax says. "I'm in.

I've been missing getting to hoop."

"Well, I haven't decided yet," I say.

"Every team needs a female. It's the rules. And you're the best, Carrie. Think about it. I wouldn't want to be on a team with anyone else."

We stand near the river, and the water bubbles over the rocks. I'm not sure how far I've come, but it has to be well over two miles, and I still need to get home.

"You don't think we're a little old? I mean, the eighteen-year-olds are going to school us."

Dax laughs. "You and I still hold every record in basketball at that school. I like our chances."

"Yeah, but that was before . . ." My voice trickles off. All that was before cancer, when I could run two miles easily instead of walking most of it, and when I spent time shooting baskets at the park or community center. It was before my knee injury.

"You'll get the endurance back," Dax says as I stand back up after finally catching my breath.

"'Cause you're the expert on cancer, right?' I want to pull the words back as soon as I say them. I'm always saying the wrong thing, and I can tell from Dax that it looks like I punched him in the gut. "I'm sorry," I backtrack. "I didn't mean—"

"I never said that." Dax pulls his leg up to stretch his quadriceps. "You look strong. The endurance will come."

My guard goes down a bit. "It feels good to be out here. I used to be able to run ten miles without hardly breaking a sweat."

"It will come back, Carrie." He glances down at the dirt before looking up and pointing. "Does that hurt?"

I look down to see what he's referring to. My two-inch port scar is red, a victim of the afternoon sun and my neglect of forgetting sunblock. It peeks out from my sports bra, and the color and texture contrast against my skin.

Dax's hand gets too close, and I swat it away. "No, it doesn't hurt. Does this hurt?" I flick at the scar on the bottom of his chin. I was there when he got it. I was a seventh grader, and he was a junior in high school. He and his opponent went for a loose ball during a contentious match and ended up hitting heads. Dax got taken out of the game because the bleeding wouldn't stop. He ended up needing a few stitches. And yes, it's pathetic that I remember.

"Sorry I asked." He tucks his hands into his shorts pockets.

"Anyway," I say, "I have a long run home. I'll see you around."

I turn to run, and Dax finds his pace beside me. "There aren't many roads in this town, Carrie. I'm headed the same way as you."

The rest of the jog back nearly kills me. So often, I want to stop and walk as sharp pain radiates throughout my body, and my chest feels like an elephant sits on it. Unlike me, Dax is in shape. His tight shirt clings to his body, and I can see the formation of perfectly formed pecs and hard abs. His muscular legs form perfect motions, both fluid and effortless. By the time we get back to town, I can't even speak, so when we reach the road for me to turn off and go toward home, I put up my hand to wave to him and then watch Dax's back as he became smaller and smaller, until he disappears completely. When he does fade, I find some long grass and vomit everything in my stomach.

Even though vomiting is my least favorite thing, I love feeling this alive.

Chapter Four

Dax

TWO WEEKS. HOW IS IT possible that the school year starts that soon? Kylie and I spend the morning setting up my classroom. She gives me ideas and states that bright colors are always best. When we're done, it looks like rainbows attacked the classroom.

Kylie even helps me with the seating chart. She has a very scientific method to it. All the desks are in groups of four, and she tries to place two boys and two girls at each cluster, arranged by alphabetizing their first names. When I take a step back, I'm quite impressed. I'm excited to start the school year.

This is about my seventh year of teaching. When I started college, the plan was to teach high school kids and then be a coach at the school. But then I realized that high school kids were kind of assholes, and coaching and teaching them would create burnout. Young kids, however, are my favorite. They're uncomplicated, tell you how they feel, and believe that the world is good and that everything will work out. I relish their innocence. Someday, they'll be my age and cynical and realize that just because we think everything will work out, it probably won't. I hate that Kylie was robbed of her innocence at such a young age.

"I'm going to head over to Sunny and Sis's and mow their lawn, sweetie. Do you want to come with me? You could play cards with Grandma Sis."

"Yes!" Kylie yells before I get the words fully out of my mouth.

Sis isn't Kylie's grandma. Not by blood. But in many ways, Sis is everyone's grandma, and her husband, Sunny, is everyone's grandpa. They're Camilla's actual grandparents and were best friends with my grandparents before they passed. That's what I like about being back in Wheaton. Leaving the city and our support system there was hard, but it was also necessary. Part of me considered moving Kylie to Atlanta to be closer to Zari's family, but selfishly, I wanted to be by my parents. I need them.

We arrive at Sunny and Sis's home on Main Street, and I get Kylie situated inside and then grab my riding mower from the truck. Jake started caring for Sunny and Sis when he moved back to Wheaton, and when I got here after Zari died, I started helping too. Sunny and Sis's kids live out of state, so they don't have family here besides Camilla.

Their entire lot doesn't take me more than twenty minutes, and I step inside, and Carrie is here now. I didn't even see her pull into the driveway.

"The lawn looks great, Dax," Sunny says as he gets out of his black recliner. "How much do I owe you, son?"

"You know your money isn't good with me." I pat his back. We have this conversation every time I stop over here to help with something. Every time, I tell him it's not necessary.

"Well, then, at least stay for lunch. Carrie cooked for us." Sunny groans as he reaches into the cupboard and takes out cups for everyone.

I go to decline, but it's no use as Sunny takes my arm and pulls me to the table. Kylie has already sat down, excited for a meal not made by me. Carrie seems to find a million corners in the room and avoids looking in my direction.

"What did you make for us today, Carrie?" Sis licks her lips and then looks at Kylie and me. "Carrie has been spoiling us with her food. It's good enough to be in restaurants."

"Sis, you're exaggerating." Carrie puts hot plates down on the wooden table and then brings in a pot. "Today's food is chicken tortilla soup, and I made some bread and a salad." She puts the bread down, and it steams as she makes the first cut.

As Carrie helps Sunny and Sis with their food, she looks at me. "I've been reading a lot about Alzheimer's and the best diet and, for the most part, am trying to serve a diet of softer foods."

"This is good." Sis moans as she takes a spoonful of soup. "Carrie knows more about my ailment than I do."

Sunny puts his hand over Carrie's. "And we sure appreciate you, Carrie."

The soup is incredible. I'm a terrible cook. I've never enjoyed it. Zari used to cook for us and even made homemade baby food for Kylie. Now, I have dad guilt that Kylie practically lives on chicken nuggets and macaroni and cheese.

"Carrie," Kylie says as she chews on her bread. "How did you get your owie? Does it hurt?"

She points at Carrie's port scar, and I wish I sat next to Kylie so I could squeeze her knee or give her some sign to shut up.

Carrie rubs her hand over the scar. "It doesn't hurt at all. It's usually not as red, but I wasn't very good and let it get sunburnt."

Kylie nods and puts her hand out. "Can I touch it?"

"Kylie, that isn't very nice to ask," I interject. Heat floods my face.

Carrie's eyes cut to mine. "I don't mind. Here, give me your finger, Kylie." Carrie leads her finger over the scar, and Kylie rubs it back and forth and then looks at me.

"The scar is just like Mommy's," she says.

The air escapes my lungs, and then I inhale sharply. Sis looks oblivious, and Sunny spoons soup into his mouth rapidly. Carrie takes Kylie's hand in hers.

"I know your mom had cancer." Carrie puts her spoon down and focuses solely on Kylie.

My baby girl nods, and Carrie clears her throat. "I had cancer too, and this is how I received medicine. Probably like your mommy." Kylie once again puts her hand up to Carrie's scar. Her small finger traces the two-inch scar right below Carrie's collarbone on the right side.

If I were an inventor, teleportation would be the first thing I'd create. I'd push a button, and Kylie and I would be on our couch, in our home, and not having this uncomfortable conversation.

"Is your cancer healed?" Kylie asks, her voice small. She takes her finger off Carrie, finally, and tucks it into her lap.

"It is, sweetie," Carrie says in a voice that puts Kylie at ease.

Kylie has so much of her mom in her and says whatever comes to mind. "Mommy died from her cancer."

Carrie reaches over and pulls Kylie into a hug. I'm watching in slow motion as she brushes Kylie's hair off her face and then puts her hands on Kylie's cheeks.

"I'm so sorry, Kylie," Carrie says. "Losing your mommy must have been very hard."

I'm still holding my breath, as I've never heard Kylie talk this openly about her mom and the cancer. I feel like I'm slowly drowning as my body slides to the bottom of the lake, and the light dims. But then, Kylie stuffs more bread in her mouth and smiles.

"She loved me the most. But don't tell Daddy," Kylie whispers from the other side of the table, and the mood gets lighter, partly thanks to Sunny jumping in to give us the fishing report.

I help clear dishes, and Kylie runs into the living room and grabs cards to play with Sis.

"You don't have to help." Carrie starts doing the dishes. "I get paid for this, you know."

"Yeah, it's one of your, like, five jobs, right?" I grab a towel to dry the dishes, despite her refusal of my help.

"Two jobs, thank you very much," Carrie responds as soapy water fills the sink.

"Come on, that was a joke," I say. "I guess I've never been here on your days."

"True," Carrie says over the running sink. She looks over her shoulder. "Next time, I'll be sure to make more food."

There isn't an edge to her voice like I'm expecting, so perhaps, she and I are fine after our bathroom encounter. I watch as Carrie puts extra food in containers and labels everything with the date and meal.

"Thanks for being so good to Kylie," I say. "With her questions and everything."

Carrie stops what she's doing and leans against the counter. "It's fine, Dax. She's a great kid." She shakes her head like she just said the most obvious thing in the world, which she did. "If you ever need help or a safe place for Kylie to ask questions, I'm always here. Really."

My heart grows instantly, and I need to grab Kylie

and get out of the house before the emotions below the surface peek through. The only people I ever let help with Kylie are family. Carrie's offer is so innocent, yet I hate feeling things.

"Anyway," I say, wanting a change of subject, "I've rented out the high school gym tonight for Malik's mandatory basketball practice, so I'll see you there."

"I can't believe I agreed to this." Carrie wipes her wet hands on her shirt.

"Malik and I knew you'd say yes." I wink at her and get back to drying dishes.

THE GYM IS A MILLION degrees because the school refuses to turn the air on until the kids return. Malik and Carrie walk in a couple of minutes after me. I've read the tournament rules, and each team will be comprised of two men and one woman, no zone defense allowed, and all games will be played to twenty-one, each bucket being worth one point, and teams must win by two points. We only play on half the court.

I'm oddly excited, and when Malik approached me, I didn't hesitate to say yes. There is nothing like the sound of a ball bouncing and squeaky shoes running up and down a basketball court. But it's more than that. Basketball encompasses every happy part of my life. When I had basketball, I felt like I had everything.

"Who's ready to win the big money?" Malik asks as he grabs a ball.

"Can we really compete against these kids? I'm so out of shape." Carrie pulls her arm across her body to stretch.

"Keep running with me, and you'll be in shape in no time," I say.

"Well." Malik puts his hands on his hips. "We have

height on our side."

He's right. Malik is the tallest, but he's also the least experienced player. He played basketball in high school but was mainly a football star. He's as tall as my brother, Jake, at over six feet, five inches. I come in next, at a little over six-foot, three inches, and then Carrie brings up the rear, at about five feet, nine inches. I've played enough intramural sports to know the advantage on any co-ed team is how strong the female player is. The woman on the team will either be the weakest link or the game-changer. We have Carrie, which is huge.

"I think I should be the point guard," I say, "And Carrie can be our shooting guard on both the wing and baseline, and Malik, you'll play with your back to the basket and be our post, main rebounder, and cleanup. Thoughts?"

Both Malik and Carrie shrug their shoulders. I grab the clipboard from the bleachers. "I created some plays that are effective for three-on-three."

Carrie laughs a little too hard. "Coach, aren't we overdoing it a bit? I mean, practice? Plays? It's a three-on-three tournament."

Malik pokes her in the forehead. "Do you know what first place gets?"

Carrie shakes her head, and Malik raises his voice. "Five-thousand big ones."

"For a charity of your choice," I interject.

"It's something." Malik shrugs. "How good would it feel to win?"

For the next hour, we shoot around and then practice plays. Pick and roll, give and go, one-on-one. We match up against each other and try to get to the basket. I find their weaknesses and try to coach them. Malik is a beast, but he's not quick, and he'll need to work on that or he'll get beat to the hoop every time.

Carrie's biggest weakness is on set plays. She's great on the run, but when we're forced to set up, she has a hard time shaking me. Granted, she'll always have the other team's female guarding her, tournament rules, but she'll need to work on her one-on-one game. I'll have to work on getting more physical. I'm tall but I'm shaped more like a runner and less like a linebacker. I'll have to fight my way in to get the boards.

After an hour, we're all red in the face. Malik pours water over himself. "First beer is on me."

"I won't say no to that." I take off my sweaty shirt and replace it with a clean one from my duffel bag.

"I feel too gross for public right now." Carrie holds up her sweaty shirt and sniffs it.

"Then, we'll go to the pool hall," Malik argues. "That's not really public."

We sit inside the stale building, and the air conditioning makes my salty sweat dry on my body, and I feel crusty. But the beer is good, and for the first time since Zari died, I'm doing more than existing and being the best dad to Kylie. It feels good to be in the gym, playing basketball again. I go for runs, and play basketball, so I'm sure I haven't been in this good shape for the past eight years.

Malik leans back in his chair, and Carrie takes her hair out of its holder and runs her hands through it. Last summer, when the town held a benefit for her, there wasn't a hair on her head. But now, it reaches her shoulders.

Malik turns his chair toward me. "Did Carrie tell you she bought the old cottage near Walleye Pass?"

Carrie looks at me and nods.

I ask, "The one half a mile south of my place?"

"I finally pulled the trigger." Carrie glances at Malik and smiles. "The first B&B on Lake Traverse."

I've always told anyone who would listen that Lake Traverse needed a bed and breakfast or cottage rentals. The lake is gorgeous and, for the most part, undiscovered, which I like. But I always thought that bed and breakfast would benefit the local economy.

"Congrats, Carrie," I finally say. "I'm sure Malik will hook you up with free labor, but I want to help out in any way I can."

Carrie scrunches her face up and then laughs. She's not subtle in how little she takes me seriously. "Yeah, okay."

She doesn't believe a thing I say and doesn't hide it. I can't blame her. Besides living in the same town and loving basketball, I don't know Carrie. Few people do. And I can only imagine what she thinks she knows about me.

"My little Meadow is all grown up." Malik pulls Carrie into a side hug, to her dismay.

"Meadow?" I ask.

Carrie shakes off the question, and a gust of wind comes into the bar as a group of women comes in.

"Oh, hi, Dax," the brunette whose name escapes me says as she walks over to the table where the three of us sit. "I've called a few times but haven't heard back from you since the party at the dunes."

Carrie puts some cash on the table, leans to kiss Malik on the cheek, and leaves, giving the brunette her chair. This is one of the many times in the past couple of years that Wheaton's smallness has caught up with me.

Chapter Five

Carrie

THE CLOSING PROCESS ON MY bed and breakfast went fast, and I already have the keys. The place hasn't been lived in for over five years and needs some love. The rooms have floor to ceiling wallpaper, and the ugly flooring, even though it's in decent shape, needs work. Not to mention the entire place smells like an animal has used it as a toilet, and the carpet needs to be removed. Malik seems in no hurry to have me out of his place, so I plan to continue living there until I tackle some of these projects.

Camilla and I went out last night for dessert, and she shared some design ideas with me. She offered many thoughts on making the space special and how to make it work as a bed & breakfast, and I can't wait for the two of us to go shopping and pick out some things.

This big part of me wants to call my mom and say, "look at how well my life is turning out. Look at the roots I'm putting down." Her reactions tend to disappoint me, though. Not because she's disappointed in me but because of her lack of caring about what I consider big milestones in my life. I'm too excited about all of this to be brought down by her.

The B&B won't realistically be ready for guests until spring, at the earliest, and having a mortgage for the first time, not to mention a heavy line of credit for repairs, is why I won't be quitting my bank job anytime soon. I'm good with numbers but have never enjoyed working there. I'm a teller three days a week, which gives me enough hours to have health insurance, but the other two days, I take care of Sunny and Sis Bergland, and I enjoy that much better.

Today is my day at the bank, but before I head to work, I treat myself to the best cup of coffee in town at the Corner Café. I'm not sure if they sprinkle magic fairy dust in, but no coffee Malik and I have made at home even come close. I walk in and wave at the regulars who sit around the tables. As I walk up to the counter, I hear Sunny and his friends discussing the weather and how cool the nights are getting as we approach Labor Day weekend. Another table I pass talks about how much the weather has shifted over the years and that if we don't get rain soon, this year's crop will suffer.

I exit the Corner Café and start toward the bank, three blocks from here, but Dax and his younger sister, Jenna, walk toward the café and stop when they see me. Jenna and I graduated from Wheaton High School the same year and were basketball teammates growing up. On the court, we felt like sisters. We knew each other's moves and anticipated where we'd run on the court next, but outside of basketball, we were nothing but friendly. Where I hid in corners, sat in the back of classrooms, and watched Hallmark movies on the weekends when I didn't have ballgames, Jenna lived like an Abram. Which meant that she was popular, outgoing, and belonged with, what appeared like, little effort. She also played volleyball, so she had all those friends too.

"Hey, Carrie," Dax and Jenna say in unison.

"Grabbing your morning cup of coffee too?"

Jenna smiles with one hand resting on the door handle. "Dax and I dropped Kylie off at an art camp at the Community Center, and then I promised I'd help him pick up more supplies for his classroom."

The tinge of coolness in the morning air reminds me that the school year is upon us. "Jenna, you played basketball," I say, switching topics. "Why didn't Dax and Malik rope you into being their female player?"

Jenna and Dax glance at each other, and she laughs. "I, fortunately, had an out. I'm exploring a few job opportunities, but not all are local. I've been traveling some for interviews and don't know where I'll be."

"Lucky." I readjust the cup in my hands and then turn my body so they know I have to get going.

Dax glances at me and then nods to Jenna. "Will you run in and get me a black coffee? I'll walk Carrie to work."

Before I can protest, Jenna nods, and I turn on my heels to walk toward the bank.

"Speaking of basketball, how's my player?" Dax matches his pace to mine.

"It looks like Jenna dodged a bullet I was unable to." I look at him. "Even if we win, which is unlikely, it's not that much money."

"I know. I just feel excited, you know?" Dax stops walking to tie his shoe. He looks up at me. "I feel like I have something to look forward to. Which I realize sounds awful, considering I'm a dad and have Kylie to look forward to every day."

"I get it." I nod. Dax stands back up, and we continue walking down the street. We pass shops that open for the day. "I'm kind of looking forward to getting back on the court too."

"Why did Malik call you Meadow?" Dax turns to me, putting his hand on his forehead to create a visor from the morning sun.

"Oh." I pause. "I don't know if we're close enough for me to divulge such information." I nudge him in the arm but hope he'll drop the subject.

"Come on." Dax nudges me back. "Now, I really want to know."

We cross the street and pass the Drug and Department stores.

"That's the name I was born with," I admit, knowing that because that Dax is older than me, he never heard the name called out on the first day of school. Jenna would have, though.

Dax pulls his lips into his mouth and raises his forehead. "Your mom named you Meadow Soleta?"

"Worse. My middle name is Lark."

Dax laughs so hard that it sounds more like a bark. His smile extends across his face, and he puts a hand on his stomach to stop the shaking. "After the basketball player Meadowlark Lemon?"

"You'd think." I stop in front of the door to the bank as we approach. "My mom couldn't name one basketball player if she tried. Totally coincidental."

"Why'd you change your name?"

"I had a grandma named Carrie, and it was the most unassuming name I could think of, so I went with it. I've had everyone call me Carrie ever since."

"Wait." Dax turns to me and tucks a leg under the other. "Carrie isn't your real name? You never changed it?"

"What's the point? That's what everyone knows me as." I put my hand on the doorknob of the bank as Dax watches me.

"I don't know if I'll ever look at you the same, Meadow."

Dax continues to laugh, and I throw an elbow into his side. "Yeah, well, don't get in the habit of calling me that."

"Meadow Lark Soleta." Dax wrinkles his forehead in thought.

"Because living in an RV at the county park with my mom, who gave massages for a living, didn't put a big enough target on my back."

Dax's hand brushes against mine as he grabs the doorknob I'm holding and opens the door. "I don't know, Carrie. I think your upbringing gives you unique complexity. People rarely surprise me. Do you have plans later?" He calls after me as I walk through the door.

Joan, one of the bank tellers, looks in our direction.

"Malik and I are heading to the B&B to do some work. We have a lot of wallpaper to get rid of." I make a disgusted face, already dreading the task before me.

"Mind if Kylie and I stop by? We can bring food. I'd love to see the place."

I feign uninterest. Lately, it turns out that it's Dax surprising me. "Umm, yeah. We'll be there. Come over whenever."

For the rest of the day, I obsess. Dax—surprised by me. My mind flashes to the bathroom with him. I shake my head, removing the memory. I thought I was following Malik's fuck it list item and going for it with Dax. But I didn't think it through. Going for someone doesn't mean hooking up once. It means getting to know a person. Someone I've been slightly obsessed with my entire life and who is turning out to be a decent conversationalist. Then, I remember I'm not interested in him anymore. No. Definitely not.

After work, I run home to change clothes, grab

Malik, and he and I head out to my new place. Malik has a steamer, and we aim to start working on the wallpaper.

We start in one of the bedrooms. The wallpaper has clearly been on the walls since the beginning of humanity, and comes off slowly. I pull about an inch off and groan when it rips. At this pace, we'll be at this for months. It would be so easy to dip into the renovation budget and hire someone to do this. As quickly as the thought enters my mind, I shake it free. I'm saving so much money by doing much of the work myself.

"Knock-knock." Dax walks in, which is a great excuse to take a break from this mind-numbing task.

Malik claps his hands together in excitement and whispers. "Is that Dax?"

"We're in here," I holler and then slug Malik in the arm.

I wipe my brow and greet Dax and Kylie as they look around.

Dax holds the bags out to us. "I brought food. And plates." Dax stands at the bedroom door. His arms hang from the weight of the bags.

"Should we go to the kitchen? I have a table and chairs." I point down the hallway.

We walk down the hallway. Two rooms sit on the right and left, separated by a bathroom on both sides. Then, the place opens up with the kitchen, living room, and sunroom.

Kylie looks around. "This place smells funny." Dax shoots her a look, and Malik and I laugh.

"It does." I take the paper plates out of the bag. "I'm hoping once we fix it up, paint it, and put in new floors, it will smell much better."

I've become almost immune to the smell at this point, but I have a feeling it comes from the dirty carpets. It smells of mold, with tinges of urine, depending on where you're standing.

"I'd love a tour." Dax puts his hand on his hips and looks at me. His eyes take everything in, and I follow his glance as he looks at the cupboards, the living and dining rooms, and the stairs that lead to my primary bedroom.

Malik starts pulling sandwiches out of the bag and motions to me. "Carrie, why don't you give Dax a tour, and I'll get Kylie started on some food."

"Let's start upstairs." I push Dax forward and follow him. The nasty carpet even covers the stairs.

Once upstairs, I show him what will be my bedroom, which looks over the lake. The upstairs bedroom is the only room with no wallpaper, but unfortunately, it has the old, dirty carpet, even the bathroom. The window takes up almost the entire wall of the bedroom, and the view of the lake is gorgeous. I can't wait to wake up to this view every day.

"This is seriously great, Carrie. The room is huge." Dax walks to the window and runs his hand around the frame. "Not that you asked, but here's my recommendation."

I fold my arms over my chest.

"You need new floors anyway. When installing them, you should have some impact barrier flooring underlayment. That will help a lot with sound. You don't want to feel like you have to tiptoe around your bedroom when you have guests here."

"I hadn't thought of that," I admit. It's a great idea. Especially since several months out of the year, people will stay below me.

I plan to open up the B&B on the first of May every year and then close it on the first of November. That will give me six months of living here alone and six months of potential guests.

"I'll talk to Jake. We just finished a job and ended up

with a lot of extra porcelain tile that looks like oak wood planks. It'd look great in here. I'm sure he'd give you a great deal. There's probably enough for the whole place."

I walk up to Dax and look out the window as he strokes the wood frame around it. "I'd forgotten that you help out with Jake's company in the summer."

"Well, being a teacher barely pays the bills, so yeah, the construction work Jake gives me is great." Dax walks away from the window and opens the door to the walk-in closet.

It hadn't occurred to me how helpful Dax could be. I knew that he helped Jake with construction jobs each summer, but I figured he did that just for something to do. I hadn't realized how much he knows. And, before recently, the guy and I hardly spoke.

"I love the idea of soundproofing." I watch Dax continue to look around the space. "I don't want to feel like I need to tiptoe around my home."

We head downstairs and into the kitchen, where Malik and Kylie are engrossed in conversation and laughing about something. Dax hands me a sandwich from a bag.

"And you'll do all the cooking?" Dax asks as he unrolls his sandwich from the paper wrapping.

"Well, I'll only provide breakfast, but yes."

"And would you keep your job at the bank?" Dax asks before he shovels food onto his plate.

I take a bite of my sandwich; turkey and provolone, my favorite. I dab at the corners of my mouth with a napkin. "That's the plan."

"No," Malik yells before I can answer another one of Dax's questions. "Quit the bank. Please. Please?"

"Eventually. Maybe. I mean, if things work out here. Before I quit, I have to ensure I can afford insurance and that the place gets booked up."

Daily, I worry about whether or not my B&B will be successful. What if no one rents my rooms? What if it never takes off? Then, I'll be stuck with a house on the lake and a much higher mortgage than I can afford. Well, much higher than I can afford if I don't work at the bank.

"We'll live so close to each other," Kylie says and then looks at Dax. "Daddy, I bet we could climb all the way here on the rocks."

Kylie hops onto Dax's lap, and he helps her open the mayonnaise packet she's been fiddling with. "If the water was low enough, sweetie, we sure could."

"We'd have Uncle Jake and Auntie Camilla on one side and Carrie on the other." Kylie takes a big bite of her sandwich, and Dax nuzzles into her neck before kissing her cheek.

After we eat, I continue the tour for Dax. I show him the main floor bedrooms, all about the same size, two with lake views and two with views of the backyard and the rolling hills in the distance.

"There isn't much work to do here," Dax says. "When you're ready to do the floors, let me know. I can help Malik. We could pound this out pretty fast."

"That's a lot to ask." I wrinkle my nose and look around the room.

"You didn't ask, and I want to." Dax shrugs.

Malik and Kylie walk in, and Dax turns to them. "I should be getting you to bed, Kylie. Are we on for practice this week? Wednesday night?"

"I have a date." Malik shimmies his shoulders, clearly proud of himself. "But you two should plan to practice without me."

Dax puts his hands on Kylie's shoulders but keeps his eyes on me. "We're on. We can work on some one-on-

one moves."

I groan. "I'll be there."

Dax and Kylie leave, and Malik and I get back to wallpaper removal. He doesn't stay silent for long. "Dax has been finding ways to see you, am I right?"

"Mmm." I nod.

"Just saying."

"I'm going with the flow, Malik," I say. "Let's not forget that interested brunette the other night."

"Everyone has a past, love." Malik shoots me a look.

"Yep." I rip inch after inch of floral wallpaper. "And some people are still living in it."

My hands throb from scraping the wallpaper when I lie in bed back at Malik's. Malik made it sound like the wallpaper would come off in big, rolling waves. Instead, I've practically had to pull at each corner, and now my hands hurt.

I think of Dax and what Malik said. He has been around a lot. Whether it's practicing for our three-on-three tournament, going for our runs, or him offering to help me out here, I feel like I'm getting to know the real Dax. Not the one I was obsessed with when we were younger, as I scribbled his name on my notebooks, surrounded by a heart. Or the Dax that I used to watch school everyone he ever played against.

There are two very different Daxes, though, and I'm not sure both of his truths fit together. There's the Dax I've seen around at parties or the Pool Hall, surrounded by women, flirting his way through the evening, and there's the Dax who is the center of Kylie's world, who is extra sweet to her, and who offers to take burdens off my shoulders.

Both of these truths can exist simultaneously. But one of them puts me at risk of falling head over heels in love with him, and the other one will be the reason he'll break my heart when I do.

I can't let myself fall for Dax. That's my truth.

Chapter Six

Dax

THE SECOND HAND ON THE large round clock that hangs on the wall is the only thing I hear. It's surrounded by banners of conference championships dating back to before I played. Carrie is fifteen minutes late for our practice. I grab my phone to text her, but then she runs through the door.

"Sorry I'm late. I got held up at Sunny and Sis's and had to run home to change, and—"

"Breathe, Carrie. It's no big deal." Her face is red as she looks around the gym, disheveled. She throws a bag on the bleachers and leans down to puts on her basketball shoes. "What are we doing today, coach?"

She looks up at me, and I realize I love being called a coach. It's a dream I still have, but being a single dad, there's no time. As much as I love teaching, becoming an educator was largely driven by my desire to coach and not be done with basketball after I graduated college.

I dribble the ball, moving it from my left hand to my right and passing it between my legs. "After we shoot around, we're playing one-on-one. It's your weakest game."

Carrie rolls her eyes but then stands straight and stretches her arms into the air. She bends to the left and right, and her shirt creeps up slightly, revealing a sliver of skin underneath. "Man, you've got me down. It is my weakest game. My college coach used to tell me all the time."

I throw the ball at Carrie, and she whips it back to me. "I've always been best at stationary shooting."

"Now you need to improve your game when you don't have a seconds lead on your opponent to get a shot off. Watch."

Carrie stands aside, and I show her a couple of moves facing the basket and then when my back is to the opponent. She then takes the ball. Her back is to me, and Carrie tries my sidestep from the left-wing, cutting to the lane. I reach around her to access the ball, but she protects it with her body. Her butt rubs against me, and my mind drifts at the proximity. Carrie is much sexier than I remember, and guarding her feels like a dance. The ball bounces against the gym floor, and then Carrie moves to the lane, fades away, and gets a shot off, but hits the front of the rim.

"I thought I had you." Carrie smacks the ball between her hands.

"Let's make this more interesting," I say, competitive spirit ignited. "How about if you score on me, you get to give me a truth or dare, and if I score on you—"

"What, are we ten?" Carrie furrows her brows and tucks the ball on her hip.

"I mean, if you're scared of losing." I shrug my shoulders, knowing Carrie can't say no to a competition.

"Me, scared?" Carrie points her index finger at her chest. "Nothing scares me."

I love that I've met my match in competitiveness. "We'll see about that."

Carrie bounces the ball to me to check it. She gets into position, and my eyes don't leave the ball. She dribbles to the right, and as she cuts to the left, her dominant hand, she's able to get a shot off. Nothing but net.

"One to zero." Carrie smiles proudly and maneuvers the ball from one hand to another. "Truth or dare, Dax?"

"Dare, of course," I say without hesitation.

Carrie puts her hand to her lips like she's in deep thought. "Okay, lose your shirt."

In one swift motion, I pull my shirt over my head and then give the ball back to Carrie. It's not the first time I've been shirtless in front of her, but her eyes stay on me before she quickly blinks and looks away. Carrie dribbles to the right and tries to get a shot off. She thinks she's bested me, but I block it.

My ball. I'm a good six inches taller than Carrie, so I use my height to my advantage. I dribble toward her, and she backs up just a step, allowing enough space for me to get a shot off. It goes in.

"One to one." I smirk. I can't help myself. I'm in my element. My happy place. Where life is uncomplicated and where people win.

"Truth or dare, Carrie?" She looks at the floor, her hand on her hip.

"Dare," she says, catching me by surprise. I always had Carrie as more of a truth girl.

"Okay. Take your shirt off." Carrie looks at me, unamused, but doesn't argue.

"I'm not going to be the only one without a shirt on," I add.

"Men are so predictable. You could have dared me to try dunking or run around the school yelling something crazy. But not Dax Abram. No. Dax is predictable."

She pulls her shirt over her head to reveal a blue

sports bra. Carrie has always been fit, but all the running and playing ball has only improved her. And now it's me that has a hard time looking away. Her smallish breasts pool out of the top of her bra, her shorts rest low on her hips, and a little hiccup gets caught in my throat.

"Look at those ab muscles, Soleta." Her skin is bronzed, and I want to look away. To not think of Carrie like I'm currently thinking of her. But I can't help it. The girl hides a lot under her clothes.

I get low and turn from the basket. I push her back, but Carrie holds her own. We're so close that I have a hard time concentrating, which is my excuse for why I dribble the ball off my foot. Carrie's ball.

She jukes me. This time, when she goes to her left, she rolls the ball behind her back and goes in for an easy layup.

"Truth or dare?" she asks me. Carrie tries to cover her smile with her mouth, but it's no use. She looks damn giddy.

"Dare," I respond without hesitation.

"Umm." Carrie doesn't take her eyes off me as she puckers her lips, deep in thought. "Shoes. Off."

"You want me to take my shoes off?" How does she continue to surprise me? I usually bore easily of people because I can calculate their next move. But not Carrie's.

"Sorry, is that not sexy enough?" Carrie grins. "I'm pretty sure this is my first game of truth or dare, so you'll have to tell me if I'm not meeting your expectations."

I lose my shoes, which turns out to be a smart move by Carrie because I'm slipping all over the gym floor. Carrie scores on me again.

"What will it be?" she asks. I refuse to find out what her next dare would be, so I go with truth.

"Hmm." She taps her index finger on her cheek.

"Who's the last person you dated?"

"My wife," I answer without hesitation. I asked her out at the beginning of my first year of college. Our first date was at a malt shop near campus.

"Really?" She looks surprised. "Not the girl from the bar the other night?"

"Nope," I answer honestly. "You said dated."

Carrie looks disappointed. She thought she had me, and this question would get me to divulge a piece of myself that makes Carrie curious.

"Work hard for the next point, Carrie, and you may get me to elaborate."

Carrie getting to ask me questions motivates her because she easily goes up four to two.

After I say truth, she asks her next question. "Are the rumors about you and your"—she coughs, and her face reddens—"escapades true?"

The ball rolls through my fingers as I give it back to her. "You'll have to be specific about what these rumors are. I'm not sure if I've heard them."

I have no intention of making this easy for her. I know what she's asking. I knew that's what she wanted to know when she asked the dating question.

Carrie bites her bottom lip and turns crimson. "You know? That you get around?"

Her neck fills with little red blotches. I don't know why I didn't realize it before, but Carrie is adorably shy.

"Define get around." I hold the ball hostage.

I lick my lips. I'm being cruel, but I can't help it. Sexual expression is a spectrum, and what one may consider loose, another may consider a normal amount of activity for a person my age.

"Do you sleep around, Dax?" The words vomit out of

her mouth, and then she covers her face.

"No." I say seriously, unflinching, and her lips twitch ever so slightly, and she looks disappointed.

"That's what people say," Carrie says softly. "Why don't you correct them?"

"It's not my job." I shake my head. "I've been with people, of course. But never more than once. It's kind of a rule."

I've heard the rumors about myself, and it's clear now that Carrie has too. Some things I've heard since returning to Wheaton with Kylie are true, but most aren't. Is my wife the last person I've slept with? Hell no. So many of the rumors I've heard about myself aren't true.

Carrie rolls her lips inside her mouth. "Well, okay then." I toss the ball to Carrie. "Let's keep playing." She's unfocused, and I easily steal the ball from Carrie, and it's mine.

When I score my third point, Carrie takes another dare. I'm so surprised by the move that it takes me a moment. She must not want to disclose anything about herself.

"Really, Carrie? You continue to surprise me."

"Well, I've never played truth or dare before. Dare seems safer."

"Safer than disclosing things about yourself to me?"

"Pretty much." Carrie shrugs. "What this time?"

I try not to ruminate on the fact that Carrie doesn't want me to learn about her.

"Kiss me." I say it instinctively before I have a chance to think about it, as it was the first and truest thing that came to my mind.

Carrie wrinkles her brow and bites the inside of her cheek. "You want me to kiss you?"

"A dare's a dare," I say.

"For how long?" Carrie takes a slow step toward me.

"Let's see how it goes." I grin. "But there is no time requirement."

She lets the ball slide out of her hand, and walks over to me, skin glistening with sweat, just like mine. Her green eyes get closer until they slowly become out of focus. It's unlike in the bathroom, where we crashed into each other. This time, she's pensive and shy. Carrie inhales, and she rolls her lips in her mouth before leaning in and kissing me.

It starts innocently enough. Carrie balances herself by placing her arms on each of my biceps, and I tilt my head down, and she stretches up to meet me. I'm unsure where to put my hands, so I stretch them across her rib cage. The energy shifts the moment the kiss goes from a prolonged peck to something entirely different.

Her hand wraps around my neck, and mine slides down to her waist. My pinky finger grazes against the elastic of her shorts. The first time we kissed, I didn't pause to enjoy it. But this time, I appreciate how soft and full Carrie's lips are. I pull her closer, and a fire ignites in me when our tongues touch. My body reacts to her mouth on mine, and even though the gym door is closed and we're the only ones in the building, I need to stop this before I lose all control. I can see the headline in the weekly *Wheaton Happenings*. "Teacher loses his job after fornicating in the school gym."

"I forfeit tonight's game," I say into her mouth, and she smiles against my lips.

"Turns out I'm not so bad at one-on-one." Carrie pulls back and squeezes my arms before taking her hands off me.

When she turns to grab her clothes from the floor, I adjust myself and whip on my shirt before she has a chance to see how affected I am. She faces the other direction but stands there, doing nothing but staring at the wall.

"You're a good coach, Dax," she says. "I already feel better."

"Ugh." I groan. "Don't call me coach after that. It makes me sound like a predator."

Carrie finally turns to me, takes off her shoes, and sticks her feet in a pair of sandals.

"Pool hall?" I ask, surprised by the sound of my words. What am I doing, and why am I playing with fire? I'm not ready for the night to end yet.

Carrie looks at the time. "Wish I could, but I have a big day tomorrow. Next time."

"Got it." I hide my disappointment. I'm not even sure why I feel that emotion. Nothing can happen with Carrie.

"Plus, I'm not sure I'm up for meeting any more of your ladies tonight," she adds, causing a stab to my heart.

Back at home, I tuck Kylie in, sit up, and click through different programs on the TV. Nothing interesting is on, and my mind isn't in it anyhow. All I can think of is Carrie and her body pressed up against mine, her guarding me, then me, her. And that kiss. It occurs to me how much truth exists, even in a dare. I wanted to kiss Carrie, but it needed to be done without expectations or pressure.

A month ago, if you had told me that I'd be thinking of Carrie Soleta, I would have told you that you're crazy. I've always liked her as a person and have respect for what she's brought to the game of basketball, but I've never looked twice in her direction.

I need to be strategic because I have no intention to date. We're coming up on the third anniversary of Zari's passing, and it doesn't feel right to move on. Not yet. Maybe not ever. I don't judge people who move on faster, but no one will ever be her. That's why I've had a strict one-and-done policy regarding women. It helps meet my needs met but never gets feelings involved. It's worked great.

If something happens between Carrie and me, it must be perfect because it can only be once. I tried telling her that tonight in so many words.

WITH THE CLARITY OF THE morning, I create a day of adventure with Kylie that may involve climbing rocks in a southern direction that may or may not lead us down to Carrie's new place.

"We're going to climb all the way, Daddy?" Kylie asks me. Her brown eyes look up at me as I strap on her sturdy water shoes.

"We are, sweetie. I'm going to bring a backpack with water bottles and snacks for the day. A Kylie-Daddy adventure."

"Yay!" Kylie yells. I put a cap on her head and then spray her with sunblock.

The lake is still and swampy. As we walk along the rocks, a carp jumps in the distance, and a pelican hunts overhead, swooping down low when it sees something.

We stop for a water break on a big, flat rock. Kylie sits down and pulls out a cookie from the bag.

"Daddy, sometimes I forget what Mommy's voice sounds like." Kylie looks out at the lake.

There are little emotions in her words, just truths spoken between a father and daughter. She finishes her cookie, stands up, and walks along the rocks again.

"We should watch videos tonight. From when you were little. Kylie, it's okay to be sad. And to talk about Mommy. I miss her too. All the time."

Whenever Kylie and I have these discussions, which are pretty much daily, her reactions surprise me. I expect tears, tantrums, or some emotion, but this time is like the others. She gets distracted by something else. Half her life was with her mom, and half has been without. With each passing day, that percentage keeps changing.

"Daddy, that's Carrie's place!" Kylie yells, unaware that this was the plan the entire time.

"I know," I say. "Should we stop in and say hi?"

Kylie excitedly nods, and we get off the rocks and head up on the lawn. As we get closer, Trey, one of Jake's construction crew guys, walks in with some supplies. It hadn't occurred to me that Carrie hung out with anyone besides Malik and me. And especially a guy.

"Aren't we going to say hi to Carrie, Daddy?" Kylie looks up at me, reading my hesitation.

"She's probably busy," I decide. "How about we climb the rocks, stop at the bay, and eat our snacks?"

"But Daddy." She puts her hands on her hips, just like her mom used to do. Then, she puckers her lips, a trait she got from her mom, and I've never been able to say no to it. I'm stuck between pleasing my daughter and looking like an ass. I'll always choose Kylie.

"We can say hi, but it has to be a quick visit, sweetie." Kylie smiles, satisfied by my response, and I knock on the screen door before we walk in.

Voices come from the kitchen, and Trey and Carrie stand around a table, looking at paint samples. They both look up at the same time.

"Dax, Kylie. I didn't hear you come in." Carrie rushes over to Kylie and hugs her.

Kylie loves every female in her life, and it scares me. She attached to Camilla so fast. She worships my sister Jenna and now Carrie. I can't help but think it is part of missing her mom.

"We climbed all the way here on rocks. It was an adventure." Kylie smiles at her.

"Hey, Dax." Trey sticks his hand out to shake mine.

"Are you helping Carrie out?" I ask, pointing to the hundreds of paint samples he's brought.

"Trying to. I thought I'd show her some color options now that the wallpaper is off in a couple of the rooms."

A foreign feeling comes over me. One I haven't felt in a long time, and it takes me a moment to recognize it. I'm jealous. It was fine when I knew Malik was out here helping, but I'm not too fond of the thought of Trey here.

I pick up some of the samples on the table. "I told you I'd be happy to help anytime, Carrie."

Trey steps forward and tries to block my view of Carrie, but I step around him. Carrie takes her fingers and pushes hair behind her ear. "I appreciate that, but you start work again next week. And you have Kylie. I couldn't ask you to help. So, when Trey asked . . ."

Carrie's voice trails off, and Trey smiles. "I can help out a couple of nights a week," Trey adds. "And Carrie offered to cook to thank me."

Kylie watches on, oblivious to the testosterone thrown out on the table. Carrie seems a bit out of the loop as well.

The subject changes when Carrie grabs Kylie's hand. "Can I show you something, Kylie? It's pretty cool."

Kylie smiles, and Carrie leads her off toward the stairs, leaving me standing there, wishing I was elsewhere.

"What are you doing, Dax?" Trey turns to look at me the moment the ladies get upstairs.

"What are you doing, Trey?" I put my hand firmly on the table, and he does the same.

"Isn't it obvious?" He runs his hands through his short, black hair.

"Don't waste your time," I pick at the day-old stubble on my face. "Carrie isn't the kind of girl you're after."

Trey laughs, unconvinced. "Well, we'll see."

Chapter Seven

Carrie

"VETO." MALIK PLOPS ON MY bed.

I stand in front of my full-length mirror, looking at the outfit I got on sale during my recent trip to Fargo.

He scrunches his face, and I spin and look at the backside of my outfit. I smooth out my top and admire the capris that hit me halfway between my knees and ankles.

Malik stands behind me, hands on my shoulder, and then twists me toward him. "Wear pants or wear shorts. Don't wear these in between things."

"Are they that bad?" I turn to check out my butt. The capris fit. Which is better than the other outfits I used to wear that were all too big.

"Girl." Malik motions for me to follow him out of the room. "You look like you're about to hike the Grand Canyon. The only thing missing from your ensemble is a fanny pack."

My white socks hit my ankle, and the capris stop a few inches short of that. "This outfit is the worst," I admit. "But, literally, all my clothes are the worst."

Malik holds his hand up to his face and taps the kitchen island with his other.

"Please, Malik," I beg. "Take me shopping. Save me from myself."

He takes my purse from the kitchen counter and hands it to me. "I thought you'd never ask." Malik's already halfway out the door, and I follow him. I spin one last time in front of the mirror adjacent to the door, and as always, Malik is right. These pants are horrible.

Clothes have always been trivial to me. My mom used to shop for both of us at local thrift stores. She'd bring the clothes to our RV and get out her sewing machine. She thought the more skin a person shows, the better. She'd hold up her designs, which barely covered my growing lady bits and would never pass a school dress code. I rebelled, saved my money, and bought clothes from a second-hand shop in town. My form of teenage rebellion was to cover every part of me. I thought if I dressed overly modestly, then perhaps no one would notice that my mom barely wore any clothes. The men loved my mom, and the women held onto their men more closely because of her. All of high school, I lived in baggy men's sweatshirts and sweatpants. It became my uniform.

Her RV massages for cash didn't help with the optics of my mother. I heard the rumors of my mom's sexual prowess. When I addressed them with her, she laughed and reminded me that she's a single woman, never has relationships with men already in relationships, and is always safe. As far as some of the other rumors about her, she told me not to give them any attention.

Kids could be cruel, though; I hated feeling like I had to defend her. As the years went on, she kept having fewer reasons to stay. In small towns, rumors are like wildfires. Once they take off, they spread and destroy everything in their path until there is no semblance of what once existed. Or of what is true.

My mom's boyfriends never lasted, which probably had to do with her preaching about the hypocrisy in the archaic ideologies of monogamy, and how we were born to be free. My mom spends her life being so extra, and I've spent my life trying to be invisible. Hiding behind others' eccentricity, physically covering myself, yet sometimes wishing my light could be half as bright as my mom's.

An hour later, we arrive at a boutique store an hour out of town, and it looks spendy and not in my budget.

"Malik," I say. "Everything is so expensive. I look fine, right?"

He coughs, pushes me through the door, and a bell rings, alerting the overly attentive sales associate that we've arrived.

"Lucky for you, I'm buying you a few outfits. And fine isn't good enough for you. You deserve to sparkle."

I don't waste my breath. I've tried to argue with Malik before. I get the impression that money was never a problem growing up because he has infinite amounts of it. The truth is, his heart is always in the right place, and these capris are that ugly.

"Besides, I have no boyfriend to spend it on currently, so I'd rather make all of your dreams come true." Malik eyes a few hanging outfits.

"With clothes?" I argue as he grabs dress after dress off the rack.

"Never underestimate the power of nice clothes." A smile spreads across his entire face.

Malik hands me a few dresses, and I shut the door. I peel my capris off and throw them over the door. Once I have the first dress on, I let him see me.

"You may not realize this, Carrie," he says, standing behind me, assessing the first sundress I try on. "But you've been a different person lately. You're talking to people, creating real friendships, and playing basketball with the town hottie, practically naked, I want to add. You're coming into your own and need the wardrobe to match your new confidence."

Malik is right. He's always right. Cancer forced me to face my invincibility in ways I've never done before. And just because I'm in remission doesn't mean it's gone. This rational fear is always lurking right over my shoulder, and with one bad test, I'm back in the hospital, on a chemo drip, promising all the higher powers that I'll live better. Do more. Be more.

"Damn, Juniper," I say, looking in the full-length mirror. "She was right."

"About what?" Malik puts his hand on my shoulder and addresses the strap.

"She used to preach to me about clothes, always telling me that how I present myself is the first thing people will see before they get to know my insides. She was right. I feel, well, pretty."

"You look like a Grecian goddess." He fans his face to dry fake tears. "That white against your skin and your auburn hair. You're going to turn heads."

I don't just feel pretty. I feel beautiful. The wide straps covers my port scar and come down, creating a deep V that shows cleavage. Actual cleavage. The elastic sinches at my waist, and the white fabric flows to my ankles, with a split up past my knee on the left side. I spin and feel light and airy. Malik grabs my arms and puts them at my side so I can't hide anymore. This dress feels like me— like a woman who doesn't need to hide or have the town's approval or someone who is still being judged because of my mom's decisions.

"I feel beautiful." I spin again in front of the mirror.

A pretty dress doesn't change everything; it probably

doesn't even change anything, but I feel confident. For now, that's enough.

"Oh, honey." Now, Malik has actual tears welling in his eyes. "You look beautiful."

Labor Day weekend in Wheaton always feels like the end of something great. The weather becomes cooler, fewer people come to town to enjoy all that Lake Traverse offers, and everything seems to move slower. The summer fishing crew leaves, and a few hunters move in for the colder months.

That's why the town gathers this weekend. For the past couple of years, Malik and I have gone to Jake's lake parties, now hosted by Jake and Camilla. Dax's brother probably has the best place on the entire lake, helped by the millions he made as a professional football player. Not only is his house incredible, but he has every kind of lake toy a person would want. Dax built a house on the property next to Jake's, and I realize I've never seen his place.

We aren't even close to the first people to arrive when we get here in the late afternoon. Cars line the driveway, including the gravel road that leads to the Bergland cottage owned by Camilla's family. There are at least fifty people standing around, and a group gathers on the lawn and plays volleyball. Coolers line their house and music blares from speakers on a table. I get out of Malik's car and smooth out my white dress.

In my imagination, heads turn toward me as I walk through the grass, my dress blowing in the wind. But the reality is that people look at me because they often don't see me in something other than a t-shirt and shorts.

"Have you seen Carrie?"

I hear a voice in my ear and turn around to see Dax,

the one person I want more than anyone to see me. Because, as fate would have it, I usually only run into people I'm interested in when I go grocery shopping in my pajamas.

He kisses my cheek. "Look at you. You look—"

My nerves don't let him finish. "Yeah, I figured I'd wear something white as Monday is Labor Day, and you know the rules around white after that day and all."

Dax chuckles and shakes his head. I reach into my purse and pop in a starburst. I always eat them in order from the least favorite to favorite. I allow myself four a day, and I've already eaten the yellow, so pink is next. It started as a nervous habit but has turned into an indulgence.

"I won't even pretend to know what you're talking about," Dax says with a smile. But his long one-over glance at me has my skin covered in goosebumps.

"You know, Carrie . . ." He runs a hand through his hair. "I'm willing to help you with the B&B. I feel bad that you brought in Trey. I know school starts Tuesday for me, but really, I'm happy to help. I want to help."

I reach into one of the coolers to grab myself a drink. "I appreciate that, but I'm good. Trey said he'd paint the place, and Jake will walk through it with me because I think I may need to convert a closet to a bathroom to create an additional ensuite."

"Fine," Dax concedes. "But I'm helping Malik with the floors."

"Deal." We smile at each other, and his cheek dimple on the right side pops out. Neither of us looks away, and I keep my eyes upward toward his face, even though gravity wants to bring them down to his chest and the missing buttons on his shirt.

Dax gets called inside, and I'm only standing for a moment before Trey joins me. I've known Trey for years.

He is around Dax's age and lived in a neighboring town. We'd play against his team in sports, and Trey seemed to be in every sport offered. This is the gift, or curse, depending on how you look at it, of growing up in a small area. Like most people in this town, I've stayed under their radar, but now he's being so kind to me I almost wonder if he remembers who I am. Scary Carrie. That's how people referred to me as a child. Although, being older and from a neighboring town, maybe he doesn't remember me at all.

"Hey, Carrie." He throws his arm around me like we're long-time friends.

"Hey." My body stiffens at his touch. "It's good to see you."

I'm not sure how many words of his I hear because all I see is Dax walking back outside and heading toward a tree where a woman waits. Her identity is not what's important as she stands there smiling and laughing at something Dax says. It's this very moment, not the one of me jumping him in Jake's bathroom, not the one of us playing basketball and making out on a dare, but this one that lets me know that my feelings for Dax growing up may have been ridiculous because I didn't even know him. Not really. But my feelings now, they're real.

Dax towers over the woman he talks to, and they seem to converse easily. Dax laughs as he brushes his hand through his already tousled hair. I want to be that hand. I want to be his blue shirt, touching his chest, the hard muscles that extend to his abs and the faint line of hair that leads beneath his pants.

Her hand extends out to his chest, and as she rests it there, an overwhelming feeling envelopes me. One that I remember all too well. We don't always get what we want in life. His blue eyes, visible from even here, are a beautiful contrast against his skin.

"What do you think?" Trey asks, turning me to him. I

realize I haven't heard a thing he's said to me. Time stood still as I watched Dax, jealous that someone else gets to share his space.

"Yeah, sure," I answer, too embarrassed to admit I haven't been listening.

Trey beams and puts his hand on my arm. "Great. I'll pick you up at seven on Thursday. They have the best food."

"Okay." I muster a weak smile. I'm going somewhere on Thursday, at seven, with Trey, and I have no idea where. My white dress made its mark, only not on the right person.

The moment the sun dips behind the hills across the lake, the fireworks begin. I look around for Malik, wanting to go. But I don't see him anywhere. I rub my hands over the bumps on my arms. The night has turned cool, and no matter how much I try to cover them, I'm not getting any warmer.

"Here, take this." Dax steps beside me, coming out of nowhere. He helps put my arms through his flannel shirt.

"Better?" Dax stands in front of me and rubs my arms.

"Thanks. The temperature must have dropped twenty degrees."

He pulls me down to one of the many blankets sprawled on the grass and looks up at the fireworks, close enough that our arms touch. Dax presses his knees into his body, and a shiver escapes him. I try to give his flannel back, but he refuses.

"Is it that easy for you?" I ask, out of the blue, and he turns to me. His hair falls in front of his eye, and he blows it off with a long breath.

"Is what easy for me?" Dax's cheek freckles are visible even in the evening light.

I motion over to the tree, where he stood earlier, to

help him remember. "Talking to girls. Dating. Being so comfortable with people."

Dax chuckles, reaches down, grabs a blade of grass, and puts it between his teeth. He then extends his long legs onto the blanket. Dax is so tall that most of his body hangs off the blanket. "Talking to women. Yes. But dating, not so much."

"That's right," I remember. "You're more of a casual kind of guy. Get their hopes up that maybe you're different from the rest, then leave them. I almost forgot."

Dax turns to me. "I've never led anyone on. Women know what they get with me and what they don't. I've never hidden that from anyone."

"Sorry, Dax," I shake my head, unable to let it go. "But it sounds miserable. For you and the women who get in bed with you and pretend it's enough but hoping you'll change your mind afterward."

Dax looks at me expressionless but moves his face so close to mine that I can smell his aftershave. "Do you want to know what the sad part is? Being madly in love with someone who is gone forever but whose face I look at every single day in my daughter's." I squirm, unable to get comfortable and unsure of what to say. "Dax, I'm—"

"If hanging out with another consenting adult helps me not feel this gut-wrenching pain, then that's my choice. Who are you to judge?"

Dax puts space between us, and I hug my knees and shiver as we watch the rest of the fireworks in silence. Clarity comes to me with relief and pain, and my realization has both of these things wrapped into the same truth. Dax Abram will never be mine.

"I'm outta here." Dax stands. He doesn't glance at me as he walks away. It's moments like this that make me miss the girl I used to be who never said what was on my mind.

"Dax," I call out after him, but he's already gone.

Chapter Eight

Dax

Morning hits with an abruptness. I'm asleep, dead to the world until I'm not. My eyes pop open, and my first instinct is to pat the space in the bed beside me. It's empty. Sadness floods me at once. Mornings continue to be the worst part of the day for me. Sleep allows escape, and when my eyes dart open, there is a moment of peace until the grief engulfs me. Nights are easier because sleep is imminent, but mornings mean I still have an entire day to survive. I often worry that it's the same for Kylie when she wakes up and remembers that her mom isn't here.

Even though Georgie from Rosso practically threw herself at me at last night's party and told me in no uncertain terms that she was mine if I wanted her, I still went home alone, as I usually do. I've never felt it's my responsibility to dispel or even address the rumors. Where there's smoke, there's fire, and although I haven't earned all the talk that has come my way, I also haven't been celibate since moving back to Wheaton. But I've been honest about where my head's at with everyone, and most importantly, I've made sure never to bring anyone around Kylie.

I lie in bed, scrolling through memories on my phone. Zari and I's college graduation, our engagement at the Sculpture Gardens in Minneapolis, our trips to Europe, and our African safari. Everything felt easy with her. We never ran out of things to say, we loved going on adventures or sitting home watching movies with takeout, and we knew this was our forever. I didn't plan to meet the woman of my dreams the first week of Freshman year, but that's what happened. Me on the basketball team, and Zari on the track team.

We didn't have a long enough relationship to go through some of the normal trials that couples experience. She was diagnosed with cancer when we were still experiencing marital bliss. Kylie was still a baby. In long relationships, there are more opportunities to remove the rose-colored glasses and see our person as a flawed, imperfect human. I was never able to see Zari like that. That's one of the issues when relationships end abruptly instead of running their course. When we lose someone at the height of our love, there is a long way to fall.

She was zapped from me before she started leaving the bathroom door open when she took a shit. Or before she got annoyed because I went for a morning run instead of feeding Kylie breakfast. I was a widower before any of her habits bothered me. When she left this world, I was as madly in love with her as I was the day I met her. More.

Self-pity is what my mind craves, but my body needs something else. So instead of lying here for another minute, I get out of bed and pull on a pair of shorts. I go to the bathroom, brush my teeth, and wash away last night's whiskey. I take a long glance at myself. I look as heavy as I feel. I strap on my running shoes, ready to run on the country roads, before heading to town to pick up Kylie at my parent's house.

I push my door open and nearly collide with Carrie as she holds her hand out.

"Carrie," I say, surprised to see her.

"Dax." Carrie raises her hand over her chest. She looks as spooked as me. "I was just about to knock."

Carrie's hair is in a high ponytail, and I glance down at her shorts and sneakers.

"What's up?" I place my hands on my hips.

Carrie assaults her bottom lip with her teeth. "I was hoping to talk."

I glance at her outfit again, and with only slight hesitation, I offer, "I'm headed for a run. Care to join me?"

Carrie looks down the driveway and then pulls her leg back in a stretch. "Yeah."

We start in a slow jog when we reach the gravel road. We head up the long driveway and then get to the blacktop highway. We run side by side until we hear a vehicle approach, and then Carrie drops behind me. It's a quiet morning, with a small headwind, birds circling overhead, and Carrie's breathing beside me.

After a mile, we reach the county park, and I decide to turn into it. Carrie follows me as I take the winding roads through the pathway. Carrie is the first person I've run with since Zari. Zari was fast and had so much endurance that sometimes I felt like I couldn't keep up with her. Carrie lets me take the lead, but our paces are similar.

The park is filled with RVs and tents, camping for the last weekend of the summer. Everyone wakes up, a few kids play on the playground, and people stand around a fire pit. I pause to catch my breath in front of the park's sandy beach. The whisky sifts through my pores.

Carrie puts her hands on her knees and takes deep breaths. When she looks at me, words pour out of her mouth. "I'm so sorry about what I said last night. I feel—"

"Not necessary." I wave her off before she has a chance to finish.

"I have to," she continues. "I was projecting. Last night wasn't even about you. I'm super sensitive about casual sex, but what you do is none of—"

"Carrie," I cut her off again. "We don't have to do this."

"Yes, we do." She turns to me and plops herself down on the sand. Her face is red, and her breathing is still heavy from the jog. She doesn't look at me when she speaks her next words. "My struggles aren't your struggles."

"Yeah, I know." Carrie is going to cross a threshold. A boundary that I've had up. And not just with women. But with everyone. I don't let people close anymore. It's easier this way.

"I was raised by a single mom. Hell, I don't even know who my dad is." Carrie continues to look at the lake instead of me. "And she made so many mistakes. Now, you're raising Kylie as a single dad, and I don't know, I feel protective of her, even though I have no doubt you're an amazing dad. Who you sleep with is not my business."

"You don't know who your dad is?" I look at her and should be offended by everything she said to me, but instead, I find myself curious about her.

She shakes her head. "No. My mom took her RV from the Southwest to Wheaton and showed up pregnant. According to her, there are a couple of options for potential fathers. She said neither is worthy, though. So classy."

"You don't have to share this with me." My voice comes out soft, and I sit next to Carrie in the sand. I pick up handfuls of it and let it sift through my fingers.

"I know." Carrie lies back. "Sometimes I feel triggered. It's so stupid."

I lie back too. The sun shines on my face, and I shut

my eyes and enjoy the warmth.

Carrie shades her face from the sun. "Anyway, this is my long way of saying that your life isn't my business, and I had no right to be all preachy to you."

"Apology accepted." I stand up, brush the sand off my body, and then remove my socks and shoes. "Also," I continue, feeling like I need to say it. "I always thought your mom was great. A breath of fresh air in a sometimes-suffocating town."

Carrie stands up and also removes her shoes and socks. She walks into the lake, takes her hands, and splashes water over her legs. When her eyes meet mine, there is sadness behind them. I don't know if it's something I said or the memory she's conjuring. "My mom is on her fourth husband, and I don't even bother to learn his name because this one won't last either. Whatever. This isn't about my mom. I'm just trying to explain why I snapped."

I go a bit deeper in the water. The surface is already warm, but each layer of water underneath is colder. Everyone talked about Carrie's mom when we were growing up. Juniper Soleta was no average woman. She'd wear crocheted bras and flowing skirts with flower crowns in her hair. She'd park her RV behind the Main Street café and offer massages and hemp products.

Juniper's beauty was memorable. She didn't look like the other moms. Her hair stretched long on her back, reddish-brown. And there were always rumors about her. But my parents reminded me that small towns could be unforgiving and sources of misinformation, so I shouldn't believe everything I hear. It never occurred to me how much this would have affected Carrie, but honestly, Carrie was never on my radar at all.

"I never knew you were so talkative," I say, and Carrie gives me the smile I was hoping for. "I always had you pegged as more of the quiet, introspective type."

"I have a lot to say," she says.

Carrie having a lot to say surprises me. I've always found her simple. Not in a bad way, but in an uncomplicated way. She's also more of an observer than an active participant, and she's never been one to speak her mind so freely, at least not around me.

I fall back into the water and let it run up over me until I'm fully submerged. The salty sweat runs down my face and into my mouth. "This feels great." I look at the few clouds that have come overhead. "Join me."

Carrie only hesitates for a moment and squeals as she dives headfirst into the water. We float, side by side, looking at the sun's shadows through the rows of weeping willows along the shore.

"I am sorry." Carrie looks at me. She floats on the water of the calm lake, and her hair stretches behind her.

"Me too." I press my open palm against her belly, causing her to submerge underwater for a moment.

"Also." I look at her. "I know it's none of my business, but I'm sure your mom wasn't as bad as you remember her."

Carrie walks back to shore, sits at the edge of the lake where it meets the sand, and lets the waves from a passing boat cover her legs. "Life didn't suck, but with every decision I make in life, I ask myself, 'What would Juniper do?' And then I do the opposite."

I sit in deeper water but press my feet against hers. A smile sneaks up on my face as I remember Juniper. "Your mom was super hot."

Carrie lunges at me before I have a chance to react, and she catches me off balance and straddles me but holds my head up to keep the water from going into my mouth.

"Watch out, Dax Abram," she says. "She's coming for a visit soon, and you are exactly her type."

Carrie relaxes her grip, which allows me to grab both of her wrists, and I flip her, so now I'm on top, holding her head above the water. Her hair flows with the current, and as I look down at her laughing, full peach lips, and straight white teeth, grinning from ear to ear, I know it's only a matter of time before every man between twenty and fifty takes one look at her, and recognizes the beauty in her.

Some man. Not me.

Carrie's beauty comes softly. Some people command all your attention the moment they walk through a room, only to become duller as time goes on. Carrie is the opposite. The more you look at her, the more attractive she becomes. She's like a Monet painting. Upon first glance, the colors appear muted and the painting seems simple. But the longer you look, the more details, like colors, landscapes, and beauty, come into focus. They were always there, but you had to study the painting to see them.

"Are we good?" Carrie asks, still underneath my body.

"If you let me dunk your head underwater, we'll be even."

Carrie closes her eyes and waits for it. I lean down like I'm going to take her head and dunk it. Instead of submerging her, I take my wet lips, kiss her cheek, and pull her to her feet.

We walk instead of jogging back to my place, where I need to change clothes and where Carrie's car is parked. With the sun high in the sky, it doesn't take long for my clothes to dry.

"With school starting Tuesday, my week will be crazy, but what are your thoughts on practicing Thursday night?"

Carrie puts her hands on her hips and bites at her cheek. Her face flushes. "I'm not free Thursday."

"What's up that day?" I ask, knowing she doesn't work one of her odd jobs on Thursday evenings.

"I think I may have agreed to go on a date with Trey."

"May have?" I raise my eyebrows.

"I wasn't really listening to his question, but I distinctly remember hearing him say he'd pick me up at seven."

"Looks like you have a date," I say.

"Yeah." Carrie fidgets with her hands. "I haven't had one in forever, so it should be interesting."

"Okay, then," I say as we reach my house. Carrie stops at her car, and I turn to her as I walk toward my house. "Let's be in touch about other days that would work."

"Got it." Carrie smiles. "And Dax?"

"No need to say it again." I throw up my hand without looking at her.

But she yells, "I am sorry."

Chapter Nine

Carrie

"My grandma used to make these cinnamon rolls in Norway," Sis says, licking the spoon and throwing it in the sink. "All the neighborhood kids would smell them from the open window and come to the door, hoping she'd have enough for them."

Sis takes the pan and puts it in the oven, and I dip my fingers into the extra icing before washing them. Sis makes the best cinnamon rolls I've ever had. She missed her calling not having a bakery. I pour us tea, and we sit at the kitchen table.

"Mom kept the tradition alive when we moved here. Every Saturday morning, she'd make enough pans for the entire block," Sis continues to reminisce.

"I know you don't share the recipe with many people, but I'd love to put these on my bed and breakfast menu. I could call them Sis's famous cinnamon rolls or something cleverer than that."

I've never had a creative bone in my body. I'll need a lot of help to make things at the bed and breakfast special.

"Oh dear." Sis laughs. "I don't have a recipe written down, but you've been watching me make them."

I jump up and grab a pen and paper from a drawer. I start writing down the steps we've already done. I want to build up enough recipes that my B&B guests who stay awhile will never have the same breakfast twice. Cooking and baking with Sis has been so good for me, but it's also been great for her. Everything we make together sparks a memory of Norway, something a grandparent or parent made growing up. Sis enjoys living in the past, and I love the richness of her stories.

After putting Sunny and Sis down for their afternoon nap, I fire up my laptop and look through my finances. The costs of getting the B&B updated have been minimal so far, but there is still so much to do. It isn't just going to be a B&B. It's also going to be my home.

I'd love to be able to pull back from my hours at the bank if I could still stay insured. I wish I could only work two days for Sunny and Sis Bergland and then focus solely on the Bed and Breakfast. I also want to start living there in the next month or two. I've been so dedicated on the main floor that I've barely worked on the second floor. The monthly income I get from Camilla renting my Main Street store does help, but it isn't much.

Most of my money goes to the costs of furnishing the B&B. I plan to have two queen beds, and then the other two bedrooms will have double beds and bunk beds. I'll need dressers and nightstands, and I need to start thinking about the outside space. Occupants will expect access to a boat, kayaks, canoes, and the like. I have none of those things.

When I lay out the plan in my head, my dream seems so attainable. But other times, the remaining projects, the cost of utilities, and running a profitable business seem daunting. After my day with Sunny and Sis, I go home, shower, wait for Malik to get home and dress me for my date with Trey, which could be challenging, considering I have no idea where I'm going.

"Oh, good." Malik walks into my room and looks at my outfit. "No capris."

"Nope. I got a new pair of jeans." I turn and show him my backside. "They feel so tight."

"That's because they actually fit." Malik admires my entire ensemble.

"Is it terrible that I want to call Trey and tell him I have a headache and can't go?" I look at myself in the mirror.

"No. Not terrible. You may hit it off, and if not, meet up with Dax and me at the pool hall. We'll shoot hoops and then head for a drink."

I rest my head against Malik as we walk out of my room. "Why now? Trey has known me for years. And now he wants to take me on a date? It isn't tracking for me."

"It was the white dress, Carrie. The white dress." Malik stands behind me as I glance in the mirror again. "Seriously, though, you've emerged as this new woman. People are noticing."

"No white dress has that much power."

Malik places his hands on my shoulder. "I'm not going to pretend why now men are realizing the catch that you are."

I pull at my shirt, and when I see the car pull into the driveway, Malik and I walk out together, me to go out with Trey and Malik to meet Dax at the gym. Oh, how I'd rather be going to the gym tonight. Or on a date with Dax.

When I get into the car, I breathe a sigh of relief that Trey is dressed similarly to me in jeans.

"Hey, there." He shoots me a warm smile. "I hope

you're hungry."

"I am," I say, and he drives on the road out of town, so I assume we're going to Dale's Steakhouse, which I haven't been to in ages.

The car ride is mostly silent. I try to think of the last date I've been on, but then my brain hurts from how far back I have to go. It's been a while. And I'm terrible on dates. I'm awkward, shy, clumsy, and all of the things that send men running in the opposite direction.

We both order a glass of red wine.

"How's the B&B coming?" Trey asks as he butters his bread.

"It's slow," I respond. "I need to sit down and make a list of what's left to do. Things are moving forward, but everything takes so much time."

A waitress takes our orders, and we settle into more small talk. Trey is nice looking, although not my usual type. He's my height, perhaps even an inch shorter. And he has more hair on his face than on his head. Trey rolls up the sleeve of his blue shirt, and his hairy forearms come into view. His arms look like he's done a lot of manual labor. They're muscular, much like the rest of him.

"How's your health?" Trey asks, "I mean, since the cancer and everything."

Subtle.

"Good." I stuff bread into my mouth. When I'm done chewing, I say, "I go back in a couple of months for my one-year scans. But I feel great."

"That's good." He smiles at the waitress as she puts our steaks in front of us. "You look good with hair."

"Yeah." I run my hand through it. "It feels good not to be bald." I smile, but he doesn't.

Why am I not better at this? Why can't I be as comfortable around Trey as I am around Malik?

Everything I say sounds forced. And stupid.

I start counting in my head how many times the word good is thrown around. Conversing with someone shouldn't be this difficult, yet here we are, talking about cancer and me not being bald again.

The entire dinner feels like this. I spend more time trying to come up with something to say next that I don't enjoy my steak and barely register any of the things Trey says. When he speaks, all I do is plan how to respond instead of listening to him. When the bill comes, I'm relieved that I've nearly survived this night.

"Do you want to go to the pool hall for a nightcap?" Trey asks me as he puts down his credit card.

I look at the time, knowing that Malik and Dax will probably be there. "Umm, Sure." No part of me wants to extend this date, but saying no feels rude.

The pool hall is full. People sidle up to the bar and spill out onto the remaining tables. The sun has set, and it's dark inside, the floor is sticky, and the music is loud. It's Thursday, almost the weekend, and everyone in town seems to be breathing easier that we've almost made it through the week.

When we open the door, everyone looks up from their drink or conversation to glance at us and then return to what they're doing. A popular song by an artist I should be able to name, but can't, blasts from the jukebox.

"There's Dax and Malik," Trey says, and we walk toward their table. I can't wait to be around people I can converse with easily.

They sit at a high top in their t-shirts and shorts, clearly coming from the gym.

"What did I miss at practice tonight?" I look at Dax and Malik as I take one of the empty chairs.

"Dax and I played some one-on-one." Malik grins. "Dax said he had more fun playing with you."

All eyes are on me, including Trey's, and I look at Dax with raised eyebrows. I told Malik about Dax and I's game of truth or dare, and by both of their reactions, Malik shared with Dax that he knows.

"I'm sure he did."

Dax glances at me, and his eyes rake my legs and chest before he moves his eyes to Trey. "How was dinner? Where'd you take her?"

"We went to Dale's. Thought we'd come here for a drink." Trey flags down a server.

When the server walks by him, without glancing in our table's direction, Trey gets up to go to the bar and asks me what I'd like.

"I'll have a beer," I say to him. "Whatever you're having."

"I'll be right back. I need to go say hi to a buddy." Malik gets up without looking at us.

As I take Dax in, my body fills with heat. His hair is tied up in the most perfect man bun, and his elbows rest on the table as he looks at me. I've barely seen him all week now that the school year has started, and although I know it's a waste of energy, I can't help how hard I'm crushing on him. Being with Trey is a waste when Dax is in the room.

"How was the date?" Dax asks, holding a beer mug between his hands. "You and Trey hit it off?"

I tilt my head and turn around to see Trey still at the bar. "It was fine."

Dax throws his head back and laughs. "That's what every man wants to hear after a date. That the lady had a fine time."

"What am I supposed to say?" I lean forward, elbows pressed into the table.

"Oh, I don't know, Carrie." Dax grins. "You can't wait

to get out of here to be alone with him. You hope he asks you out again."

"Well." I rest my head on my fists. "I barely ate my food because I was nervous, so now I'm starving. I can't remember what Trey said the entire night because I was so busy figuring out what I should say next, and I was my normal awkward self. So, yeah, the date was fine."

Dax reaches into his wallet on the table and pulls out a quarter. He darts out of his chair and hollers over the music, "Be right back."

He walks to one of the candy machines in the corner next to the popcorn machine and returns to the table with a handful of starbursts.

"I know you only allow yourself four a day. What color are you on?"

I glance up, and Dax is smiling. "Orange."

Dax places the orange candy in my hand. It's the second to last one I eat every day. I save red, the best, for right before I brush my teeth each night. I squeeze his hand, unwrap the starburst, and pop it into my mouth. I should be embarrassed by my daily ritual of eating Starbursts, but I'm not. I'm more flattered that Dax remembers.

"You've saved my life, and you don't even know it," I say, savoring the sweetness of the candy.

"Oh, hi." Dax looks up as I start to say something else. A pretty blond woman approaches our table and sits on his knee.

"Hey, handsome. I was hoping you'd be here," she says to Dax. Something shifts in him as his body stiffens.

"Sorry to be rude." Dax looks in my direction. "This is Josie. She just moved here from Iowa and had the unlucky task of giving me my latest haircut."

Josie leans into Dax as she continues to sit on his

knee. Her eyes meet mine. "Nice to meet you."

She looks comfortable, but I sense he doesn't want her there. If she recently moved here, how well can she know him anyway? Josie leans into him.

"Carrie, I'm Carrie," I fumble the words. My face is on fire, and my heart feels like it's betrayed me.

Malik has often asked me why I don't tell people how I feel. It's because of moments like this. The thoughtfulness of getting me my favorite candy momentarily made me lose my mind, and I could have easily poured my heart out to Dax, not knowing that a pretty blonde was meeting him. Or did they randomly run into each other? She is pretty. Her short hair frames her face, and her dark brown eyes pop.

"Do you want to get out of here?" Josie asks Dax, but I don't see or hear his response. Instead, I watch Trey approach with our drinks.

"Sorry it took so long." Trey hands me a beer. "It's busy tonight."

I'm nothing more than an observer as everyone sits and conversates. Josie pulls up a chair, Malik returns to our table, and the five of us sit around and talk. Well, they talk. I watch. I don't do well in groups. I tend to disappear. But after tonight, I don't think I do that well one on one either.

She's all over Dax and fiddles with his man bun. I don't know how people can do casual so well. How can Dax kiss me, even if it was a game of truth or dare, and then be out with someone else? That's not me. Or maybe I have it better. She's going to sleep with Dax and be out of his life. But me, I'll still get to be here. Maybe I have a better piece of him than she does.

"I'm tired," I say, and all eyes look at me as I get up. Trey also stands. "Trey, why don't I save you a trip to my place? Malik can bring me home." I look at Malik, and he nods.

"I'm going there, anyway," Malik says.

"It's alright." Trey shrugs. "I can drive you. Let me finish my drink first."

"No, no," Malik says, saving me, in a way only a best friend can. "Carrie and I had some B&B business to discuss, so I'll take her."

"As long as I can take you home next time," Trey says, and I nod.

"Can you swing me by my parents'?" Dax stands. "I need to get Kylie home and in bed."

"You got it." Malik nods, and I don't miss Josie's shoulders drop in disappointment.

We say our goodbyes, I get in the back seat of Malik's car, and Dax gets in front. We drive to his parents' house, where his car is parked. Malik and Dax talk basketball in the front, and I stare at the back of Dax's head, and my mind tries to process the hundred of thoughts that pop in my brain at once.

I get out of the car to get in the front seat.

"Here." Dax holds out his hand. I look down at the red starburst he placed there. His fingers graze mine as he lets go.

"My favorite." I unwrap it before I can consider saving it for later.

"And mine." We look at each other, and I know he's in the middle of the bathroom memory, just as I am. "I have a question for you, Carrie."

Hope flutters around my heart. Maybe Dax left the pool hall with Malik and me because he wanted to be alone with me—he wanted to ask me out. He laces his fingers together and glances at me.

"Ask," I say, happy that it's dark because I feel my face flush.

"Well, I know Fridays are your short days at the bank. Is there any chance you could pick Kylie up after school? This week? Like, tomorrow?"

My heart drops, but I hide my disappointment.

"Yeah," I say. "Is everything okay?"

"Yes, but I have a teacher meeting, and my mom is in Fargo all day, and Camilla and Jake are headed out of town tomorrow morning. Jenna is out of town, and my dad sees patients all day tomorrow, and—"

"Dax," I interrupt. "It's fine. Put me on whatever list there is at the school, and I'll be there at three."

"Ever since being back in Wheaton, I've never had a situation where everyone who loves her is busy. And it will look bad if I flake on tomorrow's teacher meeting. School just started, but I already feel like I'm working fewer hours than—"

"I'm not busy. And I'd love to pick Kylie up," I say again.

"I owe you. Big time." Dax gives me a brief hug. "Honestly, Carrie, I'm so happy to have you as a friend."

The word stings me. Dax gives me a playful punch on the shoulder before walking away.

Before Malik has a chance to ask me about my date, I say, "Not interested in Trey."

Malik turns at the end of the road to head to his place. "But that hug with Dax looked like something."

"Oh, you mean with the guy who just had a woman sitting on his lap and staring longingly at him?" I look out the window. "Nope. I'm afraid not."

"Well, I like who you are around Dax." Malik rounds the corner. "You're you, Carrie. Sweet, sarcastic, quirky. The list of people you let see the real you is so small."

"I love you, Malik," I say as we pull into his driveway. "But I was doing fine. Now I've started to crush on the guy again, and I already sense it's leading to heartache. I don't have it in me."

Malik takes my hand as we walk inside. "Or it's leading to something beautiful."

Chapter Ten

Dax

CARRIE MEETS ME AT KYLIE'S first-grade classroom promptly at three.

"Thank you, thank you, thank you." I take her hand in mine. "Again, I owe you. Name it. Anything." Gratitude pours out of me.

Kylie walks out with her class, single-file, everyone looking for the parents who will take them home after the first week of school. Carrie stares at me longer than she usually does. I adjust my glasses that I had to wear today because my contacts were irritating the shit out of my eyes. Her mouth opens slightly and then she moves away from me.

Carrie waves at Kylie, who smiles and runs to her. I see how I rank in this. "Dax, honestly, I had nothing else going on. We'll head to your place and see you after your meeting. No rush."

"You're good?" I ask one more time, squeezing Kylie's shoulders. Then, I squeeze her hands and pull my girl into another hug.

"Daddy, we'll be fine." Kylie holds me and Carrie's

hands at the same time.

I've kept the orbit around Kylie small since Zari died. She's mostly with my family, Zari's, and then she has some people around town that she knows well. Kylie has always been around Carrie, but today feels different because it's only Carrie. Usually, it's Auntie Carrie and Uncle Malik.

The teacher meeting seems to take forever, and time stands still as I incessantly check the wall clock. We report on the first week of school. Highs, lows, what we need to watch out for, and what we can do to make the days go smoother.

Every teacher has a story they want to share from their week, and when the clock hits five, I start to get antsy. I want to be at home, talking to Kylie about her first week of school. I don't know if it's being a single dad or if all parents feel this way. But having a child, I feel like my heartbeat is always outside my body, and I'm never in the right place if I'm not with her. At five-thirty, the meeting wraps up, and I rush to my car and drive home. The sun is low in the sky and sets further south than usual.

My hurry isn't because I don't trust Carrie, yet, gravity pulls me out here like I don't remember happening before. I want to be with them. I walk through my front door to a waft of deliciousness. I need to know that Kylie is happy and taken care of.

Kylie runs to me and grabs my leg. "Daddy, you're home!"

Carrie turns and waves as she stirs something on the stovetop.

"I am. And what are you ladies cooking? It smells so good."

"Me and Carrie went to the grocery store, Daddy," Kylie says proudly. "And then she taught me how to cook spaghetti and meatballs, and we even made you dessert, but that part's a surprise."

"A home-cooked meal." I walk into the kitchen. I open the saucepan, go to dip my finger in, and Carrie slaps my hand. "Yum."

"No peeking. It will be ready in five minutes. Will you help Kylie set the table?" Carrie once again glances at me. It's got to be the glasses. I take them off, wipe my eyes, and then put them back on. I'm blind without them.

Kylie runs over to me, grabs my leg, and pulls me toward the table. Friday nights have become very predictable in our household. I either stop and get Kylie fast food on our way home from town or pop chicken nuggets into the oven. I give her strawberries and green beans to supplement the meal and help with my guilt. We then plop in front of the TV, and Kylie picks a show while I catch up on emails and texts on my phone.

This Friday night is so much better. Eating a homecooked meal at a table is something we haven't done in a while. When Kylie and I moved to Wheaton, my mom cooked for us constantly, but I finally had to ask her to stop. Camilla also brings us food, but I want to be self-sufficient, so I try to ration the help I receive from others. Which means Kylie is one nugget short of becoming one.

I set the table with Kylie, and Carrie brings the food to the table. There's a salad, her homemade bread that I think about for an inappropriate amount since I tried it for the first time, and her spaghetti and meatballs. She dishes us up, and I go into the fridge and grab a bottle of wine.

"Does the cook allow us to drink with the meal?" I hold up the bottle for Carrie.

"You do you." Carrie grabs her purse. "We're in your house."

"Wait." I grasp Carrie's wrist. "Aren't you staying?"

Carrie pauses and looks at me.

"Please, Carrie, you have to stay." Kylie pulls her arm.

Kylie looks up at me, and we are desperate, grabbing at Carrie's arms, begging her to stay with us. She looks around before she puts her purse down and grabs another plate from the cupboard.

"I figured—" Carrie blows out a breath. "Of course, I'll stay."

Kylie claps her hands together. I love every moment I'm able to spend with Kylie, but adult conversation over wine sounds amazing as well.

The smell doesn't do the food justice. It's hands-down the most incredible pasta I've ever had. I open a white wine bottle, pour Carrie and me a glass, and Kylie drinks her spicy water, which is what she calls sparkling water.

"Where'd you learn how to cook, Carrie?" A noodle sticks in the large gap between Kylie's two front teeth. "It's yummy."

"Well." Carrie puts her napkin on the table. "Can you believe it, but my mom didn't know how to cook. And I love to eat good food, so I decided to teach myself. I went to the library and got books on cooking, and then I experimented with different recipes until I perfected them. Once I got good, I'd cook all the meals for the two of us."

"You cooked for your mommy?" Kylie asks, eyes bright.

"Every meal." Carrie takes a sip of her wine and smiles at Kylie. "I bet your mommy was a really good cook."

Kylie's eyes light up, and I'm happy that Carrie finds a way to bring Zari into the conversation. So many people avoid talking about her like it will make us sad. But the people acting like she never existed hurt us the most.

"My mommy was the best cook. She liked the spicy food. But Daddy doesn't know how to cook at all."

Carrie stifles a laugh and looks at me. "Well, no one can do everything, right, Kylie?"

"Right," she agrees. "Daddy knows how to do other stuff pretty good."

After dinner, Kylie whispers something to Carrie and then Carrie pulls an apple pie out of the oven.

"I taught Kylie how to make a Grandma Sis apple pie. Which is a very secretive, exclusive recipe. Never to be shared with anyone. Under any circumstances."

Kylie looks so happy, doing normal family things, learning how to cook, and being around another woman who isn't a relative. I've tried to convince myself that I can be everything she needs, but I know I can't. My mom helps so much, and my sister Jenna. My sister-in-law Camilla has become one of Kylie's favorite people, but it still doesn't matter. Kylie needs this level of normal every day. Not only when I have a meeting and need to phone a friend.

I insist that Carrie and Kylie relax, and I do clean-up duty. Carrie made plenty of food, so I put the leftovers in Tupperware and stuff it in the refrigerator. Kylie gets her dolls, and Carrie sits on the floor and plays with her. Kylie walks into the kitchen and grabs at my pants.

"Can Carrie spend the night?" She says it loud enough for Carrie to hear, and we lock eyes. Carrie's face blushes, and I clear my throat.

"I'm sure Carrie wants to sleep in her bed, but if you ask her, maybe she'll stay until bedtime."

Kylie nods, satisfied by that response, and I hope Carrie doesn't have plans. Kids have a way of making things awkward but don't know they are doing it.

I pop the popcorn, bathe Kylie, and get her into pajamas, and then Kylie sits between us, and the three of us watch a movie while Carrie and I polish off the bottle of wine. Kylie only stays awake for the first forty-five minutes, and then her head falls into my lap. If I know anything, it's the heaviness of a child's head when they've dozed off. I turn the TV off, pick up Kylie, and carry her to her bedroom.

Carrie stands by the door when I get out of Kylie's bedroom. "I feel like I overstayed," she says, almost in a whisper.

"Overstayed? Hell, if it were up to Kylie, she'd have you spend the night."

Carrie puts her hands over her red cheeks. She's red at the thought of sleeping over. My face even flushes a little.

"Gawd, please stay longer. It's 7:30, and I'd like not to go to bed yet. I kind of feel like a real human person tonight," I joke. Yet, I mean it. The nights after Kylie goes to bed are the quietest. I hate it—almost as much as I hate the quiet mornings.

"If you're sure," Carrie wrings her hands and licks her lips.

I motion to the couch. "I'm sure."

We sit back on the couch, and I make myself a drink, but Carrie declines. She leans her elbow on the back of the sofa, and words pour out of my mouth before I can overthink them.

"You're incredible," I tell her, and my reward is her smile. "Is that a true story about cooking for your mom? You're so self-sufficient. Your childhood sounds so—"

"Traumatic?" she asks.

"No, just different."

Carrie's upbringing was the opposite of mine. Many

say their parents are the best in the world, but mine are.

"Adulthood has made some childhood things come up for me." Carrie shrugs. "But honestly, so much of it was great. My mom took me on adventures. There were no screens, only playing and imagination."

"That does sound nice." I glance at the space between us.. "My mom stayed home with us, and my dad worked long hours. We came home daily to homemade cookies, and a homecooked meal served promptly at six."

"Zari sounds incredible," Carrie says, pivoting the conversation. "I wish I could have met her."

I scroll through my phone and show her pictures. "Yeah, she was the best. Larger than life. She was an athlete like you. Track was her sport. A sprinter. She was something."

"I bet she graduated from college, though, unlike me." Carrie adjusts her body and pulls her leg onto the couch.

"Carrie," I say, tempted to put my hand on hers. But I pull back. "You need to be less self-deprecating."

The stories go on for an hour, and Carrie listens, laughs, and asks me more questions. I share about Zari's Freshman roommate forgetting that she put hardboiled eggs under her bed until it stunk up their entire dorm room. I tell her about our honeymoon in Tanzania, going on a safari, and then traveling to South Africa for an additional week.

By the time I quit talking, Carrie knows Zari almost better than anyone who isn't related to me in this town.

"You would have loved her," I conclude, leaning my head back on the couch.

I'm also aware that I wouldn't be sitting on a couch with Carrie if Zari were still around. Carrie wouldn't have picked Kylie up from school, made us dinner, and watched a movie with us. Carrie can only be here because Zari isn't. And as much as I wish Zari was the one here, the reality of this truth hits me. I love the friendship I'm developing with Carrie, but our friendship and my relationship with Zari wouldn't have simultaneously existed. It couldn't have.

Carrie presses her lips together and whisks her hair behind her ear. "Did you two ever talk about what she wanted for you after she was gone?" My mouth opens, but Carrie puts her hand up. "I'm sorry. Too personal."

"No, no," I say. "We did talk about it. Zari was adamant that I move on. Made me insist on it. As long as the woman would be good for Kylie. Her words. She knew me better than anyone, though. I'm a mate-for-life kind of guy. I imagine she's looking over me, disappointed as fuck."

Carrie licks her peach lips, grabs my drink from my hand, and takes a sip. "What's your sign?"

"My sign?" I lift my head and watch as Carrie's lips touch the glass.

"Your sign," she repeats. "Astrological."

"Capricorn."

She hands the drink back to me and her smile extends across her entire face. "That makes so much sense. And I know I'm going to sound a lot like my mother, but Capricorns have tall, impenetrable walls. But once they let you in, you're in."

"Is that so?" I take a drink.

"It is. Capricorn men are pretty much considered the Eeyores of the zodiac, but I think most are just misunderstood. You're some of the most loyal people in the world, and I bet Zari knew you wouldn't be keen on moving on."

How is Carrie so spot on with all of this, I wonder. Our knees touch, and I don't pull back. "But if she knew the other shit."

"She knows?" Carrie looks down at the couch. "Just don't let your self-reliance get in the way of building relationships. Many think that Capricorns don't have emotional depth. But I think most are simply into self-preservation."

"How do you know all of this?" Instinctually, I put my hand on her knee and she stiffens beneath me, so I pull my hand back.

"My mom may not have taught me to cook, but she taught me many other things, like astrological signs and what sign goes best with a Taurus. You know, to help me on my journey."

"You're a Taurus? What does that mean for you?" I'm intrigued by the conversation. It's one I've never had, and a territory I've never entered.

"Read up on it and let me know if you have questions." Carrie smiles and squeezes my knee before standing up. "I should go. It's late."

The time on my cell says that it's late. Unlike my teacher meeting from earlier, where time didn't move, tonight, time sped on by, like I was robbed of it. I don't want the night to end. I want to hear about what being a Taurus means. I want to learn more about Carrie. She's easy to talk to, interesting, and different from anyone else.

"How can I pay you back?" I ask her as we stand by the door. My arm leans against it.

"No need." Carrie's hand rests on the doorknob.

I push the door open and follow her out the door to walk her to her car. "But what if I want to?" I press further.

We reach her car, and she opens it and leans forward. The moon is directly behind her, and the silhouette of her auburn hair glows.

"If I were you." She flicks a mosquito off my shirt, and she's so close, that I can smell the perfume on her neck. "I'd do the most Capricorn thing you can think of."

Carrie pats my face, gets into her car, and I close it. She rolls down her window, and waves at me. "Have a great weekend."

Back inside, I check on Kylie, who sleeps soundly. I look at the clock again and realize that all I did was talk about myself, Zari, and our life for over two hours. Me, me, me. I barely asked Carrie a question.

I lie back on the couch and start looking up: *how does a Capricorn repay a favor?* The ideas are endless, and I know exactly what I'll do next.

Chapter Eleven

Carrie

"WHAT'S JUNIPER'S ETA?" MALIK ASKS, his legs thrown over mine, a full glass of bourbon in his hand.

I reach to the floor for my glass of wine and turn our TV off. "She said something super specific. She'll be here after the waxing gibbous moon but before the moon turns full."

Malik laughs into his glass, and I pinch his foot. "It's not funny. She's going to show up in her rackety-old RV, and the entire town will start talking before she parks out front of your house."

"What?" Malik sits up. "She's staying here?" He looks around his place, with the open floor plan and modern layout.

"See? Juniper isn't funny when she's in your space." I also sit up and push Malik's legs off me. "And no, she's not staying here. She suggested she'd park the RV at my B&B. I didn't argue with her."

Malik lets out a breath in relief. I feel it too. When I moved back to Wheaton after my Sophomore year of college when I blew out my knee, which ended my basketball career, I felt like the time I was gone gave me the space and separation from my mom. She divorced her third husband the summer after my senior year of high school, and after driving me to college in the old RV, she never went back to Wheaton. She kept on driving until she finally settled in Apache Junction, Arizona.

I don't think I would have returned to Wheaton if she was still here. I feel bad thinking that, but I can't help myself. She made everything hard for me growing up. I wanted stability and conventionality. I needed to feel like I fit in. Belonged. Yet I never did.

There are too many situations that I've yet to heal from. Like when I finally felt like I connected with a teacher in the fourth grade, Mr. Jenson. My mom met him at Fall conferences, and a month later, I walked into our RV to them kissing. Things got awkward for me at school when she ended it with him.

Or the time she served my friends alcohol when I had them over, and when their parents found out, they were forbidden to hang out with me ever again. Or the time at Eagles Drug Store when she announced loudly that her daughter Meadow would most likely die a virgin but that she still wanted me to be on the pill, just in case.

The stories replay in my mind, one after another, like the most embarrassing moments that could ever happen to a girl growing up. Except these things did happen. They aren't hypotheticals or worst-case scenarios. The last friend I ever brought to the RV was Scottie. He was a guy in my grade, and I had a little crush on him. My mom sat us down to talk about the birds and the bees, which was mortifying enough, but then told us she needed to run out and wouldn't return to the RV for two hours.

Nothing happened in those two hours. The RV door shut with a bang, and we sat there, avoiding eye contact, mouths still open from the conversation. I knew Juniper loved me, but I craved normal. I wanted a life like everyone else's I saw—a house that wasn't on wheels, dinner served at five, and boundaries. I grew up with no rules and wanted Juniper to care enough about me to say no. Just once. Because sometimes, there is no greater gesture of love than that.

"You need to let me know how I can support you while she's here," Malik says as he walks into his room. "I got you."

I'M AWOKEN THE NEXT MORNING by the sound of a scraping muffler on the street. I sit up, the blood drains from my face, and I know that Juniper Soleta is here. Malik is at my door the next instant, with sheer horror on his face. He's never met her, but we've spent hours unpacking all that encompasses Juniper.

"Is it weird that I'm nervous?" Malik looks back and forth between me and the front door.

"Don't be." I throw a sweatshirt on. "Get ready to be entertained at my expense."

The RV is like I remember it. The white is discolored, rust brimming at the corners—a wide mustard stripe down the center, the door painted with a meadow of flowers. There are no RVs quite like this one, and seeing it brings me back.

"Is that my Meadow Lark?" my mom says as she walks around the RV and faces me. Her reddish-brown hair hangs in two braids, and her yellow dress falls off her shoulders and down to her ankles. Her skin is tan from the Arizona sun, and she's as fit as I remember her. Her beauty always takes my breath away, and today is no exception. She walks toward me with her arms extended.

"Hi, Mom." I sink into her. She's not tall, and my chin rests on her head as we hug.

"Look at you." She holds my hands and has me do a little spin. "You've gained some of the cancer weight back. And your hair is so beautiful. So grown out since the spring. And you must be Malik." She turns to him.

He stands there with a look of bewilderment on his face. "Hi, Juniper. It's nice to meet you."

"You didn't bring . . .?" I blank on her fourth's husband's name.

"Oh, honey, I got rid of him this summer. Your mama is single once again and ready to mingle." She laughs. "I'm going to take a long nap this afternoon, but then we need to have some fun tonight. Right, guys?"

Malik still wears a goofy grin on his face. He looks like he's seen an alien, but he can't look away.

"Mom, I'll follow you out to my bed and breakfast and get you situated, and we can meet up later. I have a bed in there now too, and the water is turned on, so you should stay inside. It'll be more comfortable."

"I may take you up on that, Meadow." She walks back to her RV.

"Oh my gawd," Malik mouths silently the moment she looks away.

"I know," I mouth back. "I know."

When we pull up to the pool hall later, after her afternoon nap, I moan when I see how busy it is. A large part of me hoped to hide Juniper out at the lake and people wouldn't even know she was in town. But when I see this crowd, I know that won't be the case.

Malik opens the door for my mom and me, and all eyes are on us. My mom doesn't just walk through the door—that wouldn't be a big enough statement. The moment she hears the music from the jukebox, she starts moving her shoulders, swaying her hips, and stomping her feet to the beat. Juniper has arrived.

"This place hasn't changed a bit." She turns to me. "It still smells like cheap beer and broken promises."

We grab a drink, and I pour mine down my throat too fast and then order another. My feet stick to the floor as my mom pulls us to the back room where the pool tables are. All eyes look at us, and when I think I couldn't be more on edge, Dax walks through the door with some buddies, and when he sees me, he walks in my direction. My mom has already pulled Malik off in another direction.

"That's your mom?" he asks, motioning to where she is helping herself to popcorn.

"The one and only," I respond, keeping my back to her.

Dax glances over my shoulder, and I take another gulp of my beer. The more I drink, the less her presence overwhelms me.

"My memory of her is pretty sketchy. She's, like, really hot," Dax says, and the blood drains from my face for the second time today. I square my body up in front of his and enunciate my next words.

"If you ever say that to me again, we can't be friends," I say. There isn't a bit of sarcasm in my voice. I mean every last drop of it.

Dax wraps his hand around my wrist. "You look just like her, Carrie."

I soften, but only a little. "I'm nothing like her."

But he doesn't back off. I wear my armor thick, and it covers all of me. He puts his hand behind my head and whispers into my ear. "You're the more put together, better, hotter version of your mom. Is that better?"

My face flushes, and I'm grateful for the bad lighting and the loud music, so Dax can't hear my heart thumping against my chest, attempting to escape and land right in his hand.

"And who is this?" My mom points to Dax right as Trey approaches us as well.

"This is Dax, and this is Trey."

My mom insists on being extra and pulls them both into a hug like she's known them forever. "Well, aren't you two the cutest things I've ever seen." My mom points to a table, and we all sit around it.

I do what I always do in my mom's presence. I cease to exist. There has never been room for both of us. I sit back and listen to my mom flirt with Malik, Dax, and Trey. "Oh my goodness, Dax, you are the cutest person I've ever seen." She laughs, and I hold my breath as her hand goes to Dax's knee. "And which of you lovelies is dating my little Meadow Lark?"

Before anyone can answer, I say, "Mom, please."

"Oh, honey, you are still so shy," she says. Like me wanting not to be embarrassed is a bad thing.

"Arizona is a long drive, ma'am. You must be tired," Trey adds, and my mom puts a finger up to him.

"Honey, no calling me ma'am here. I'm a young forty-five, and it is a long trip, but no one's tired."

I excuse myself to go to the bar, order a beer, down it, and then bring the next beer back to my table. Malik is the only one that looks uncomfortable. Dax and Trey are eating out of her hands, and I hate how I instantly feel transformed back to high school when I was miserable, and she was the main source of it.

When I reach the table, my mom holds Dax's hand palm up and reads it.

"Oh, this is interesting. This line tells me that you've had some hard things happen to you that have hardened your heart. And this line here . . ." Her voice trails off, and she gives Dax a sideways smile. "This line here tells me you're a very passionate lover. Very giving in bed."

"Mom," I interrupt. Dax's eyes move to mine. "I'm sure these guys don't want their palms read."

Trey sticks his out. "Will you read mine next?"

My mom reaches across the table to grab Trey's. I squeeze Malik's knee under the table and motion to the door. I want to get my mom out of here when we still have our dignity intact, and as the moments tick away, I lose confidence in our ability to do that.

My stomach is tied in knots, and I feel vomit threatening to come up through my chest and out of my mouth. Juniper is just being Juniper, and I should be used to it by now. The awkward school conferences, the men she dated in town, and the things she would say in front of guys I was interested in all come to the surface like unresolved issues usually do. And I can't take anymore.

"I'm going home," I announce, standing up, unsteady on my feet. "Malik," I slur, "make sure Juniper gets home."

"I can take you." Dax places a hand on my shoulder.

I try to wave him away, but I feel his hand move to the small of my back. When I try to resist, the pressure gets stronger. When we get outside into the fresh air, I turn to face him.

"I'm fine walking." I stumble on a rock I hadn't previously seen. I try to calculate how many drinks I threw down tonight, but I can't remember.

"Yes, I can see that." Dax takes my hand and leads me to his car. He opens the door for me and helps me get in.

We drive to Malik's place in silence. I hate how my mom makes me feel. I hate who I become when she's here. I despise that she's the most interesting person in every room she enters. I loathe that I become invisible.

Dax parks in front of my place, walks around the car, and opens my door. He helps me get inside, lets me lean on him the entire time, and grabs me a glass of water once we get inside.

"Do you want to talk about it?" Dax asks, but I take my water and walk to my bedroom. Dax follows.

"You tell me, Mr. Mom Flirter." I take off my shoes and throw them across the room, narrowly missing Dax's head.

"Umm, I did not flirt with your mom," Dax barks. He stares at me, opening his mouth until words finally come out. "Do you think you're making her out to be worse than she is?"

He sits next to me on the foot of the bed, and thoughts swirl through my mind. His jeans rub against mine. His stupid shirt makes his eyes look even bluer. When he puts his hand on my knee, I brush it off.

"No, I'm not making her to be worse. Whose side are you on?"

"Sorry, Carrie. I didn't realize there were sides."

I think of my mom's hand on Dax's knee under the table, and I know I'm not overreacting. I didn't imagine those childhood memories. And who is Dax or anyone else to tell me how I feel is wrong? It's how I feel.

Dax stands up and starts removing the blanket from my bed, and I have a moment where I realize that Dax is in my room. My actual bedroom.

"Do you want me to stay?" He leans over the bed and pulls the sheet down. "I can hang out in the living room until Malik comes home."

"No," I say too fast. "Go back to the bar and flirt with my mom more. Or better yet. Have a one-night stand with her. You're both into those. Hell, you're a perfect match. Neither of you wants to screw someone more than once."

The words spew from my mouth, and I picture them hitting Dax square in his stomach.

"You're a lousy drunk." Dax shuts the lights off.

"Sleep it off, and maybe you won't be such an ass in the morning."

Chapter Twelve

Dax

TWO WEEKS INTO THE SCHOOL year and routines have been established. Most mornings, Kylie and I have breakfast, leave the house around 7:15, and arrive by 7:30. She stays in my classroom for the first thirty minutes while I prepare for the day, and at the first bell, she walks down the long hallway to her first-grade classroom.

I'm lucky to see her many times throughout the day. When my third-grade class stands in line waiting for gym class, her class walks by on their way to the cafeteria. She always gets out of line for a moment, squeezes my leg, and then giggles as she gets back in line.

Most teachers stay until 3:30 each day, thirty minutes after the last bell, but I run down to Kylie's classroom, pick her up, and we head home. I'd love to be able to wrap up my day like everyone else, but it isn't fair for me to make Kylie arrive early for school and then stay late. The routine works.

"Daddy, can Carrie pick me up from school again tomorrow?" Kylie asks. I've managed to avoid Carrie all week.

I lace my fingers through one of Kylie's curls. "I can

ask, but her mom is visiting, so she might have plans."

"But Daddy," Kylie pleads, lips pouted. "She was going to teach me how to make her tortilla soup."

The truth is, I could use the extra time at school tomorrow, but things didn't end so well with Carrie a few nights ago, and although I'm not sitting by my phone, waiting for an apology, I still want to hear one.

"I'll tell you what, sweetie." I pull into the school parking lot. "I'm going to see Carrie later for basketball practice. How about I ask her?"

"Yes!" Kylie claps her hands together. "And remind her that I want to learn how to make her soup."

Later that evening, Carrie walks into the gym first. She continues to put on muscle, and her lean legs look tan under her black shorts.

"Hey." She plops on the floor and pulls her shoes out of her bag.

"Hey." I watch her tie her hair on top of her head. I grab a hairband and tie my hair up too.

Carrie takes her outside shoes off and replaces them with her gym shoes.

"I haven't seen you all week." Carrie looks at me as she ties her shoe. "Is everything okay?"

When I look into her eyes, I wonder if she remembers anything.

"We haven't seen each other since I drove you home from the pool hall. And then tucked you into bed."

Carrie's face scrunches up in confusion. She puts her hand over her mouth and shuts her eyes. "Did I say something stupid?"

"Carrie—"

"Dax," she interrupts. "I admit, I did have a crush on you, but I'm way over it now. I don't like you. At all."

"When you were in eighth grade?" I ask.

Well," she stutters. "More recently than that."

"You have a crush on—"

"Had," Carrie cuts me off again.

She remembers nothing, and I refuse to be the ass who reminds her and makes her feel worse. At least right now. They say alcohol is the liquid courage, and now I know what she thinks of me. She puts me in the same category as her mom. But when was this more recent crush?

"I guess we're good," I say, and then I think of Kylie and how much I don't want to disappoint her. "And if we're good, I'm hoping you could pick Kylie up from school again."

Carrie responds, "I promised Kylie I'd teach her how to make the tortilla soup I served at Sunny and Sis's. Does that work?"

"You don't have to cook," I say.

"But I promised Kylie."

Malik walks into the gym with his bag strewn over his shoulder. "What up, players?" Malik throws his bag on the ground and gets right to stretching. "Ready to get your asses kicked tonight?"

We're starting to play well together, and I don't want to jinx anything, but I think we have a real shot at winning this thing. We've all improved our game and have been committed to shooting around and running some plays at least once a week. I'm in the best shape I've been in for a long time. Being in the gym clears my head.

"Beers after?" Malik asks within the first five minutes of practice.

I shake my head. "Nah, I need to get Kylie in bed for school tomorrow."

"I'm in," Carrie states. "I need a break from my mom."

"Fuck it list," Malik says between shots. He then says, "Oh, yeah, that's right. Never mind."

Curiosity piqued, I ask, "What's a fuck it list?"

Malik and Carrie share a look, and I catch Carrie shaking her head. "Nothing. Cancer stuff. It's nothing."

"I see," I respond. "If I make this shot, you have to tell me." Carrie shrugs her shoulders, non-committedly.

I line up for the shot behind the three-point line and let it go. It looks good all the way to the basket, but it bounces off the back of the rim and falls away from the hoop.

"Guess you'll never know, playa," Malik says through a laugh.

A LITTLE AFTER FIVE ON Friday, I walk through the door, excited for whatever the evening holds. Kylie stands on a stool in the kitchen with Carrie, and her mom, Juniper, sits on the couch with a bottle of wine on the table beside her. Juniper. I hadn't considered she'd be here too.

"Hi, Juniper. It's nice to see you." I throw my bag on the bench by the door.

Juniper jumps up from the couch and pulls me in for a hug. "Dax, it's so good to see you again, kid." She sits back down and takes a drink of her wine.

Juniper is an attractive woman. She's a few inches shorter than Carrie, but they have the same olive skin and bone structure. Juniper wears her hair a lot longer than Carrie's, and it's got reddish tints throughout. Carrie also has much fuller lips, but they have the same cheekbones. Most would mistake them for sisters, and if I ever put them next to each other, Carrie is the more attractive one. However, Juniper's attractiveness is in your face, and Carrie's is more subtle.

"And how's my girl?" I go into the kitchen and give Kylie a squeeze.

"Daddy, this soup is so easy, even you could make it," Kylie declares, and Carrie covers her mouth and laughs.

"I've been writing down recipes for you, Dax, and I agree with Kylie. You can handle this one." Carrie turns from the oven to face me.

"Wine?" I ask in response and hand her a glass. "Have you had a nice trip so far?" I turn my attention toward Juniper as we all sit down for dinner.

"It's been so great. I've been working on some paintings at the B&B. What a neat place that is. I don't know if Carrie told you, but I paint." Juniper scrapes at her fingernails. "And during the day, while Carrie works, I putz around. I visited my old stomping grounds, the county park, and caught up with old friends. It's good to be back."

I spoon the soup into my mouth, and it's as good as I remember it. "How long will you stay?"

"Oh, Dax, one never can say for sure. I go where the wind takes me, and today, I'm happy. I don't think beyond that."

Carrie and I exchange a look, and it again occurs to me how different the two are. After dinner, Carrie tries to leave, but I ask her to stay, and the four of us play a game of Trouble—Kylie's favorite. She manages to win each game.

"Dax, we really should go," Carrie says once again.

"Daddy." Kylie pulls at my pant leg. "Can't Carrie put me to bed tonight?"

"Oh, sweetie, not tonight. Carrie and her mom need to leave."

"I don't mind." Carrie takes Kylie's hand and leads her to her bedroom. A few minutes later, Kylie comes out in pajamas, hugs me, and returns to the room. Every day, she grows up a little more.

"Your daughter is gorgeous," Juniper says as I walk to the sink to rinse the dinner dishes. "What's her sign?"

I turn back to look at Juniper. "Her birthday is July second."

"Oh my," she responds right away. "She's a Cancer. Watch out for that one. They tend to have real big feelings. Yet they are also beautiful creatures."

I turn back to the sink and feel Juniper's presence behind me, and then she grips my waist and flips me around. I turn the sink off and face her. My hands are still wet from rinsing the dishes.

She takes my hand in hers and traces a line down my palm.

"When I was younger, you were exactly my type, Dax." She looks at me.

"Umm, thanks?" I swallow, saying it more as a question. I back up against the counter.

Juniper leans in, and I hold my breath again. She reaches over me, and I'm pretty sure her breast rubs against my arm. She grabs a towel. "Here, let me dry."

"I should check on Kylie." But unless Juniper moves, I'm boxed in.

"I'm sure she's fine." She grins.

"She's down," Carrie whispers, coming into the kitchen from the dark hallway. She looks at her mom, then me, and back to Juniper. "Let's go." She grabs her purse from the couch and her mom walks beside her.

"Carrie," I call after her, but she puts her hand up and then calls out. "See you soon." Carrie takes Juniper by the wrist and barely glances in my direction as they leave.

I want to run after Carrie and say she was right about everything. Maybe I didn't notice that her mom was flirting at the pool hall, but there was definite flirting tonight—even a little rubbing. But I don't run after her because she's with her mom, and this is not a conversation I want to have in front of Juniper.

Now that I've hung out with Juniper twice, I'm ready for her to leave town so I can have some semblance of the old Carrie back.

Chapter Thirteen

Carrie

"FUCK IT LIST."

Malik waves his finger in the air, and for whatever reason, when he says those two words, I fall under a spell and can't say no. I don't know if it's his cute southern accent, how he's so invested in my happiness, or how he gets giddy saying the eff word—but I fall under a trance every time he says it.

"I'm about to tell you to take your list and shove it up your—"

"Now, now, Carrie, that's a bit much." Malik taps a button on his phone, runs to the office, comes out with a piece of paper, and hands it to me.

"You take this list, put it in your room, and look at it daily. There is only one thing you haven't even started on that list. Why is that?"

The words *repair relationship with my mom* scowl back at me.

I take the list he hands me and stare at it. This is the one item that makes me feel physically ill. The majority of my being wants to move forward and be closer. But there is this other part of me that has a long memory, and not only can I not forget things from the past, but I can't get over the resentment I feel when the memories flood me. "I want to. But she keeps messing up. I mean, she flirted at the pool hall. You should have seen her with Dax. I walked out of Kylie's bedroom, and the vibe was off. She hasn't changed. Never will."

"Ask Dax if he thought your mom was being inappropriate with him." Malik slams the fridge shut and pours himself a cup of juice.

"I can't." I shake my head. "Because if I'm wrong about this, I'll look like the world's biggest jerk for even thinking it. Who thinks that about their mom?"

"Someone raised by Juniper, that's who."

After work at the bank, I head out to my bed and breakfast. Progress has slowed down since my mom's arrival. She parked her RV in the expansive yard but has been staying inside the B&B. Because of my efforts to avoid her, I haven't been out here finishing the painting as much as I should.

"Hey, Mom." I walk inside to announce my presence. "I'm here."

"In here, Meadow." She still refuses to call me Carrie after all of these years.

My mom has a canvas set up in the living room, and when I step around her, the picture is breathtaking. It's the view from the lake of my new home. There's a sign off the house that says *The Meadow Lark*.

Instead of grass, it's a meadow of flowers, in my favorite color. Red.

My mom puts down her paintbrush and admires her work. "I thought you could put this at the end of the driveway. So everyone knows about this place."

"What if I don't want to call it that?" I put my hands on my hips and study the picture.

My mom glances at me with a hint of disappointment on her face.

"You can call it whatever you want, but that is your name, and it's a fitting name for a B&B with all of these wildflowers around."

I don't tell her this, but the name fits this place's look and feel. "It's beautiful. Thank you, Mom," I muster up the strength to say.

I think of the list, now clipped to my bedroom mirror so that it can stare back at me. I've put effort into every aspect of it except this one. My mom's and my relationship, at times, feels too broken. I have great relationships with almost everyone in my life, but this one eats at me the most. No matter what I do, it's the hardest one to get right.

It's a control thing, as in, I have none. Our relationship is full of thorns, and they prick me. Every time Juniper apologizes, I let her back in, only to be hurt again. How many times are we expected to forgive people? Logic tells me one more time than we've been hurt. But the pain is exhausting. Being the bigger person time and time again zaps me of all energy. I'm the child in this relationship. Not her.

"Mom, I thought it would be fun to pack some food and go up on the hills like we used to."

Her entire face lights up. She stands up and grips my face with her paint-colored hands. "I love that idea." "

When I was younger, we'd climb the hills, and when we'd get to the top, we'd lie in a field of flowers and look at the lake below. It felt so far away. I'd bring some flowers back to the RV when we were done, and my mom would put them in her crystal vase and place them on our little square table. For a moment, our house on wheels felt like home.

We reach the top of the hill. I lie back and squint at

the sun that burns above me.

"I loved doing this when you were little." My mom lies next to me and wraps her pinky in mine.

"Me too." I smile at the memory of wildflowers in the vase.

My mom sits up, and I follow. She folds her legs, feet on top of her lap, like only a yogi could do. "You know, your childhood wasn't all bad."

I pull my bottom lip into my mouth and let the grass tickle my fingers. "I know."

"We had good times too. Mostly good times. It was Juniper and Meadow against the world. We never needed the suffocation of male energy, and we never answered to anyone. I liked that about us."

"Mom." I hesitate but think of the fuck it list. If not now, when? "I know we had good times. I haven't forgotten those. But we had hard times too."

She rests her open palms on her knees and shuts her eyes. "I could have bought you a house and painted your bedroom pink. I could have worn an apron and cooked three meals a day. But that sounds like conformist bullshit that I never wanted."

"I know."

But what she described sounds like my idea of happiness. It's what everyone else seemed to have, and I spent my childhood jealous and ashamed that I didn't have it too.

"We always had enough money for what we needed, and I felt the freedom that we could up and move if we wanted to. We were best friends. I miss that."

"I wanted a mom more than a best friend." I sharply inhale through my nose and hold all the air inside me for a few seconds.

Juniper extends both hands out, and I take them in

mine. She smiles at the sky and then at me. "I had only a mom growing up, never a friend, and that wasn't so great either. I'm sorry if I wasn't everything you wanted me to be, but you're grown now. Your resentments aren't hurting me, Meadow. They're hurting you."

Damn, I hate when she's right. But she is. I've let my resentments control everything, mostly my ability to move forward with life and allow myself to be happy. I hate feeling this angry at her. I don't know how, but I must start letting things go.

"You are part of me," my mom says. "And when I thought I could lose you to cancer, well."

My mom was even somewhat helpful when I had cancer. She showed up in her RV early during my treatments and drove me to my chemo appointments. She also rubbed me up in oils, just in case western medicine wasn't the answer. We stayed out at the County Park, and I holed up in that old RV for a couple of weeks before she got on the road again.

She chokes up but then continues, "We aren't that different, you and me. I'll always be your biggest fan."

Juniper extends her arms and pulls me into them, and I let her. The conversation doesn't feel like enough. But I also don't know if I need to say more than this. Who will it help if I go through every wrong I felt like she ever did toward me? Every ounce of pain or embarrassment I've felt. Will I even feel better by saying it? Because I know my words will only make her feel worse.

THE NEXT MORNING, I WAKE up with renewed energy and purpose and decide to go on my morning run after missing more than a week. I'm not surprised when I don't see Dax waiting for me, so I keep running.

The weather is perfect this morning for a jog. It's

cool, with the promise of frost in the coming days. My legs feel strong as they take me out of town and down the gravel roads of the country before I cut over to the river. I almost run right past Dax, but then I see him sitting under the willow tree, and he wipes his face when he sees me.

"Hey, Dax." I wave, and he pulls his shirt up again and wipes his face.

"Sorry, I thought I was alone." Dax stares straight ahead, and when I study his face, it looks broken. His eyes are red-rimmed, and his shirt is wet from where he wiped his tears.

"Is everything okay?" I sit beside him on the bank of the stream.

"Came out here to think." Dax leans back on his elbows and stretches his long legs out in front of him.

"And to be alone, I bet." I nudge him in the shoulder, and he smiles. "I'm sorry I'm here. I'll leave. Say no more." I go to get up, but he pulls me down.

"Four years today." He doesn't need to say more. Zari.

"Dax." I wrap my arms around him and hold on tightly.

He lies his head on my shoulder, and it strikes me how comfortable I've gotten with Dax. It's like we're old friends, and I know I wasn't supposed to find him out here, but maybe this is where I'm supposed to be. A supportive friend to give a shoulder to cry on.

"She was only twenty-six, Carrie. Twenty-six. Your age."

It's impossible for me not to tie my mortality to Zari's. Cancer struck both of us, yet I'm here, and she's not. Cancer has taken so much from so many people. And although I'm alive, it's taken away the hope I used to have in a future because I'm always too scared to go there. It lurks everywhere and reminds me that it can come back any time and take more from me.

"What do you like to do on milestone days like today? Do you and Kylie have a tradition? Do you like to look through pictures? Tell stories? Does Kylie know what today represents?"

Dax stays silent for a while, picking at his knee, and then picks up a pebble and tosses it in the stream. "She was so young. I don't know how much Kylie remembers her mom or only thinks she does because of the stories. Today is another day, and I don't want to rob her of that."

I take his hand in mine, and we look at the river. Dax squeezes it, and I don't know what's in that squeeze, except perhaps he's thanking me for being here.

"I miss her. But the sadness is fading. It's changing. That scares the shit out of me. When she died, I honestly thought I'd be miserable forever. But with each day, it all fades. Her voice. Expressions. The way she held Kylie. The way she held me. Fading. And I'm no longer miserable, and that scares me more than anything."

"I didn't know Zari, but I can't imagine she would have wanted you to stay unhappy."

"But if I'm not grieving, who am I?" he asks with a furrowed brow and trusting eyes, like I may have the answer.

"You'll always be grieving, but you don't always have to be sad. You get to live life, Dax. Why waste that? What happened wasn't fair. But you're here. And there's a reason for that."

We sit quietly for a few more minutes, hands wrapped in each other's, looking at the water flow over the rocks. Dax finally looks at me and gives me a sideways smirk. "You should have been a therapist."

"Hearing other people's problems all day? No, thank you."

We laugh, and the mood is instantly lighter. Dax gets

up first, puts his hands out for me, and helps me get off the ground. It takes a while to get back to town because we walk instead of jog. Neither of us say anything, but there is comfort in the silence.

When we get to town, Dax stands in front of me, and I go to say something, but he puts his hand on my shoulder. "I feel like I need to tell you something."

"Go on." I raise my eyebrows, and my mind sprints in one hundred different directions in the few seconds it takes Dax to speak.

"Friday night, when you and your mom were over—"

"Yeah." I cross my arms across my body.

"Well, I should have listened to you," Dax says, as if that's enough for me to understand what he's talking about.

I know where this conversation is headed, but I want to stop it. I don't want it to go there. "Meaning?"

Dax's eyes plead with mine, silently asking me not to make him say the words. But I'm wrong about so much that I need to hear what he has to say. His mouth opens, then closes, and I can see his mind spinning as he chooses his next words.

"I think your mom has unhealthy boundaries. She made me uncomfortable the other night."

The world stops spinning on its axis for a brief moment. My mom and I made up, and things feel good, or at least better. Dax has been the person trying to tell me that maybe she isn't so bad. And I'm finally starting to believe it, and now he says this.

"Could you have misread things?" I put out into the world what I want. I try to manifest a situation where, if I say it out loud enough, it will become the truth.

His face drops, and his mouth hangs open. "I'm not misreading how I feel. Juniper doesn't interact with me like a friend of her daughter's. That's all I'm saying."

Resentment. Disappointment. Anger. It all bubbles up. I'm allowed to think poorly of my mom, but no one else has permission. I will always be on team Juniper. I will always defend her. If you look up toxic relationships in the dictionary, a picture of my mom and me will come up first. I am her biggest enabler.

I should choose my words as wisely as Dax tried to pick his, but I don't. "Well, be careful with her, Dax. She's a heartbreaker."

Dax grows pale, and I know I've said the wrong thing. In matters of my mom, I'm always saying the wrong thing. He turns to walk away but looks at me over his left shoulder.

"I'm sorry that things suck with you and your mom, but I thought we were better friends than that, Carrie."

He's right, and there is nothing else for me to say.

Chapter Fourteen

Dax

I GLANCE AT KYLIE IN HER booster chair in the backseat, kicking her legs to the beat of the music, waving her hands every time the chorus echoes out from my car's speakers, and it occurs to me... Kylie is going to be a woman someday. She'll have big emotions that I won't even pretend to understand, and she'll accuse me of not understanding her as she slams her bedroom door, and she'll be right. I don't understand women.

We pull up to Jake and Camilla's place, fifty yards from mine. Camilla comes out in leggings and an oversized sweatshirt, and her baby bump is unmistakable.

"Auntie Camilla." Kylie runs to her. Kylie will be as tall as Camilla in another two years or so.

"Where's Jake?" I look around the place.

She nods to the gazebo. "Jake and a few of the guys are hanging out. You should join them. I want to take Kylie apple picking."

Kylie's eyes light up, and she pulls at Camilla's arm. "Are we going to make pie?"

"We can." Camilla smiles. "Then, I'll put on a show

to do your hair."

Everyone in my circle contributes to bettering Kylie's life in some way. Camilla, it turns out, does hair like I've never seen. She knows what to do with Kylie's curls and buys all the products, so we have the right things in our house. I couldn't raise Kylie without the village. Moving to Wheaton was the right decision, and I'm constantly reminded of that.

In the gazebo, Trey and Malik are having a beer, and Jake tells a lively story about a recent job. They acknowledge me, and I sit down and grab a beer.

"Anyone want to shoot pool later?" Malik stretches his long legs out in front of him, still wearing his dusty old jeans from his day of work.

"My eyes are set on other things." Trey grins, then smashes his empty beer can against the wood floor before grabbing another one.

"What'd you have in mind?" Jake leans back on the cushioned bench he sits on, folding one leg over his other.

Trey interlocks his hands and puts them behind his head. "After I shower, I'm heading to Carrie's bed and breakfast. She invited me over for dinner, and if things go the way I'm hoping—"

I toss my empty can toward his head. "You're disgusting."

"And she's my best friend." Malik kicks up his boot in Trey's direction.

Trey laughs, unbothered by Malik and I's non-joking faces. Trey is reliable and does a nice job on the construction sites, but I still don't know why Jake puts up with him. Jake has created a great business and makes a point to hire standup guys. I wouldn't put Trey in that same category.

"All I'm saying is Carrie offered to cook me dinner, and we all know what that means."

"It means dinner," Malik, Jake, and I say simultaneously.

Jake opens the cooler, throws me another beer, and then stands and looks at the lake. "The fish started biting again. Camilla heard it when she was at the café this morning. A last surge before the first freeze."

Malik and I nod at each other, thankful for the change in subject, but I can't help but think about Carrie. She doesn't strike me as someone who does casual dating and hookups. And not with people like Trey. Carrie wants passion, stability, and longevity. She wants the opposite of what Trey is offering up. At least, I think she does. Carrie and I are still in a precarious position building a friendship. We don't discuss dating.

After putting Kylie to bed for the night, I decide that I'll take her fishing the next morning to test if they are biting. If I catch a few walleyes, I could offer to cook for Carrie. It's the one meal I'm good at, which is a way I could pay her back for all the meals she cooks for us. Although, I am still mad at her. I prepare me and Kylie's poles, so everything is ready when she gets up.

The next morning, I pull an excited Kylie out of bed to go fishing. I haven't done this for too long. I fasten her life jacket over her sweatshirt and put her hood on, as it's a cold morning in Minnesota. The grass is damp from the night's dew. I put everything in the boat and triple-check that everything is in order.

The water is so calm. It looks like glass when the sun peeks out behind the clouds and lights everything in its path. My fishing boat glides through the water, breaking the structure and pushing the water to the side in a kaleidoscope of colors. Kylie's pole bends first.

"Daddy, Daddy," she yells, waving her arms all over the place and almost dropping her pole. "Something's on it."

I put my pole down and help her reel in. Kylie's hands are small as I wrap mine over hers. She grunts with each crank, and I get the net ready. When I pull it in, we both gasp at the perfect walleye before us.

"Kylie! You caught your first walleye!"

Her eyes are huge with amazement, and her hands go over her mouth.

We high five, put it on a stringer, and go on to catch three more. Father and daughter, out on a peaceful lake and my six-year-old didn't complain. I've brought Kylie into my fishing boat thousands of times, but she's always observed and never been interested in holding a pole.

We troll past Bergland's point, and I continue south on the lake. First, there's the Bergland cottage, and a little further down the shoreline is Jake and Camilla's A-frame. Fifty yards from that is my new build, and I keep going.

Carrie's bed and breakfast come into view, and it's one of the best views of the lake. It sits in a bay; the water is shallow and doesn't get deep until quite a ways out. It has a sandy bottom, perfect for swimming or launching a kayak. Once she gives the outside a fresh coat of paint and does some landscaping, this place will be gorgeous.

"Daddy, who is that?" Kylie points to the shore at the very moment that Trey walks out of the B&B. I look at my phone. It's only 6:30 in the morning.

Trey doesn't see us, but he looks around, pulls his cap lower on his head, walks to his car, and dust flies up as he peels down the gravel driveway.

"Carrie must have had a sleepover," Kylie says with such innocence, not realizing what she's insinuating.

"Maybe," I respond. "Let's reel in. We have enough for a meal."

My heart suffers a foreign kind of pain because I have no right to feel it. Carrie has every right to date. Hell, men would have to be stupid not to notice her. Why do I feel this lump of something directly below my sternum? It's there and makes it hard to breathe. Carry is so funny and smart, and she's not bad on the eyes. But liking Trey makes me think there is something wrong with her. Trey's an ass.

"Are you okay, Daddy?" Kylie brings me back to reality. I smile at the sight of her pulling at her life jacket.

"Yep. We caught some fish, and now we need to get ready for school."

My brain has difficulty concentrating at work, and I snap at Tommy, one of my third graders, at one point. He's had it coming, but I'm not a teacher who loses my cool. I pride myself on it. The day is long, my eyes hurt from being open, and I want to get home and tune out all the thoughts that won't get out of my head.

We don't have a basketball practice scheduled tonight, so instead, I ask Kylie if she wants to have dinner with my parents, and I suit up to go to open gym at the high school. You never know who will show up, but tonight, a few guys from the boys' varsity basketball team are here, a couple from the girl's team, and some former players, like myself.

Basketball helps me forget. The sound of a ball bouncing in a gym, echoing off the walls, and the sound of brand-new sneakers squeaking on the freshly swept floor. The sweet smell of sweat, mixed with deodorant and perfumes. I need all of it tonight.

But then Carrie and Malik walk in, and my mood shifts back to agitated.

"Hey." Carrie hangs her head low, hands on her hips. She holds a closed box and places it on the bleachers.

"Hey," I say back.

We both tiptoe around the awkwardness. The last time we talked, I walked away hurt, and I haven't stopped thinking about her words ever since. We need to talk it out, but things keep compounding. I don't even know where I'd start with her at this point.

After we shoot around, we break into teams. Five on five, as there are exactly ten of us here tonight. I don't match up with anyone right away, and then the only person who is left to be guarded is Carrie, so I guess I'm on her tonight.

Her team gets the ball first, and she catches the ball underneath the basket, her back to me. I push into her, and she tries to fake me to the left and go right into the lane. She goes up to do a hook shot, and as she releases, my hand catches hers, and the ball falls short. She gives me a look but doesn't call the foul.

The game remains physical and isn't the stress reliever I thought it would be. Malik misses a shot on the other end of the court, and the ball gets rebounded. I run down the court for a fast break. I catch the ball on the run, and as I'm going up for a layup, Carrie gets between me and the basket. I shift my body to lob the ball into the basket, and my elbow connects with her face.

"Charge!" someone yells from behind me. I turn to see a pimpled face high school boy looking back at me. I ignore him and turn to Carrie.

"Shit, are you okay?" I remove her hand from her face so that I can get a good look, and it's obvious she's going to have a shiner. "You need to get ice on that."

"Do you think?" She huffs at me as someone hands her a bag of ice.

I sit on the sidelines with Carrie as the game resumes, four on four now. "What can I do?" I ask, feeling helpless. "I'm really sorry. I didn't see you there. I never would—"

"Nothing." She stands up from the bleachers. "I'm going to head home and put a proper icepack on my eye so it doesn't swell shut."

She grabs her bag, walks out of the gym, and I follow. She hands me the box that she brought, and I take it, but don't open it up.

"What's your deal? You were all over me tonight. And that was before giving me a shiner."

"Did you ride with Malik?"

Carrie nods her head.

"Let me drive you home." Carrie doesn't fight me as she gets into the passenger seat.

When we get to Malik's house, I fill a bag with ice and toss the melted bag in the sink. Then, I put her on the couch. My elbow met the bone right under her eye. I hold the ice, and she lies back.

"I didn't hurt you on purpose." I press the pack to her eye. "You came out of nowhere, and my momentum took me to the basket. I'm sorry. That's the game."

"I know it wasn't on purpose." Carrie keeps her eyes closed and puts her arm behind her head. "But the thought crossed my mind that you're retaliating against me for the stupid comment I made about my mom."

My brain tells me to stay quiet and not say the words on the tip of my tongue. It feels like I have an angel and a devil on my shoulder. I know how I should conduct myself, but I can't help but say what I want to.

"Did you have fun with Trey last night?" Her good eye opens for a second to look at me and then closes again.

"It was fine. Nothing special." Confirmed. Carrie was with Trey. But I suppose I didn't need confirmation. I saw him walking out of her place this morning.

"What'd you guys do?" I continue to hold the bag over her right eye.

"He came to the B&B, and I cooked. It wasn't that exciting."

Carrie's shirt comes up, revealing her flat stomach, and with both eyes closed, I stare at her. She pulls at her shirt.

"I'm soaked. Will you go to my room and grab me something dry?"

I walk to her room and open the top drawer. Full of panties. I should have guessed. On the mirror, a piece of paper is stuck in the corner. I get closer to read it, and I see my name.

With a shirt in hand, I go back to the living room and wave the list in front of Carrie. "Why is my name on this list?"

Carrie removes the bag from her face. When she sees what I'm holding, she lunges for me and pins me down on the couch, but I keep the paper out of her reach. Carrie is fast and stronger than I would have guessed.

"Dax. Threesome. Clothes. Mom." I stare at the typed list. Carrie straddles me as she tries to grab it. "What is this?"

"Nothing." Carrie jumps over me and grabs the list. "Nothing," she says even louder, crumpling it up, and then stuffs it in her bra. "Nothing." Her neck turns splotchy, and her face bright red.

"You want to have a threesome with your mom and me?" I shift Carrie off of me so I can sit up. "How do clothes come into play? I'm so confused."

"Ugh." She moans, leaning back on the couch. "That is officially the grossest thing I've ever heard. Gawd no. To all of it. My mom? You? Eww, Dax."

I lean back too. Arm to arm. I look at Carrie, and her chest moves heavily, in and out. She's breathing hard after wrestling me for the note. I turn and look at her. Face to face. Heat floods my entire body. Of course the note means something else, but what?

"As a friend, anyone but Trey. You can do so much better." I bring the topic back to Trey because that's easier than moms.

Carrie crosses her legs at the ankle. "Who, then? I

threw myself at you, and you were repulsed."

"Quit changing reality." I grab the ice bag to put it back on her face, but she dodges me. "I know I have no right to care, but I still can't believe you'd hook up with Trey. You think I have a reputation? Nah. That guy has a reputation. Only his is warranted."

"Hooked up with Trey. Umm, no." Carrie takes her hairband out and runs her fingers through it. "Never happening."

Dax. Threesome. Clothes. Mom. Trey. You'd think I was the one who took an elbow to the face because I'm confused and not even sure what I'm talking about anymore. "I saw him walking out of the B&B early this morning. At 6:30. I assumed—"

Carrie shoots up and puts her head in her hands. "Oh, my gawd." And then she looks at the wall and speaks louder. "Oh, my gawd."

"What?" I stand up. It looks like she's seen a ghost. "What did I say?"

"You need to go, Dax. Now." She walks to the door and opens it, and in case it isn't clear that she wants me to leave, she pushes me forward.

I go to say something to her, but she slams the door in my face.

When I get to my car, I notice that Carrie left the box she carried on the front seat. I contemplate whether to bring it to her door, but instead, I decide to open it. It's a cookie cake with a big basketball on it, and in the center, it says, *"Dax, I hope you'll give me a pass for being an ass."*

An apology cookie cake. With an original quote by Carrie. If I had seen this earlier in the night, things could have gone so differently between us these past couple of hours. I want to laugh at her thoughtfulness, but instead, I glance at the house and wonder why we're butting up against each other so much lately.

Chapter Fifteen

Carrie

I DRIVE OUT TO THE LAKE with one eye swelling shut and the other on the road. I've been happy the past few days. My mom and I's relationship was on the mend. We were moving forward. At least, that's what I thought.

Dinner last night was good. I made chicken pot pie. Trey, my mom, and I sat around, laughed, and had a good time. I only have one bed at the B&B that my mom uses, so I said goodbye and drove back to town. Trey stood at the door with me. I assumed he was right behind me.

But he stayed. Is that what Dax was telling me? That he saw Trey leaving the house in the morning? I pull over on the side of the road to vomit. I'm unsure if I'm concussed, disappointed, or in a rage. Everything comes out of me when I reach the B&B and whip through the door to find my mom at the kitchen table, smoking weed, like always. There are two types of people in this world— those that wake up and drink coffee and those that wake up and get high.

"Did you sleep with Trey?" I ask, not having the patience for small talk.

My mom's eyes widen, and she holds a joint out to

me, so I shake my head.

"It's an easy question, Mom." I cross my arms in front of me, and she stands up and tries to rub my swollen face, but I brush her away.

My mom's long hair is pulled up on the top of her head, and she wraps her sweater tighter to her chest.

"Oh, Carrie," she says. "Why so dramatic?"

"We had such a good talk the other day," I cry. "I thought things were getting better. That we were moving forward. You'll never change."

My mom walks to the kitchen window above the sink and looks out at the lake. "No, I don't suppose I ever will. I didn't realize our talk was about me changing anyway."

"Answer my question."

My mom tries to put her hands on my face again, but I back up. I need her to tell me what happened. She takes a long puff of her joint, holds it in her mouth, and then exhales it in one long blow. "No, I didn't sleep with Trey. After you left, he asked if he could stay. We smoked, listened to music, and he was in no shape to drive—"

"What happened?" My tone becomes more urgent as saliva fills my mouth, and I fear I'll be sick again.

"I'm the parent in this relationship, Meadow. Don't you forget it."

Tears prick the back of my eyes, and I blink them away. "Just tell me."

"Your little boyfriend tried to kiss me, but don't worry. I didn't let anything happen. Is that what you want me to tell you? Someday, you'll thank me. He's not good for you, and now you can stop pretending you feel any sort of way about him."

Juniper offers me her chair, and I sit and put my head between my knees. I'm not sure whether to laugh or cry.

I am relieved on all counts. One, that my mom didn't do anything with Trey, but also that Trey tried something. I've had this nagging feeling about him, and now I know. There is so much peace in the knowing. "Why can't you just be my mom?"

"You're making yourself hysterical." She runs her fingers through my hair, but the touch makes me stiffen, and I feel like I'm suffocating.

"Look," she continues. "You two had no chemistry. Trey's a Gemini. He couldn't be more incompatible with you."

I wipe the back of my hand across my snotty face. "This isn't about Trey. This is about you. I thought we could move forward, but you come into town like a tornado. And you make messes for me. Then, you leave, and I'm stuck having to clean them up. I need to know I have friends here because they like me. Not because they want to sleep with my mom."

Juniper stands up, grabs a bottle of wine from the counter, and pours me a glass. "What else, baby? What else?"

I haven't had a chance for my morning coffee yet, but I accept the glass of wine anyway.

"Dax told me how you acted around him and that it made him uncomfortable."

I expect a mocking reply, but instead, she pounds her glass of wine and then tops both of our glasses off. "Now, we're getting to what's eating at you." Juniper places her hand on my knee. "This is about Dax. The actual boy you like."

The sound of Dax's name coming out of my mom's mouth infuriates me.

"I don't think Wheaton is big enough for both of us. I want a mom. Someone I can leave a friend with, or someone I thought I was kind of dating, and not worry that when I turn around, you'll cross every boundary." I continue through the sobs. "You have no boundaries. None. You are spending more time gaslighting me for feeling this way than owning up to how your actions affect me. Why do you keep disappointing me?"

My mom blows smoke into the room. When she glances at me, her eyes look tired and sad, and her lips stay in a straight line. "Your expectations aren't fair."

"They are fair," I say, rejected. "I expect you not to entertain men I'm sort of dating. I expect you not to hit on my friends. It seems like an easy request."

We talk for another hour. Nothing new is said or can be when someone doesn't own their part of the story. I've spent my life apologizing for things that weren't my fault—for owning not only my mistakes but my moms' too. It was the only way to stay in each other's lives. If I held her accountable, she'd walk away, and I'd be alone. I refuse to do it anymore. I want her in my life. She's the only family I have. But if I don't have standards, I'll continue to be eaten up by her.

I get home late and try to sleep, which is hard because my eye throbs. When I wake up, she'll be gone. She'll slip out into the darkness of the night and never look back or reflect on what she did to create this mess. When she's called out, she retreats and makes herself the victim. I've seen it so many times before. In a few months, she'll reach out, and we'll never discuss this again. The pattern is set. It's happened so many times before.

The bank is understanding when I call in sick the next day. Malik offers to stay home from work, but I brush him off. I'd rather be alone. I take a long, hot shower, wrap myself in my robe, and fall asleep.

"Is anyone home?" I hear someone call out from the living room, and in my groggy state, I assume it's Malik checking if I'm still in bed.

"In here," I respond, kicking the blanket off me.

The door pushes open, and when I see its Dax, I jolt up and pull my robe more tightly around myself.

"Sorry." He stands in the doorway. "You said to come in." He hesitates at the door. His hand rests on the doorknob, his eyes drift to me and then comb over my body, and I once again grab my robe and pull it closed. His other hand holds a gift bag.

"I thought you were Malik."

Dax takes his hand off the doorknob. "I brought you something."

Dax walks over and sits on the bed next to me. My naked skin fills with goosebumps under my robe. He wears a backward cap, and his blue shirt matches his eyes. "Your eye looks horrible." He points to my face.

I continue to fidget. I really wish I was wearing clothes.

"What are you doing here? It's Friday. You were supposed to have alone time with Kylie. Wait. Is school already over?"

Dax tucks his leg underneath himself and turns to me. "She begged me for a sleepover with Jake and Camilla. I couldn't say no." He smiles. "Plus, you haven't been answering my calls."

Dax's eyes look like they've been possessed. He glances at my legs. Then, he closes his eyes. He looks at my chest and then darts them back to my eyes.

"I'm under the weather. I think my phone is dead somewhere."

I lean back against my headboard and pull the blanket over me. Dax follows and leans back too. He holds the gift bag out to me. "This is for you."

He nods, and I open the card first. It reads, *"I've been a jerk, but being your friend is such a perk."*

I peek inside the bag, where there is a large bag of Starbursts. I smile at Dax and hold the Starbursts against me.

"So cheesy, Dax."

Dax playfully hits me in the shoulder. "You started it with that ass cookie cake."

We both smile. Then, I remember what Dax thinks happened with Trey.

"It wasn't Trey and me."

I'm embarrassed to say the words out loud. To Dax. It would be less complicated if it were Trey and me out at my place. That would have felt more normal than this. Just a twenty-something year old enjoying a night in with a man she's dating. But the reality of the situation feels too complex for words.

"I know," Dax admits. "That's why I'm here. I wanted to check on you. To see if you're okay."

"You're right. The woman has no boundaries."

Dax cups my face. He's taking no pleasure in being right about my mom and how she made him feel. "I didn't want to be."

He strokes my eye, which is much less swollen than before but still tender and discolored. I turn to him. To lighten the mood, I say, "Please never hook up with my mom, Dax."

Dax runs his hand through my wet hair. "Middle-aged moms have never been my kink."

Dax's lips turn up in a smile, and I can't help but follow suit. He brushes a strand of hair behind my ear. I hold my breath for a moment.

"You have no idea what it's like." I shake my head, trying to get the million images that flood me out of my head.

Dax smirks, and his cheek dimple pops out. "To have

Juniper Soleta as my mom? You've got me there."

I lean my head further into the headboard and close my eyes. "To never matter or be important. Most of the time, when she's around, I feel invisible. I bet your mom was perfect."

Dax's arm brushes up against mine, and neither of us moves. We turn our heads to each other. I can make out the tiny, subtle freckles that sprinkle his cheeks.

"My mom is pretty perfect. I'm not going to lie. And this isn't the same, trust me, I know, but I've always been a bit of the black sheep of the family. Try being the baby brother of an NFL star. I've felt invisible in life too." He never glances away from me, but he grows quiet again. He presses his lips together, forming a thin line and his tongue flicks out to wet them. "And then Jenna was the baby. The only girl who could do no wrong. And then she ended up being an amazing athlete herself."

"You went to a division one school to play basketball. On scholarship," I remind him.

"True." Dax nods. "A state school. Because I didn't get the national recruitment attention, and now I sound like a whiney frat boy, so I think I'll stop here. But know, Carrie, if you ever want to talk, I'm here."

"Same, Dax." I bite my lip to suppress a smile. "If you ever want to talk about this middle child syndrome that plagues you, I'm your girl."

Our heads inch closer to each other. Dax once again wets his lips. His hand is a blur as it comes up and cups my face. One more inch, and we'll be connected. And not because of a list that brought us into a bathroom together or because of a game of truth or dare. But a real kiss.

"How you feeling, Carrie?" My door swings open, Dax jumps and puts space between us, and I pull the covers up to my chin. Malik grins at Dax and then at me. "Oh good, you seem to be much better. The color has come back to your face." "Great to see you, Dax." Malik still stands in the doorway, in no hurry to leave. "Seeing that you're both here, should we do some basketball strategizing?"

"Malik, can we catch up later?" I nod toward the door. But I know that even when he leaves, it will be hard to recreate the moment.

"You guys sure?" Malik comes over to the bed and pretends he's about to get in but then walks out of the room, laughing.

Dax throws his legs over the bed. "Malik has impeccable timing."

I sit up too. "He always has."

Dax stands at the foot of the bed. A minute ago, I thought I would get kissed, but now, Dax acts casual, like nothing was about to happen. "I am sorry. For what happened. And I'm here. As a friend. If you need me or want me to be."

The word friend hangs in the air between us. That's what we are. That's what Dax can offer me. But I'm not imagining this thing between us.

"Thanks, Dax. And same."

He walks to the door and pauses with his hand on the doorknob. Then, he turns to me. "I need to get going. There's a get-together, and I'm meeting some people there."

My mouth feels too dry for words, so I purse my lips and wave.

"Okay, then," Dax says. But he stands a moment longer, looking at me, and then shakes his head and walks out.

When I was an eighth grader and was put on the varsity girls' basketball team, sometimes the girl's and boy's teams would both have away games on the same night, and the two teams would share a bus. I was always relegated to the front of the bus, near the coaches and managers, and Dax would walk by me and go to the back of the bus with the other cool older students.

I was caught staring at him more than once when he walked by. Back at the RV, I hid a yearbook under my pillow, and when my mom wasn't around, I would pull it out and stare at his picture. One day, I got bold, took a black sharpie, and drew a heart around him.

He wasn't like the other high school boys. He opened doors for the ladies. He went out of his way to smile and say hello. I never heard him say a bad word. I crushed on him so hard. The thing about crushing on someone in high school is that it's sometimes the only version we get of them. We all peak at different ages, and many people crest at eighteen and never become a different version of themselves.

Dax is different. He went away to college, experienced life, traveled, got married, became a dad, and went through grief. He became a better version of the person he was, and he was already pretty great.

Yet, as I lie back in bed, pull the covers up to my chin, and pull my knees up to my chest, I can't help but think of that girl on the bus. Her having the opportunity to be friends with someone like Dax would have been enough. It would have been everything. But the twenty-six-year-old me doesn't feel that way. I'm not imagining that we have some chemistry that pulls us to each other. To the old me, it would have been enough. But it's not anymore.

Chapter Sixteen

Dax

"YOU AND CARRIE LOOKED COZY the other day," Malik says as we kneel, laying the new floors in Carrie's bread and breakfast. I was right. Jake was more than willing to give the leftover porcelain tiles to Carrie at cost, and the floors are starting to come together.

I toss a towel at his face. "It's a good thing you came home when you did."

Malik throws the towel back at me and wipes his brow. "What does that mean?"

"It means I was thinking with the wrong head. Do I need to spell it out for you?"

Malik laughs but shakes his head. "I'm a guy. I get it. But what's wrong with that?" Malik lays the tile down, pounds it in, and goes to the next one. "You could do a lot worse than Carrie. A lot."

"So many things. Kylie loves Carrie and needs her around." I line up the next tile for Malik. "We've become such good friends. I need stability for Kylie, and well, sex ruins things. And I'm nowhere near ready to date."

"Or it doesn't," Malik snaps back.

I work my way to the edges, tile by tile. "I saw you and Carrie's little list. Did you have anything to do with Carrie jumping me in the bathroom the night before Jake and Camilla's wedding?"

Malik stops what he's doing and looks at me. "I shouldn't say anything, but—"

"Out with it, Malik," I snap. I'm finally going to get to the bottom of this list.

Malik stops what he's doing and looks at me. "Carrie is saying *fuck it* to cancer and taking charge of her life. What that looks like is completely up to her."

"Meaning?" I grow more irritated. I want someone to interpret that list for me. I've been curious about it since I first saw it.

"Meaning she can figure out what a fulfilled life looks like. Carrie is the strongest woman I know. Scratch that. The strongest person I know."

My mind flashes to us in the bathroom. It wasn't chemistry that was lacking. But I care about Carrie enough to treat her well, and I'm not in a position to treat anyone great right now. The more I think about it, Carrie may be my best friend. I talk to her about things. About Zari. I'm not willing to lose that. I need friendship more than I need anything else.

"Carrie and I are meant to be friends." I rub my knee that falls off the foam pad. "We're building a real friendship."

"Then, quit messing with her." Malik turns his back to me.

"I'm not messing with her." I stop working to look at Malik.

He stops the tile pounding. "Have you ever considered that being just friends isn't enough for Carrie? So, if this is how you feel, quit playing strip basketball with her. Or almost making out."

"Malik—"

But he cuts me off. "She's strong, but she's also sensitive. You have the ability to crush her, Dax. Be careful with her feelings."

There is little I can say in response. I didn't know Malik saw it this way. It's not how I've seen things. I don't know if Carrie wants more with me. I don't get the impression she does. We enjoy each other's company. We're friends.

After Malik's and my heart-to-heart, we work beside each other in silence.

I get the house in order at home, and the guestroom made up because Zari's sister Amina arrives tonight from Atlanta. She wanted to fly in and visit Kylie and me. We haven't seen her since our trip to Atlanta this past summer. She's two years older than Zari. Well, two years older than Zari should be, which is thirty. But Zari will forever be twenty-six, and now Amina is thirty-one. Dying stops everything, and we all continue to age without her.

"Kylie," I say as she sits on the couch watching a cartoon. "What do you think we should do while Amina's here?"

Kylie looks up at me with big brown eyes. "We could play with dolls and fish and take her to a restaurant."

"Those sound like fun—"

Before I have a chance to finish, Amina comes barreling through the door, bags in hand, and runs toward Kylie.

"Is that my baby girl?" Amina plucks Kylie off the couch and holds her.

"Auntie, you're here!"

Amina spins her around. When she puts her down, she comes and hugs me. "Hey, Dax. It's good to see you."

Her arms wrap around me and hold me for about five seconds too long.

"You too." As Amina continues to cuddle Kylie, I grab her bags and bring them to the guestroom.

I need a moment to myself. Amina looks like her, and all my oxygen is gone. She wears her hair in long braids, just like Zari did. They both have the same dark brown, almond-shaped eyes. Their voices even sound alike. Seeing her is a lot, and I know it isn't her fault, but it always sets me back.

"What should we do tonight, Kylie? I want to do everything while I'm here." Amina sits on the couch and pulls Kylie onto her lap. She examines her hair and looks pleased with the state of it.

"Tonight, we should watch a movie and eat popcorn." Kylie rests her head on Amina. "And then play dolls. And you should sleep in my bed so we can cuddle."

Amina looks back at me. "And maybe we could give your dad some time to hang out with friends, and we could have the house to ourselves."

"Amina, you don't have to," I begin to say. I have nowhere I want to go anyway.

"Dax, I know you have help here, but you're doing this alone. Go. Have fun. Tomorrow, the three of us can spend the day together."

There's no point in arguing with her. Amina enters every space and takes over. I say goodbye, call Jake and twist his arm into going into town and grabbing a drink. I drive the minute to his house, and he takes us in his truck.

We switch it up, drive past the Pool Hall on Main Street, and go to the Tasty Tavern instead. It's quieter, and the beer is better. We sit at a round table by the window, and I order a tall beer, and Jake orders a soda water.

"What's Camilla doing tonight?" I ask between sips.

"She already had pajamas on and couldn't wait to watch some reality TV nonsense. I was happy to get out." Jake's eyes smile when he talks about Camilla. Like he's always thinking of a memory that brings him joy. It's endearing and nauseating all at once.

"Yeah," I say. "Amina acted like she wanted alone time with Kylie and practically kicked me out of the house. I didn't know where to go and didn't feel like going to the parents' house."

A server comes by, and I order another beer. "How's Camilla feeling?"

"For the most part, good." Jake adjusts his weight on the chair. "The nausea has gone away, but now she's tired all the time." Jake looks at me and sees through all the bullshit in a way only an older sibling can. "How are things with you?"

"It's hard to see Amina," I admit. "Kylie needs her family in her life. She deserves to be surrounded by love. But damn, Jake, she looks just like her. It's like seeing Zari's ghost. When I see her, I start the grieving process all over."

Jake leans back and puts a toothpick between his teeth. "I'm not going to pretend to know what this feels like. If anything happened to Camilla . . ." He leans forward. "I know I'd never get over it. I'm here for you. However that looks. We all are."

Four drinks later, all for me, Jake peels me out of my seat. "I'm going to use the bathroom," he says. "I'll meet you outside."

I nod, throw down some cash, stand outside in the brisk evening, lean against the building, and wait. Voices come down the sidewalk, and it's Trey with a few people. He separates from the group.

"Hey, man," he says. "You should have come to the pool hall. A lot of people were there tonight."

"Yeah. I wanted something quieter." I'm hoping he'll continue on his way. Trey is the last guy I want to see right now.

He leans against the brick building and puts his leg up against it. Trey chuckles. "Carrie was there tonight. She gives me such hot and cold vibes, man. I can't figure her out."

"You want to talk to me about Carrie?" Blood rushes to my face.

"Just making conversation, man," Trey says. "I've been interested, but I can't read her."

My chest tightens, and I push off the wall. "I'm no expert on females, but I hear they don't take kindly to men who make passes at their mom."

And then, the blur of Trey's fist taking a swing at me comes into focus, but all the beer I've drunk causes me to have a slow reaction time, and his fist connects with my face. The sting of contact with my cheekbone causes me to wince.

"What the hell?" I I charge him and take him to the ground as his arms still throw punches at my face.

Somebody pulls me off of Trey. "What is this?" Jake shouts, standing between us. He may be my brother, but he's also Trey's boss. "Two grown-ass men fighting on Main Street. Is this who we are?"

"I'm sick of your mouth," Trey says, and I spit blood on the ground and try to charge him again, but Jake stops me.

I take a step closer, but Jake pulls me back. "Bullshit. The only reason you're upset is because I know. You're a loser who couldn't get anywhere with Carrie, so you went for her mom."

Trey connects with my face again, even though Jake stands between us. I reach around and punch Trey in the gut.

"Enough!" Jake yells, this time louder. "You guys are embarrassing yourself." Jake grabs me by the arm and pulls me to his truck. He then turns back to Trey.

"We'll discuss this tomorrow."

"If I ever hear the name Carrie come out of your mouth again, you'll be sorry," I yell as Jake shoves me into the truck.

Jake gets in and slams the door but doesn't say anything. I hate how my older brothers can make me feel like I'm still a kid. He turns to me when he pulls into my driveway at the lake. "I'm sure you were in the right, Dax. But he's my employee. You have to settle things better than that."

"He's an ass." I spit blood through the open window. The taste of iron fills my mouth.

"I know that. But when you stoop to his level, you're no better than him. And you're a dad. You don't get a pass, Dax. You have to be better than this."

"He tried hooking up with Juniper Soleta. When he was trying to date Carrie."

Jake looks at me, mouth open. "I'm going to pretend I didn't hear that. Go sleep it off. Camilla and I'll check on you in the morning."

Because luck isn't on my side today, Amina lies awake on the couch, and when I walk in the door, she flips on the lamp.

"Dax, what happened to your face?" She rushes to me, and I try to brush her away.

"It's nothing, I promise."

"It's not nothing. You're bleeding."

She grabs my hand, brings me into the bathroom, and shuts the door. I sit on the counter, and she pulls a washcloth out of the drawer and starts wiping the blood off me. "Are you going to tell me what the meaning of this is? I certainly hope my niece's dad isn't going around getting into fights. Kylie deserves better than that." Amina puts pressure on my face and looks at me. She and Zari have the same disappointed face.

"I know, Amina. I know. Would it be better if I told you I was defending my friend's honor?"

"Maybe," Amina says. "Is that what you were doing?"

I tell her all about Trey. And Carrie. And Juniper. Amina listens to me without speaking a word. When she's sure I'm done with the story, she puts her hands on her hips.

"Is that all?"

I nod. "Pretty much."

Amina pulls me off the counter and walks me into the kitchen, where she grabs a tall glass of water and hands it to me. "Who is Carrie to you?"

"A friend," I answer without hesitation. "I've known her forever, actually. The friendship is a newer thing."

"I see." Amina puts her index finger over her lips in thought. "Do I get to meet your friend Carrie?"

"Wheaton's a small town. It's likely."

We sit in the living room on the couch, and whatever Amina was watching when I came in is on mute, and all I can hear is my breath. We stare ahead at the TV and the shelves full of books and photos.

"It looks like a shrine in here," Amina says, breaking the silence but never looking at me.

Photos adorn the entire room. Zari and I at a college party. Us at an event for the college athletes. Arms around each other at graduation. Our engagement. Our wedding. Zari pregnant. Zari in the hospital, holding Kylie.

"I don't want Kylie ever to forget her." I rest my ankle

on my knee. "She was so young. She's forgetting stuff."

"Look, Dax. I get it. I do. I lost my sister. But it looks like a mausoleum in here. At some point, you have to move on."

"No—"

"Yes," Amina interrupts. "We're all worried about you. Zari wouldn't have wanted this nonsense. She wouldn't have wanted you to be miserable. And she sure as hell wouldn't have wanted you to get your ass handed to you like you did tonight."

Amina looks at me, raises her eyebrows, and I chuckle. She's probably right. Maybe tomorrow, I'll remove some of the older pictures. But moving forward feels too much like moving on. Kylie was so young when Zari died. If I don't give her constant reminders, she will grow up not knowing her mom. There are no new memories to have with her.

Amina turns to me. "I know you love Kylie's therapist. Maybe you need to get some therapy too."

"I'll take everything you said into consideration. But for now, I need to sleep this off."

Chapter Seventeen

Carrie

"GUESS WHAT ALL THE GUYS were talking about at work?" Malik leans against the shopping cart as we pick up a few groceries.

"Hmm." I put my hand up to my chin like I'm thinking about this hard. "You and the crew want to come to my B&B and paint the exterior for free? 'Cause you all love me so much?"

"Umm, no." Malik swats me. "I guess Trey and Dax got into a fight. Trey threw the first punch, and then Jake broke it up. It's literally all people were talking about at work."

"For real?" I throw noodles into our cart.

"Sure am." Malik shakes his head. "I know it's true because Trey confirmed it. He wouldn't say what it was about, though. Dax hasn't told you?"

"We haven't talked."

"Speaking of the freaking devil." Malik rams the cart into my side. "Here he comes."

I glance up, and Dax walks toward us with a beautiful

woman who looks familiar. Her face. That smile. I've seen her somewhere.

"Hey, guys." Dax looks at us and then at the woman he's with. "This is Amina, Zari's sister. Amina, these are my friends, Malik and Carrie."

No wonder she looks familiar to me. She looks so much like Zari. Not only has Dax shown me pictures, but he also has them displayed all over his house. They could be twins.

"It's nice to meet you both." Amina's smile widens until I can see all of her teeth. "I'm here for the long weekend. I flew in yesterday from Atlanta."

"Hi." Malik pulls her into a hug. "You are gorgeous. It's so nice to meet Zari's sister."

Amina turns to me. I stutter. I'm not worthy of being in her presence. "Yes, it's nice to meet you."

I look at my outfit and have never felt more underwhelmed about myself until standing in a supermarket next to Amina.

"We're picking up food. Amina has a couple of meals she wants to cook for us." Dax looks down at the food in his cart.

"Yes, and speaking of cooking, are you two doing anything tomorrow evening? I'd love to have you over to Dax's for dinner. Jenna is coming. And I think Jake and Camilla as well." Amina folds her hands under her chin. She's so charming, and there will be no way to say no to her.

Malik and I look at each other and shrug. There is part of me that wants to get to know Amina, but there is another part of me that wants to run.

"I won't take no for an answer," Amina continues. "My jambalaya recipe is to die for. Please, join us."

"We don't have plans, do we, Malik?" I ask.

This is a moment where I hope Malik will save me. He'll swoop in and create plans that I wasn't aware of.

"None. Tell us what time to be there and what to bring, and we'll be there." Malik looks from me to Dax and then to Amina.

"Come at six and bring yourselves." Amina beams. "Isn't this exciting, Dax? We're having a dinner party."

Dax doesn't look excited, though. He seems as struck being in Amina's presence as I feel.

"See ya'll tomorrow," she adds, and I wave as we continue grocery shopping.

When we get to the other side of the aisle, I nudge Malik. "Dax looked super uncomfortable. No?"

Malik tosses pop tarts into our cart. "Did you see his swollen lip? Trey did a number on it."

How ironic that as my black eye is almost healed, Dax now has a fat lip. He and Trey fighting makes no sense. Trey called me a couple of days ago and acted as if nothing had happened and that my mom didn't suddenly leave town for a reason. She was on her way back to Arizona the day after I confronted her. Typical. I never mentioned that I know anything because I don't want to say the words out loud. The conversation felt creepy. He wanted to try to date me after making a pass at my mom—what a dirtbag.

"Can I just say that you actually put together a very nice outfit?" Malik leans into my bedroom door as I get ready for dinner at Dax's.

"Don't look so surprised."

I'm starting to feel more confident dressing for my body. Tonight, I chose a pair of jeans that Malik bought me. They hit me at my ankle, and I paired them with a flat. And on top, I have a casual denim shirt. A few years ago, I would have rolled my eyes at a woman who takes so much time getting dressed. But I was wrong. Investing in what I wear has done wonders for my confidence. Old Carrie may have been wrong about this. Maybe about a lot of things.

Even though Amina told us not to bring anything, I grab a bottle of wine from the fridge and the collection of books that I found for Kylie. When I was young, the Ramona Quimby books got me interested in reading, so when I came across this antique set at the local bookstore, I had to buy them. Maybe they'll instill a love of reading in Kylie as they did for me.

"Hi, honey, we're home," Malik calls out as we walk through the door. Kylie gets up from playing on the floor, Amina rushes over like she's known us forever, and Dax waves from the kitchen.

"It smells great in here, Amina," I hug her back and hand her the bottle of wine.

"Thanks. The jambalaya has been cooking all day. It's an old family recipe. You're going to love it."

"Hey, guys." Jenna gets up from the couch and takes my jacket from me. "I'm so happy you could come."

The door is still open, and Jake and Camilla come up behind us. Camilla pulls me into a hug. "It looks like a party."

"Here. Give the jackets to me." Jake takes the coats from Jenna, and we all work our way inside.

Malik lifts Kylie and spins her, and I go into the kitchen to see if I can be helpful and grill Dax on what happened.

"Your lip looks terrible."

Dax feels his lip when I say it. It's cut on the corner. Only one side of it is swollen, and the side of the face is also bruised.

"You should have seen it a couple of days ago." Dax grabs plates from his counter. "It feels like it's growing its own heart."

I lean in and quiet my voice. "What'd you say to Trey to piss him off?"

Dax lets me put my hand on his lip. It's warm, and I grab an ice cube, and hold it to his lip. "I didn't say anything untrue. He's a tool."

"Such a tool."

We both smile.

Dax leans against the counter, looking out at all the guests in his home. I lean back, too, and look at him. "Are you doing okay? You seem off to me."

Dax hands me plates and then grabs cups, and I follow him to the table. "It's been a very long few days. Having Amina here stirs up about a million feelings that I can't seem to articulate."

I set down all eight plates. "Dax, I always knew you married someone beautiful, but knowing that Zari looked so much like Amina. Umm, wow."

"What are you two talking about in there?" Amina comes to the table with a glass of wine and hands it to me. "When you whisper, it makes it hard for me to hear you."

"Nothing." Dax and I say in unison, and Amina raises her eyebrow and stares.

Jenna grabs a pitcher of water from the fridge. "Do we have everything? What else can I help with?"

"Nothing." Amina brings all the food to the table, and we sit down. "Let's eat."

Amina dishes us all jambalaya and cornbread. I stare at her. I can't help myself. I feel like a fangirl in the presence of someone I'm not worthy of being around. Like I'm looking at the sun. Everything about Dax losing

Zari and his grief becomes clearer for me.

Amina catches my stare and smiles. "What is it?"

"It's just . . ." I hesitate, but all eyes are on me. Well, except for Kylie, who is already ripping into her bread. "I never met Zari, but you look so much like her pictures."

Amina smiles. "I know. Literally, everyone thought we were twins growing up."

"You're stunning." Malik moans while taking a bite of food. I'm not keeping count, but this may be the fifth time he's told her. "I always knew you wouldn't waste your beauty on someone ugly, Dax."

"We have good genes," Amina says. "Our mom was runner-up for Miss Georgia back in the day." Amina turns her attention to Kylie. "And speaking of Georgia, we need to get Kylie down there this fall so Mama and I can teach her all of our recipes."

"Yeah, Daddy," Kylie chimes in. "I want to go to Atlanta."

"We'll make that happen, sweetie." Dax pats the top of her hand.

Amina looks up from her plate. "What's this about a three-on-three basketball team?" She looks at me, Malik, and Dax.

"Temporary," Dax cuts in. "It's a tournament, and the winner gets to choose a charity to donate the winning funds."

Amina adjusts herself in her chair. "That's amazing. You could donate to breast cancer awareness. That cause was so near and dear to Zari."

Dax nods and puts his fork down. "It's a contender. We've also thrown out lymphoma cancers. Or maybe even domestic abuse survivors. We have options."

"Honestly," I say. "For me, it's more about playing the game again. I missed it. It's been good."

"Same." Dax nods. I missed the competition. It's been fun."

Jake puts his fork down and places his hand on Camilla's belly. "It seems like a good way to get hurt if you ask me."

Camilla laughs. "I can't wait to watch you guys play and relive the glory days I hear so much about."

After dinner, Jenna, Camilla, and I help Dax clean up. He and I get dishes duty, so I grab a towel and stand by him.

"You haven't been running." I close the door to the dishwasher after rinsing everything.

He turns the water off and leans against the counter. I throw him the towel to dry his hands. "Now that the school year has started, and we're losing daylight, it's harder to get out in the morning."

Dax reaches up and touches my eye. The bone still feels bruised from his sharp elbow, but it looks so much better than it did.

"It's healing." I touch his lip once again. "Your face looks worse."

Dax continues to poke around my eye with his finger. "I feel horrible that I did that."

"Dax." I swat his hand away. "It's not the first shiner I've gotten playing ball."

Amina walks into the kitchen, and Dax and I jump like we've been caught in a conversation we shouldn't be having.

"Carrie, I thought us ladies could go for an after-dinner walk. We could bring a glass of wine and have some girl talk."

"Can I come too?" Kylie runs to us in the kitchen.

"Yes," Amina says. "You're a young lady, after all."

Dax grabs the towel, puts it in his back pocket, and nods toward the door.

"Sure, let's do it," I say.

We fill our wine glasses and head outside. It's a cool evening, and I wish I had grabbed my jacket before heading out. October is in a few days, and the tops of the trees are already starting to change color. The days have started to get noticeably shorter too. When my alarm goes off in the morning, it's still dark, and an hour or so after dinner, the sun sets for the day.

We walk down the long gravel road that leads to Jake and Camilla's home and eventually reach the bench near a few apple trees. Kylie runs ahead to pick up apples that have fallen on the ground.

"Where does this road lead to?" Amina turns and asks.

"That road leads to my grandparent's house." Camilla sits on the bench. "I lived there until I moved in with Jake. Now, we take care of it, but it sits empty."

Amina nods and then sits on the bench, and I follow. Jenna and Kylie take a seat on the grass, but Kylie only sits only for a moment and then runs off to chase a Monarch butterfly she sees. I take a sip of my wine, and it warms my stomach. Amina leans back.

"Kylie is so loved. She's lucky to have the three of you."

"She's lucky to have Jenna and Camilla." The words pour out of me, and it takes me a moment to realize I said them out loud. I love Kylie, but I'm not anyone special to her. Not like her aunties.

"Come on." Jenna picks at the grass. "Dax told me how much you've been helping out on Fridays after school. Kylie loves you."

"She reminds me so much of her mama." Amina smiles. "She's headstrong and determined. She may be all cute and innocent now, but you wait. Dax will have his hands full with her someday. I'm already imagining her teenage years."

"The whole town looks out for Dax. And Kylie. They are well-loved here," Camilla says.

"I know, I know." Amina takes a slow sip of wine and holds the glass against her lip. "But I want Dax to have someone. He acts like he's happy and content with his life. But it's been almost four years since Zari died. Four. And he's not happy. I worry more about him than I do about Kylie."

Amina removes her glass from her lip and puts it between her legs. "I go back to Atlanta, so I won't be here to help anything along. But I know the three of you care about Dax. Don't you all have any friends you could set him up with? I want him to be happy. Does he date at all?"

Jenna and I make eye contact, and then she speaks. "Dax and dating? No. But he's not sitting at home crying, either. He gets out, has a lot of friends, and maybe he's into someone. I'm not sure. It's not something he'd probably share with me anyway."

Everyone looks at Camilla. "Don't look at me. I married into the Abram family. No one tells me anything."

All eyes turn to me. "He doesn't talk to me about girls, so I'm also clueless," I finally say.

"He's stubborn," Amina says. "That was Zari's only complaint about him. His stubbornness."

"How do you think Kylie is doing?" Jenna asks. "We see her all the time, so it's hard to pick up on changes."

Amina takes a long drink of wine. "It's sad, but she got so little time with Zari. And the entire time, Zari was so sick. Don't get me wrong, it's a loss, and Kylie is sad. But she was so young."

Jenna stands up and brushes the grass off of her

leggings. "I know Dax still brings her to therapy."

"Well, I'm being the typical big sister and getting involved where I have no place. I've just never seen a man so in love as Dax was with my sister."

What Amina may not realize is that Dax is presently in love with Zari. He's not over her, and I don't think he ever will be.

When we get back to Dax's, he gives me a look, but I smile, letting him know that all is good.

"We should go, Malik." I walk over to Kylie and hug her. "Thanks so much for dinner, Amina. It was incredible."

"Let us know when you're in town next." Malik pulls her into a hug. "You can cook for us."

"Deal." Amina walks us to the door and gives us both one last hug.

I say goodbye to Jake, Camilla, and Jenna, who sit around the table and share a laugh with Dax.

We get into the car, and before the engine is hot, Malik turns to me. "How was the girl talk?"

"Amina is worried about Dax. She wants him to move on." I roll the window down a crack to get some fresh air. "She's wondering if any of us know of any possibilities."

Malik pats my knee. "Did you volunteer yourself as an option?"

"Yeah," I say. "'Cause that sounds like something I would do."

"Fuck-it list, Carrie. You need to tell him how you feel."

I wave him off because this is not something I'll ever do.

Chapter Eighteen

Dax

TODAY IS WHEATON'S FALL FESTIVAL, and it's all Kylie has talked about since the school year started. Several blocks of Main Street are closed for tonight's street dance, and it looks like the town has thrown up pumpkins, hay bales, and cornucopias. The first time Zari ever visited Wheaton was for the fall festival. We'd only been dating about a month, and I brought her here to experience all that is small-town Americana. She both loved it and felt culture shock.

It's unseasonably warm for October, so we're plenty warm when we walk out of the house, me in the only flannel shirt I own and Kylie in a checkered coat.

"I want to pick my pumpkin first." Kylie takes my hand and drags me down the road toward Main Street. I can barely keep up with her short little legs.

"How about we do that last, or Daddy will be carrying a pumpkin all day. Let's start at the petting zoo, or you can bob for apples."

Kylie pouts her lips, stops walking, and puts her hands on her hips. I know I've lost this battle. Jenna always tells me that Kylie will be spoiled if I continue giving her everything she wants. She thinks I'm overcompensating for the loss of her mom. I know I'm overcompensating, but Kylie is the farthest thing from a spoiled brat, and I choose my battles wisely with her. So, we go to the pumpkin patch, and she touches a few before deciding on a perfectly round one. "This is it, Daddy."

I pick up the pumpkin for her, knowing I'll be lugging this ten-pound beast around for the next few hours.

"I knew it the minute I saw it." Kylie squeals as she jumps up and down.

I pay for the pumpkin, which costs a dollar a pound, and the cashier tells me it's sixteen dollars. Correction. I'll carry a sixteen-pound pumpkin around for the next few hours.

"Ponies next!" Kylie leaps down the road as I support the weight of the beast of a pumpkin in my arms.

She rides a pony, pets some goats, rolls around in a pool of corn and then eats a caramel apple, which is no small feat, seeing that as of recently, she's missing her two front teeth.

"Look, Daddy! There's Emma." I see her friend Emma from school walking around with her parents. "Can I go say hi?"

When I nod, Kylie runs over and hugs her school friend, and then I spend the next hour talking with Emma's parents as Kylie and her friend enter the sack race, then use the sack to go down the big yellow slide. It's almost dark when Kylie quits running and decides she's ready to go home with my parents and watch a movie. My arms ache, even though I set the damn pumpkin down at every attraction we visited. I hand it to my dad and say goodnight to my girl.

"Kylie. I'll hang out here a bit longer. But I'll see you soon."

She barely looks back at me as she walks away, my

dad on one arm and my mom on the other.

"We're going to watch something fun and eat popcorn. Don't hurry, Daddy."

Propane heaters line the street as it's gotten a few degrees cooler and the band warms up. I debate following my parents home and watching a movie with them, but instead, I decide to stick around for a bit longer.

"What up, man?" Malik joins me at my table, and when I look at his outfit, my first reaction is to laugh.

"Look at you." I point, and Malik spins for me. He wears cowboy boots with jeans, a flannel shirt, and a cowboy hat to finish the look.

"Don't forget, I'm all country." Malik stops spinning and takes a drink. "I'm from Oklahoma, remember?"

"Did you see the email?" I ask Malik as Carrie approaches our table with Camilla and Jenna. "We got the three-on-three matchups for the next weekend. We need to strategize."

Carrie puts her hand to her ear, and the music starts up. "I'm sorry, did you say something? I can't hear you."

I move closer to Carrie and speak into her ear. "Did we decide on the name Next-Gens? Should we get a few practices in?"

Carrie barks a laugh. "I came here to dance. If you want to talk basketball, you'll have to do it on the dance floor."

"I'm not dancing," I call out, but it's too late. Carrie takes Malik's hand and runs to the dancefloor while Camilla and Jenna stay with me.

"Unfocused. Completely." I lean forward on the table and watch Malik spin Carrie, and she laughs as he picks her up. Everyone is decked out in their best fall gear today, and Carrie is no exception. Her jeans are tight, her boots reach halfway up calves, and her red and black flannel shirt is tied at the waist.

"It's a dance, Dax. Enjoy it." Camilla puts her arm on mine. "Don't feel like you have to stand around with a pregnant woman."

Jenna loops her arm in mine and puts her chin on my shoulder. We both watch the dance floor. "I like Carrie. You should ask her out. You need to put yourself out there."

"You're one to talk." I shake Jenna's chin off my shoulder. "I don't see you putting yourself out there."

I regret the words as soon as I say them. Jenna was engaged to her high school sweetheart and called it off while at University. Then, she started dating some mystery man last fall, and she doesn't talk about it much, but that relationship went south, and Jenna has been in a slump ever since.

"I'm sorry." I wrap my arm around her waist. "I didn't mean that. I'm feeling all this pressure to move on, and I'm not ready."

Jenna puts her head on me. "I know. I'm sorry. You don't need your baby sister telling you what to do, either. But I think she's so perfect for you. There, I said it, and now I'll drop it."

"Maybe I will dance." Camilla and Jenna point me to the dance floor, and I'm so desperate to end the conversation with them that I'm willing to dance to get out of it.

"It's time for a square dance," the lead singer on stage yells into the microphone. "Line on up."

Malik grabs my arm before I can beeline back to the comfort of my table. We stand in a circle. There are about eight of us. The announcer says, "All join hands and circle, circle to the left."

Carrie is on my right, Malik on my left, and we join hands. I've never wanted to be anywhere else more in my life.

"Take your partner, swing her high, then low." Malik partners up with the woman next to him, which means Carrie is my partner. She takes my hand and puts it on her waist and shows me what to do.

"Now promenade with a heel and a toe!"

Carrie throws her head back, laughing at me, as I look like a deer caught in headlights. "Go with it, Dax. You might have fun."

"Ladies, go in the middle. Now, the gents. With your right hand, circle to the left."

Malik and I, and two guys I don't know, circle in the middle one way, then the other, while the women stands around, waiting for their turn. I've never square danced in my life, nor had the desire to, but here I am.

"Break that star and swing." Carrie takes my hand again, and I swing her.

I'm a step or two behind the entire dance. Most of it involves Carrie pulling me along for the ride, placing my hand on her shoulder or waist, or spinning me to face the other way. The longest square dance known to man finally ends, and I nearly run off the dance floor. When I get to a table, Carrie joins me and continues to laugh.

She puts her elbows on the table, and her body shakes from laughter. "You weren't half bad."

"So says your hysterical laughter." I finally let out a breath and smile. "I came out on the dance floor to discuss basketball. I got more than I bargained for."

"I guess being coordinated on the court doesn't mean you are on the dance floor."

I'm not bad, but who knows how to square dance? I hadn't done it since gym class in the fourth grade.

When the next song turns slow, I want to show Carrie that I'm not that bad of a dancer. My mouth opens to ask

Carrie to dance, but before I have a chance, another man approaches her.

"Care to dance, Carrie?"

She puts her hand out, and he leads her to the dance floor. But I'm not in the mood. Instead, I watch Carrie talk easily to the guy she dances with. He's into her. Another guy can tell these things. Although I have no right, I feel a tinge of jealousy.

I like Carrie. I always have. When she was younger, even though the two of us never conversed, I looked out for her. She was the youngest on her basketball team, and when the men's and women's teams traveled together, I always looked on from afar.

We never talked, though. Even after I moved back to Wheaton with Kylie after Zari died, we'd wave and say hi to each other. I even attended a couple of fundraisers for her when she was undergoing cancer treatment, but it never went deeper than superficial conversation. Everything changed when we kissed in the bathroom at Jake and Camilla's house. I told Carrie it was her that came onto me, but I wanted to kiss her too.

There is no playbook for dating after a spouse dies. But for the first time since losing Zari, I feel like I'm cheating on her. Everything up to this point was physical, but with Carrie, I think about her more than I should.

"Hey, there." I turn to see Blake standing next to me, and she's the last person I want to converse with.

"Hey." I inch to the side, putting more space between us.

Blake was my first girlfriend. She and I dated from tenth to twelfth grade. I don't remember who broke up with whom, but I was headed to one city for University, and she was headed to another, and it made sense. We ended things at our class graduation party and spent that last summer in Wheaton doing our own things.

"It's such a beautiful night, isn't it?" Blake puts her hand on mine.

When I moved back to Wheaton, I knew I'd see people from my past. But I recently heard Blake and her husband divorced, and she's texted me on more than one occasion since then.

"It was great to see you, but I'm being summoned." Blake looks disappointed, but she nods.

The rest of the night, I stand around with some of the guys and avoid the dance floor. I look for Jake when it's time to leave because I could use a ride, but he's nowhere in sight. I start walking in the direction of my parents' house, and the streetlights show me the way.

"Hey, partner, you need a hand?" Carrie loops her arm in mine and steadies me.

She's everywhere, which makes it impossible to avoid her and process how I'm feeling.

"Going to my parents' house to crash." I kick a rock down the road. "Kylie is there already."

There's a small park on the way, and I lead Carrie to a picnic table and take a seat.

My ass finds the top of the table, and I sit down. "I'm going to have to tiptoe when I get to my parents' house. Like when I was in high school."

Carrie sits next to me and hands me her bottle of water. "I didn't see you on the dance floor after your square dance."

"You were out there a lot." I take the water and pour it down my throat.

"The music was great." Carrie looks at the sky and smiles back at me. "And the night is clear, and the stars are so bright. What a fun night."

"The beer was stale. It got chilly. The music was only average."

Carrie jumps off the picnic table and holds her hand out to me. I slide off the edge, and we walk again in the direction of my parents' house. Neither of us speak, but a big sigh from Carrie comes out.

"What is it?" I ask, continuing to look down, focused on the road beneath my feet.

"Oh, it's nothing." Carrie continues to lead the way.

"Out with it."

Carrie folds her arms over her chest and rubs her fingers across her shoulders. "I was thinking of how different you and I are."

We reach the front of my parents' house, and all the lights are off except the outside one, illuminating the sidewalk that leads inside.

"We're not that different." I glance at my parents' house, and an upstairs light flicks on.

Carrie looks up too, and we're both aware that we're most likely being watched. "Cancer has taught me to look at life differently. To lie in the grass, look at the stars, and dance. To live life."

"Is this about your fuck-it list?" I think about that list with my name on it.

"Not really." Carrie shrugs. "But I guess that list is related. But that wasn't the point I was trying to make."

"What are you trying to say?"

Carrie walks up a step, and I follow until we stand in front of the door. "You use grief as the reason not to go for anything. To not feel. You stand back and judge how everyone else is living and make excuses for why you'll never move forward."

I place my hand against the cold metal of the doorknob. "Not fair. Your life has been easy compared to mine."

Carrie surprises me when she pinches my cheeks

between her hands. She forces my gaze on hers. "Dax, nothing about my life has been easy."

"I meant—"

But I don't have a chance to speak as Carrie continues. "Don't. You are choosing how to move forward. Or how not to. Don't act like your life has been harder than mine. You lost someone. And I was faced with my own mortality. Maybe yours was worse. But things have sucked for me too."

Thoughts flood me. Words that I want to say. Apologies I could and should make. But instead, I do what I do best. I lean forward with an urge to feel physically close to Carrie. To have her lips pressed against mine and to numb the overwhelming feeling of sadness. I'm almost there when I feel her hand against my chest.

"Umm. No." Her voice is cold and distant.

"I thought . . ." I begin to say.

But I don't finish. My head is a mixture of different thoughts, but none are coherent enough to say aloud. Do I want to kiss Carrie? Or do I want to feel the hope that being close to her brings? The possibility that life won't always feel like it does in this exact moment.

"I'm not some escape for you to deal with your feelings, Dax." Carrie folds her arms across her chest and looks at me.

She opens the door for me and then walks down the sidewalk away from me. "You need to figure things out."

The reminders that I'm not doing well surround me as I stand there and watch Carrie walk away. I want to be happy, but I'm not sure I deserve it. I have moments where I feel hope for a joyful future, but then I have nights like tonight where I think about Zari and what she would want for me and what she would say. Then, I have nights where I hardly think of her, and I feel like I'm betraying her and all she meant to me. My mind is heavy as I crawl into bed with Kylie and kiss her forehead before dozing off.

Chapter Nineteen

Carrie

"ARE YOU GOING TO TELL me what the mail from the hospital said?" Malik stands over me as I lie on the couch, trying to get a few minutes of sleep, but he has other plans for me. The envelope sits on my chest, opened.

"It's a reminder to set up my one-year scans." I keep my eyes closed. The couch dips by my feet, and Malik places them on his lap.

He doesn't say anything, and I concentrate on my breathing. One breath in through my nose, followed by a deep exhale through my mouth. I've been doing so well lately. Getting a cancer diagnosis is life changing. Every pain, cough, or shortness of breath stops me in my tracks, and I become convinced that the cancer is back.

One-year scans post-remission are a huge milestone in my cancer journey. The recurrence rate after this point goes down considerably. And my scans are coming up. I feel good for the most part. I'm tired a lot, but that's because I've been getting physical activity for the first time since my diagnosis. Not only running, but playing rigorous basketball, something I haven't done since college. Naturally, I'm tired.

My life is also fuller than before. I'm socializing for the first time in forever. I'm spending some time with Dax and Kylie, getting out more, and I've been busting my butt, getting my dream of a bed and breakfast up and running. At the same time, I am working with Sunny and Sis. My schedule is packed. It makes sense that I'm tired.

"Get out of your head, Carrie." Malik puts his hand on my shin, reading my mind. "Your scans are going to confirm that the cancer is gone."

"But what if—"

"No," Malik interrupts. "It's only going to be good news. You've never been more active or looked healthier."

Malik never allows me to talk about the what ifs. He's a superstitious guy who thinks that if I bring up the possibilities, I'm somehow bringing cancer back into my life.

"Let's talk about something else." Malik claps his hands together. "How's the list coming?"

"Well, I think we can mark number one as complete." I sit up and cross my legs. "I no longer dress like a teenage boy."

Malik checks out my current outfit. Pajamas.

I hit him on the arm. "Okay, my jammies don't count. For the most part, I look good. Or, at least, better." We laugh, and I continue, "Let's skip number two—"

"No way. I want the details. How are things going with Dax?"

"Never better," I say. But I don't mean any of it. We're two ships passing in the night, heading in opposite directions. There is this part of me that wants to change him, but I don't want to be one of those girls.

"But you like him, don't you?" Malik pokes me in my side.

"Ugh, Malik. Why do you do this to me?" I lie my head on his shoulder. "I was happy before you opened up that can of worms."

"But . . ." Malik's big, brown eyes stare at me. "You think he's so dreamy?"

I throw a pillow at his head. "I'm attracted to him. Who's not?"

"Very True." Malik puts his hand to his face and grins.

"Except Dax is unavailable, and he reminds me of it constantly. He isn't ready to move on yet, and he's made it clear to me that he hooks up with women once, and that's it before anyone develops feelings."

Malik plops his head on my shoulder and sighs. "But haven't you ever wondered—"

My face fills with heat. "Not at the cost of not getting to be his friend anymore. No."

We stand up. It's getting late, and I'm exhausted and need to get to bed. Before Malik goes into his bedroom, he turns to me. "I think this is different. There's a spark, and Dax feels it too. I can tell."

I stand in my doorway, chewing on the inside of my cheek, thinking about what Malik says. "I think you're giving me hope where none exists."

THE TOURNAMENT STARTS TODAY, AND a million texts have already been shared between Dax, Malik, and me; a reminder to wear our jerseys, a dark purple hue. I don't know if Dax knew it when he chose this color, but it represents support for lymphoma cancers.

Another text reminds us what time to be at the gym, to eat a good breakfast, to be sure to hydrate, and finally, a reminder that if we win the first game, we'll end up in the winner's bracket and can expect a full day at the gym. There is almost nothing I hate more than being on a group text.

This three-on-three basketball tournament means different things to all of us. Malik is a born competitor and has missed being part of a team. Dax feels like he's going through a contemplative time where he's trying to figure out what role basketball will have in his life. For me, it's symbolic of moving on and forward in a direction where cancer will forever be in the rearview mirror. Sure, it would be great to place in the top three and get some money, but we all realize this tournament has taken on a life of its own.

When Malik and I walk through the school doors, the smell overwhelms me and brings me back to the days when I was part of a team. The concession stands open, cooking hot dogs waft in the air along with the buttery, rich smell of popcorn and coffee brewing. Candy is laid out in rows, and the sound of squeaky shoes echo on the gym floor.

It's already packed when we walk into the gym as a game nears completion. People sit on the bleachers, and two women sit behind a bench and run the scoreboard. Two referees, who look like recent high school graduates, officiate in their zebra-striped shirts and black shorts.

Two games go on at once, and a row of folding chairs separates the two courts. I make eye contact with Dax, and he waves us to the corner where he stretches.

"These teams look pretty weak." Dax nods toward the courts. "We'll have no problem beating this level of competition."

Dax looks good in his purple jersey, with the words Next Gen across the front and his last name Abram on the back. Dax still looks like a basketball player. Tall, lean, muscular, and I'm brought back to when I used to sit on the bleachers and watch him play. I barely remember who that girl was anymore.

"We're playing them." Dax points to the opposite corner, where two men and a woman in red jerseys with Dollar Store written across them. I don't know any of them. They must be from a neighboring town, but the woman doesn't look very tall, and my height will give me a huge advantage.

Jake and Camilla walk in, with Kylie between them, and she waves to us, and then they take a seat on the bleachers. The final whistle blows, and it's our turn to warm up. After a few minutes, the whistle blows again, and it's time to start the game.

We dominate from the first minute. We utilize our speed, and the competition can't keep up. Malik rebounds the ball, and I take off running down the left side, and he finds me. I take two dribbles and launch the ball to Dax, who sprints up the right side of the court, and he catches it on the run, dribbles once, and puts the ball up for an easy layup.

The game ends up being a lopsided humiliation for our opponents, and then we have a break for an hour and start game two. The pace is a little slower, but we still dominate. I catch the ball on the wing, fake to the right, like Dax showed me, drive to the lane, and throw a fifteen-footer that goes in. Malik is dominant underneath the basket, using his skills as a football player to get in position. And Dax, sometimes I watch him play instead of actively playing alongside him. He's all finesse, executing a small juke with his head. The person guarding him jumps up, and Dax dribbles once to the right and shoots the ball. Nothing but net.

After our second game, we have a couple of hours to wait, so we head back to Malik's house for lunch. "Carrie, are you drinking enough water? You look tired." Dax opens the fridge and throws me a bottle of water.

I stuff the turkey sandwich in my mouth. "I'm exhausted from all of the winning," I say, and Dax rolls his eyes.

"This feels so good, doesn't it?" Dax's smile beams as he looks at Malik and me. "I know the teams will get harder, but it feels great to be playing again."

"Agreed." Malik downs his water.

"When we win the next game," Dax says, popping a grape into his mouth, "We'll be done for the day, but we'll play the first game tomorrow. Assuming we win that, we'll only have one more game later in the day, and then we'll advance to championship Saturday, a week from today."

"We got this," Malik says, pumped up.

"And Carrie, you're feeling okay?" Dax asks again.

"Dax, I'm good. I promise."

Our last game of the day is a little more competitive. Dax and Malik have decent people guarding them, but their female is weak, so I get the ball a lot. She's slower and shorter than me, and I use speed and height to my advantage. When the game is over, with another win by us, I'm exhausted. Sweat drips down my face, and my muscles feel like jelly. I want to stand underneath the showerhead and let the water remove every salty bead of sweat.

We walk out of the gym with my duffel bag slung over me. Dax puts his hand on my shoulder. "Drink a lot of water and get some potassium. Eat a banana or something."

I turn to Dax, his face riddled with concern. "Okay, coach."

"I don't know about you guys," Malik chimes in. "But after I shower and eat, I'm heading to bed. My muscles are getting old."

The warm shower feels great against my sore body. We've been practicing for a while, but nothing compares to playing non-stop basketball all day. I stretch my neck and arms and do ankle exercises as I stand there and lather myself with soap.

When I play basketball, I feel like I can do anything. I don't think about how bad my relationship with my mom is or how many resentments I hold toward her. I don't think about my one-year scan, cancer, or the fear I've lived with since my diagnosis. The court makes me happy, and although everything hurts right now, I can't wait to get back at it tomorrow.

"Did you leave me any hot water?" Malik asks when I walk out of the bathroom with a robe around me and a towel over my head.

"Umm, I think so." I turn to Malik. "And I know I told you this, but I'm going to start moving some of my things to the B&B this week. This girl is moving out."

Malik pouts his lip and fake cries. "That makes me sad."

"Me too." I also do a pouty face. "Living with you has been—"

"Don't make me cry." Malik walks into the bathroom.

I lather my body with some CBD lotion. My tight muscles ache, and I should stuff my face with food after the calories I burned today, but I don't have the energy to eat. I wrap myself back in my robe, pull the covers high over my head, and pass out for the night, dreaming of squeaky shoes on the court and balls going through the net.

But my last thought before I sleep is Dax's purple jersey against his tan, smooth skin, his blue eyes, and his sexy man bun.

Chapter Twenty

Dax

AFTER TWO WINS ON SUNDAY, I rest. My muscles feel remarkably good, and after playing two days straight of basketball, I still have energy in the tank. When we resume playing the following Saturday, we're only two teams away from winning the grand prize.

"Daddy." Kylie pauses, coloring for a moment to look at me. "When I grow up, I'm going to play basketball like you."

"Or . . ." I sit down at the table with her and open another coloring book. "Maybe you'll run track like Mommy."

"Maybe." She wrinkles her little forehead.

"Or maybe, sweetie, you'll do both."

Kylie's eyes get big, and she grabs the blue crayon and colors in the sky. "Can I do both? That way, I wouldn't have to choose."

"You can do both or none at all. You get to decide."

Kylie grins from ear to ear, and we sit across from each other and color. These days, she brings up more about what she wants to do as she gets older. I've been trying so hard to talk about Zari more. It used to make me too sad, but then I realized not talking about her makes me feel worse. I want Kylie to know her and to take all of her goodness.

I look around my place, and pictures of Zari are still everywhere. Amina thought it would be good to remove some photos, but it doesn't feel like it's been long enough. And if there aren't reminders everywhere, how can I be sure that Kylie won't forget everything about her?

"It's bath time, and you need to get to bed. It's getting late."

Kylie moans but puts down her crayons and coloring book. She takes my hand and leads me to her bedroom, where she grabs her frog towel, and then we trudge to the bathroom. After her bath, I lie in bed beside her.

"Can we read my mommy book?" Kylie puts her head on the pillow and cuddles up to her bunny, Pinky.

I grab the book from the shelf and open it to page one. My parents had the book made for me when Zari died, and we read it frequently. The first pictures are of Zari as a baby. Kylie looks so much like her. Then, it fasts forwards to photos of Zari and me together, and our wedding. The book tells our love story: a short but beautiful tale.

"When baby Kylie was born, Mommy and Daddy were the two happiest people in the world. She had her Mommy's complexion, lips, and eyes but the Abram's nose. She also had Daddy's long fingers."

Kylie holds her hand up to mine and compares. Her hands are still so tiny in comparison.

"Is this when Mommy got sick?" Kylie hugs me tight when the next photo shows Zari and her, and Zari has no hair from the chemo.

"Yep, sweet girl. Now, Mommy is sick."

Kylie's face changes. Like it always does at this part of the book. "I don't like this part as much."

"Me neither." I choke back my emotion.

The additional pages are scattered with pictures, as we took photos of everything in those last couple of years. Zari and Kylie at the park. The three of us at a restaurant. Us bathing Kyle. Zari reading to her. Kylie lying in bed with Zari as she was in a hospital bed. The last picture is of Kylie, Zari, and I, lying in bed at home, Kylie in the middle of us, and Zari and I holding hands on top of her. It's the last picture we ever took. Hospice was already called, and three days later, Zari was gone.

We parented together for such a short time. Almost the entire time, Zari was sick. She tried to do everything she could for Kylie, but there were nights when she couldn't even stand because of nausea and pain, and I would go to Kylie's nursery and give her a bottle and cry in the dark room, so scared that we would lose Zari.

"Does this book make you sad, Daddy?" Kylie wipes a tear from my cheek, and I hadn't even realized I was crying.

Kylie snuggles closer to me, and I wrap her in my arms. "I miss your mommy, that's all."

Kylie thinks about this for a moment. "I miss her too, but I know she's okay and protecting me. She said she'd do that."

I kiss Kylie's forehead. "I know she is too. Now, goodnight. Tomorrow is a school day."

Since Zari's death, the pain has changed, but it's also constant. Instead of stabbing me, it's more of a continuous, dull ache. It feels good and hurts at the same time to talk about her and see her pictures everywhere. Most of my sadness comes from what I fear Kylie is missing out on. She seems so happy but will always be the girl whose mom died.

A WEEK HAS GONE BY, and championship Saturday is here. Malik, Carrie, and I stretch in the corner and watch our opponents warm up. Carrie wears her hair in two pigtails, rolls the waist of her shorts, and then pulls her shirt over it.

"We should be able to get past this team, no problem," I tuck my leg behind me to stretch my quadriceps. "As long as we stick to our plan."

We didn't have a chance to practice much this week. Carrie spent most of the week moving her stuff to her new place, and Malik was busy finishing a job for Abram Construction.

"She's tall." Carrie leans on me for balance as she stretches and points to the girl on the opposing team.

"She's also slow," Malik adds. "I've been watching her play."

The whistle blows, the game starts, and we can play at our own pace. Carrie is forced to play away from the basket because of her opponent's height, but she barely misses a shot. She's in a zone, and one after another sinks through the net.

I dribble the ball from half-court and toss it to Carrie on the left wing. She dribbles toward the lane, and the person guarding Malik goes to step in, leaving Malik open underneath the basket. Carrie puts the ball in her right hand and tosses it with force in his direction, and he goes in for an easy layup underneath the basket.

After winning, we get a break before playing the Ross' Rhinos. They look young, barely out of high school, but short. Malik cleans up under the basket and dishes the ball out to Carrie and me.

"I'm open," I yell when Malik gets a defensive board. With both hands, he chucks the ball toward me, and I take a dribble and, with my right hand, bounce the ball to Carrie, who charges the basket. She goes up with her left arm, and in mid-air, the person guarding her checks her with her body, and Carrie goes down hard.

Both Malik and I run over to her as she grabs her ankle. "Are you okay?" I ask and then turn to the other team and mouth, "What the hell?"

"Where does it hurt?" Malik feels around her ankle.

"It's fine. I landed awkwardly. I'm fine." Carrie gets up and sinks her two free throws, but I watch her, and she's not putting much weight on her left ankle.

We squeak by the team and break before the final game, which is against a team that already has one loss, so if we win, we're the tournament champions.

"Are you sure you're okay?" I sit next to Carrie. She stretches her legs straight out in front of her.

I take her leg, undo her shoelaces, and pull down her sock. Her ankle is swollen and a purplish-blue color.

"Malik, will you grab ice?" I ask.

"Honestly, it's fine." Carrie pulls back her leg.

"You say fine too much," I add. "I'm going to at least tape it."

The gym fills with people for the championship game. Between the entrance fee to join, the cost to watch, and the concessions, there will be a lot of money to donate to charity. I hold Carrie's ankle in my hand and, with the athletic tape, form figure-eights until I'm confident it's stabilized.

The game starts out physically. The two men on the team graduated high school last year and were good athletes. I don't know the woman, but she seems to have game too. I throw the ball to Carrie, and she tries to fake her opponent but can't shake her and passes the ball back to me. Carrie hobbles toward the basket, and I can tell she isn't alright.

After the other team makes a shot, I get in Carrie's ear. "You should sit out. I can't stand to see you in so much pain."

Carrie brushes me off. "And what? You and Malik will play two on three?"

"We'll have to. You're hurt, and it will get worse if you don't take it easy." I raise my voice. I'm annoyed by her stubbornness. She can barely walk.

"I'm fine," she shoots back at me and sets herself on the right baseline.

"You are not fine," I fire back.

The leaderboard keeps changing. We score a bucket, and then they do. The lead has changed fifteen times already.

We're down by one point with thirty seconds left on the clock. Malik inbounds at halfcourt, and I dribble down the court.

"Three." I hold up three fingers with my left hand, keeping my dribble low with my right.

Malik posts up under the basket, and Carrie hobbles to the wing. She struggles to get open, cuts toward the basket, and out to the wing again, and I toss the ball her way. It's my only option, as Malik is completely covered. Carrie glances at the clock, which is down to ten seconds. She holds the ball low and takes two dribbles to the right, and Malik clears out from underneath the basket.

Carrie crosses the ball through her legs until it's in her left hand. She cuts through the lane and throws up a hook shot. As she jumps, her opponent fouls her with her body, and Carrie crashes to the ground.

She grabs her ankle and rolls on the court. You could hear a pin drop in the gym. All eyes are on Carrie as she grimaces, but not a sound comes out of her mouth.

"Two shots," the ref yells, with no time on the clock.

"She's hurt, ref." I walk over to the teenage kid in the black and white striped shirt. "Can someone else take her free throws?"

"Nope." He holds the ball and stands at the free-throw line. "You know the rules of basketball, Abram."

I hunch over. "Carrie, it's fine. Second place is still really good. You did awesome. Your shot was going to go in."

"Not quitting," she murmurs and puts her arms out to me to help her get up.

"You can't, Carrie." I help her to her feet, and she only places weight on her right ankle. "Malik, tell her that she can't."

Malik runs over to Carrie. "If we get you to the free-throw line, do you think you can shoot it with one foot?"

I scowl at Malik. "That wasn't helpful."

"What choice do I have?" Malik and I put her arms around our shoulders and bring her to the line. The other team stands at half-court. The time expired, so there's no reason to line up. It all comes down to these two free throws.

Carrie balances on her right foot and grimaces when her left foot touches the ground. Her face is red, and I'm unsure if it's from the pain or the exertion. She takes the ball, bounces it once, lines up, and shoots. The crowd screams out when the ball goes in, but Carrie screams in pain when her ankle touches the ground again.

"You don't have to do this." I pat her butt as the ref hands her the ball. "Please, Carrie. This is insane."

"I do. This game can't go into overtime, 'cause I'm done. I just have to make this one shot." She grimaces. It's no use trying to talk her out of this. Carrie is determined.

It's at this moment that I realize how stubborn

Carrie is. She's as big of a competitor as I am. She takes the ball and bounces on her right foot, and her left leg bends at the knee. She lines her hands on the ball's seams and releases. It goes up with a huge arch, bounces off the front of the rim, and then the ball's spin brings it back and goes through the net.

The gym erupts. But I barely hear any of it. I motion to my parents to take Kylie and yell for my dad to meet me at the hospital, where he's one of the town doctors.

"We did it." Carrie switches between a smile and a grimace and leans her weight into me.

"You're more competitive and stupid than I thought." I stand next to her and let her put all her weight on me. "Malik, grab her things. I'm having my dad meet us at the hospital for x-rays."

I pick Carrie up and bring her to my car. Her arms wrap around my neck, and she's light, and her body long. I place her in the back where she can stretch out.

"On a scale of one to ten, how bad is the pain?" I ask her, looking through the mirror.

"A nine." Her eyes meet mine in the rearview mirror.

"You could have really hurt yourself, Carrie. I don't know whether to be mad at you or kiss you."

We arrive at the hospital a couple of minutes later, and Malik is behind us. I carry her in, and Malik grabs a wheelchair by the entrance and places her in it.

"You guys beat me," my dad says, coming through the door. "Carrie, I'll wheel you back and see the damage."

My dad takes Carrie into an exam room, and she glances back at Malik and me before they go in.

We sit in the waiting room, and Malik turns to me. "I heard something pop when Carrie went down. I can't unhear it."

"Yeah, it didn't look good." I replay the foul and how

she landed on her ankle.

Malik looks up at me and raises his eyebrows. "Man, we won. I can't believe we won."

We give each other a fist pump. All thanks to Carrie, we have thousands of dollars to give to a charity of our choice. I can't believe we pulled it off. And I hate that she's hurt, but I dislike even more that our reason to hang out so frequently no longer exists. Basketball is over.

"We moved all her stuff to the B&B. She doesn't have a bed at my place anymore." Malik puts his head in his hands.

"The B&B is probably better anyway. Your place has too many stairs." We sit in the bright orange chairs of the hospital lobby. "Kylie is spending the night at my parent's house. I can get Carrie back to her place. There are beds in the main floor rooms, right?"

Malik nods. "Just the one. We moved her bed upstairs. There is a bathroom right there too. I can come tonight and help look after her."

"I've got this."

The urge to take care of Carrie runs deep, and I hope Malik doesn't insist. She'd probably rather have him anyway. They're closer. But I want to do this. I'm surprised at how much.

Malik gives me a side-eye. "Are you sure? Don't make me regret this."

"I'm not going to screw anything up. Let me take care of her."

Malik gives me a long look, but I know I can do this.

Chapter Twenty-One

Carrie

THE MEDS START TO KICK in, so the constant throbbing gets better. Dr. Abram comes in with the slides and holds them up.

"Carrie, you have a very bad sprain accompanied by an avulsion fracture." He points to my bone on the film and explains that the ligaments separated from my bone, and a small piece of bone came off too.

"You probably won't need surgery." He continues to study the slide. "But you're also not going to be on your feet for a while."

Blake, one of the hospital nurses, comes in with a boot, and Dr. Abram sits in the chair. "I'm going to put you in this boot, but you are not allowed to put any weight on it, do you hear me?"

"Ugh," I moan. "Like, no weight at all?"

"None. And you need to rest, ice, compress, and elevate, Carrie. Did you hear me? I said rest."

"This is so inconvenient." I cover my face with my hands and shake my head.

Being injured doesn't fit into my schedule. I just started moving into my new home, but I have so many projects to do, many of which I was going to do on my own. I work at the bank. I can't leave Sunny and Sis in a bind. I'm frazzled thinking about how much this isn't going to work for me.

He puts the boot around me, and Blake comes in with crutches. We adjust their height, and then Dr. Abram hands me a prescription for pain pills to take as needed.

Blake turns to me. "Do you have someone who can help take care of you?"

"Not sure yet, honestly," I respond.

"Well, it looks like you have some options in the waiting room," she says.

I hobble out, and when Dax and Malik see me, they stand up. Dr. Abram walks beside me. "The patient is doing well, but she'll need a lot of rest and ice. Can I trust you boys to take care of her?"

"I'll stay with her at the B&B tonight, Dad. You're good with Kylie, right?"

"Good? I'm going to go cuddle my granddaughter right now." He smiles and then turns to me. "I want to see you in a few days. I need the swelling to go down, or I'm going to get you into a compression ice boot."

"We thought because you moved your stuff out, and the B&B has sleeping options on one level, you'd be more comfortable there," Malik says. "Dax offered to look after you tonight. Are you good with that?"

The pain makes me indifferent to most things. I don't care who brings me home. I want to be clean, in my bed, and with my foot elevated. Dax drives me to my new home, and when we arrive, he helps me get inside. The place looks so good, and I've only slept here two nights so far, but I already love it and waking up and looking at the lake. But there is still so much to do.

"I need to shower." I pause in front of the bathroom door, and Dax's face has a look of panic.

"Is that a good idea? You could slip and fall, and you shouldn't remove your boot, but it can't get wet."

"I'm showering." I smell my shirt to further my point. "All my clothes are upstairs. Will you go into my top drawer and grab my underwear? My pajamas are in my bottom drawer."

Dax's face reddens. His eyes shift from the stairs leading upstairs and back at me.

"Sorry, but it's not too late to back out and call Malik."

Dax shakes his head and runs his hands through his hair. He then hops up the stairs, two at a time. "No. No. I've got this."

He comes down with a few pajama options and a handful of underwear that I take from him. I should be embarrassed, but the pain has made it impossible to feel anything else, including embarrassment. Dax helps me get situated in the bathroom and starts the shower, and when he leaves, I do my best to clean myself while standing on one foot and leaning against the side.

I put on pair of pajamas and then use the crutches to get back to the bedroom, where Dax gets me situated with ice and pillows for elevation. I'm so happy I got the internet set up here, as I don't think I will do much except lie in bed for the next couple of days. Dax drives the mile to his place to grab clothes, and then he comes back here and uses my shower.

"Dax, I'm fine alone, I promise." But he ignores me and props the pillows behind my head. I'm sure he has no idea how self-sufficient I am from a life of being alone and doing things for myself.

"I'm not leaving, so get used to it." He plops down on the bed next to me, making sure not to bump me. "My dad told me to stay on top of your pain meds, and we need to ice once an hour. I've set all the alarms on my phone."

My wet hair dampens the pillow, and I try to turn to my side, but it hurts. Everything throbs, and aches, and the pain stabs my ankle and runs up my leg.

"You were the MVP. No doubt." Dax grins, tucking my hair behind my ear. "I can't believe you could shoot those free throws."

"Well, anything to be better than you." I swat Dax in the arm, and he smirks at me.

"You're such a smart ass, Soleta." Dax smiles as he looks at me and seems stuck in thought.

He gets me ice water, and we settle on the bed together and agree that we should only watch scary movies because it's the month of October. We turn on the Shining, and Dax lies on my right side, away from my injury, and cuddles into me. I turn to him, close my eyes, and feel sleep start to take over. I'm both in pain and content with where this night has taken me.

"Carrie," Dax whispers, shaking me from my thoughts. "Do you have any extra blankets out here?"

Dax already brought my blankets from my upstairs bedroom to this room. I don't open my eyes when I speak. "I have nothing extra. Go home. I'm fine. Seriously."

Dax sits up, and my eyes are slits as I watch him look around. "I'm going to grab a few towels and sleep on the floor."

The floor? With towels? My breath catches in my chest. I didn't know Dax was planning to stay here? With me? All night? "Don't worry. You're safe with me. Sleep in the bed. I promise I won't try anything."

The bed vibrates with Dax's laughter. I love the sound. He doesn't laugh often, so when he does, it's everything. "These pain meds are making you a bigger smart ass than usual."

Dax lies down and puts a couple of pillows between us. "So I don't accidentally hit your ankle. Not to protect me from you."

We hold each other's gaze for a long moment. His mouth opens, but no sound comes out. His eyes pierce into mine, and he plumps the pillow underneath his head, leans over and turns the light off.

When the pain overtakes me in the night, I go to yell for Dax. I'd forgotten that he's right next to me, sleeping. I shake him awake, and he groggily opens his eyes, grabs me a pill, ice, and more water. Maybe his phone alarm isn't working, or I need pain relief sooner than expected. He rubs my arm until the medicine makes me sleepy, and I'm able to pass out once again.

The sun wakes me the next morning, as I still don't have curtains on the windows. Dax is beside me, curled up in a ball, and looks peaceful. His hair falls over his eye, and his lips look kissable, closed, and soft.

He lost his shirt at some point in the night, and the blanket is pulled up to his chin. He looks so childlike, not like the thirty-year-old man he is. I stare for longer than I should, but Dax Abram is in my bed, here because he wants to be. He's taking care of me. None of this feels like real life.

My meds are on the nightstand on his side of the bed, and the pain is coming on strong again, and I want to stay on top of it. I lean over him, and he catches my arm and smiles without opening his eyes.

"Are you getting frisky?" Dax asks. His fingers extend across my upper arm. "I knew you had a ploy to get me to sleep in your bed with you."

I grab the bottle and shake it. "Not this time, sorry. Grabbing my meds."

Dax pulls me into a hug, rubs my back, then my hair, which I'm sure is a disaster after going to bed with it wet. I lie over him and feel his skin against mine. For a moment, I forget how much my ankle is throbbing and instead focus on his heart, beating directly beneath mine. I didn't have Dax as a cuddler, but he holds me and melts into my touch. Our hearts are in sync as they beat against each other. Fast.

Dax releases my arm, and I go back to my side of the bed and sit up. "How's the pain?"

"Not great." I take a pill and down it with water. "You probably need to go get Kylie. I'll be fine."

"I've already texted my parents. They'll bring her by after dinner tonight. You aren't rid of me yet."

"Sorry." I look at Dax as he reaches down to grab his shirt. I have seen him without a shirt a million times, but for some reason, it hits differently when he's in my bedroom.

"I appreciate everything you're doing for me. But I know you have a million other things you should be doing. I don't want to put you out."

He leans into me and kisses my forehead. "You aren't. I assure you."

Dax goes to my upstairs living quarters and brings the dresser drawers full of my clothes down so he can quit fetching things at my request. I was so excited to be moved in, but now I'm living in chaos again.

He helps me get situated on the couch, runs home, gets some tools, and begins fixing a few things throughout the place, mainly in the kitchen, like the leaky faucet and the refrigerator noise. I observe. Like, how the toolbelt hangs low on his waist or how he looks at me every couple of minutes to make sure I'm watching, and he smiles when he realizes I always am.

He then brings me back to the bedroom, where I lie down for a nap, and he settles next to me and reads a book. He tells me his eyes are dry from his contacts, and he puts a pair of glasses on to read, and somehow Dax manages to get better looking. Or maybe it isn't the glasses at all, but instead, Dax holding a book. Whatever it is, I like having him be the last person I see as I doze off.

When I wake up and look at the time, sadness washes over me. I don't want Dax to leave, and I don't want to be alone. Dax brings an energy to this place that didn't exist before, and I like how I feel when I'm around him. I enjoy feeling cared for.

I've lived with Malik for so long that I hadn't considered how I would feel being out here alone. I can't wait until the place is ready for guests. Then, I'll never be alone. But it's Sunday, and I know he must be with Kylie and get prepared for her week of school and his week of work. Dax looks at me and notices I'm awake.

"What's the matter?" he asks, closing his book. He takes his glasses off, squeezes his eyes, and then puts them back on.

"Nothing," I lie. "But it's about dinner time. You should probably get home before Kylie arrives."

Dax nods in agreement but stares down at his book and then at me. "I don't like you being here alone. Should I call Malik and ask him to come?"

"I'll call if I need him." I push my hands into the bed and sit up. "The worst of it is over. I can handle the night, and you've already brought my stuff down here. I'll call you if I need anything."

"Promise?" Dax stands up. "I don't like leaving you."

"Promise."

Dax puts some things in his bag. "I'd stay if I could." He lingers in the doorway, his arm pressed against the door and his bag around his shoulder.

We say goodbye, and I promise I'll call him later. I email my boss at the bank and let him know I won't be in tomorrow due to my injury. He emails me back, saying he knew already because he was at the game.

Malik calls a hundred times, and I insist I want to sleep without company. The truth is, I'm sad. In moments like this, I wish I had a normal mom. I'd call her up, and she'd come over and make me chicken soup, help me in and out of the shower, and push fluids on me. She'd clean my house while I recuperated, tiptoe room to room, making everything better than when she found it.

I don't even have a mom I can call and tell about this. Juniper doesn't care. If I did call her, she'd instruct me to find weed as it heals everything. She'd give me unhelpful advice and then turn the conversation to herself and everything going on with her.

A tear trickles down my face, and I can't believe I'm this sad. Maybe because I got to feel what it was like having Dax here, in my bed, in my kitchen, helping me with everything, and now that he's gone, the void I didn't know was there feels bigger. I somehow feel more alone than I ever have.

Or maybe it's these stupid pain pills that are making me emotional. Yes, that's most likely it. My phone rings.

"How are you feeling?" Dax asks.

"I'm going to stop the pain pills," I answer. "They make me feel loopy. I'm hoping aspirin will be enough."

"I wish I was there to take care of you." Dax breathes into the phone. "I put Kylie to bed, though, so I'm sitting here alone. I wish I could bundle her up, put her in the car, and come and see you."

You and me both, I think.

Then, Dax asks, "Do you want to watch a scary movie? I'll video call you, and we can start a movie at the same time."

"Sure," I say, suddenly unaware of the pain in my ankle. "My pick. Hmm. I've been dying to watch Amityville

Horror. And not the remake. The original."

Dax chuckles. "That shit is scary, Soleta. Are you sure you'll be able to sleep alone in your place after watching it?"

"Who says I'll be sleeping alone? If I'm scared, I expect you to have me on the video call all night long in your bed."

Dax laughs again. That laugh that could light up an entire room. "Deal."

We hang up, and he calls me again, this time on video. He moves from the living room to his bedroom, a space I've never seen. From what I can see, it's nice with hardwood floors and a large bed anchored by a fluffy rug. It's a manly space with no obvious female touch. He shuts the door behind him, and we queue up the movie.

The movie starts, but I steal glances at Dax. He lies on his side, propped up by his elbow, and his arm flexed. His headboard has dark wood planks, and his bedroom screams guy. Dax takes a break at one point to make popcorn. When I look at the phone, Dax stares at me.

"You're supposed to be watching the movie?" I prop myself up further with pillows.

"I'm trying, but you look scared. I'm worried I'll have to bundle Kylie up, go to your place, pick you up, and bring you here."

"Did you know this is based on a true story?" I ask as Dax takes a pillow and puts it in front of him.

"Not until you just told me. I may have to crawl into Kylie's bed," Dax grins.

"Wimp," I joke.

Dax grins. "This shit is scary."

My eyes are tired, and I don't know when I fell asleep, but it's before the movie is over. I wake up with the sun, just like yesterday, and jump when I see Dax staring back at me through my phone.

"It looks like you slept much better than the night before." Dax readjusts himself in bed. "I was afraid to wake you up. But I didn't want to hang up without saying goodbye."

"Yeah, sure." I blink rapidly, waiting for my brain to catch up with being awake. And I'm still on the phone with Dax. "You slept too, though, right? You didn't watch me sleep all night?"

"We slept together again. I promise I didn't watch you sleep all night." Dax says, and I feel my entire face fill with heat. "I have to get Kylie up and ready for school."

"Yeah." I wipe my mouth, hoping there's no drool. "I wanted to stay up for the whole movie."

"You fought hard. I could tell. I didn't want you to be alone, so I kept the call going all night. I can't believe your phone didn't die."

"Go. Go." I struggle to get out. "We'll talk soon."

"Ice the shit out of that ankle today, Doctor's son's orders."

"Bye, Dax."

The weirdest thing happens when we hang up. I cry out of nowhere. A dam breaks, and it's not only tears that come out of me. It's gasping—ugly crying.

I call Malik, trying to catch him before he heads to work. He picks up on the first ring. "Is everything okay, Carrie?"

"Ugh. I like him," I say, followed by a gulp from Malik. "And I can't unlike him. And it hurts. My chest actually hurts, Malik."

"Oh, honey," Malik sighs into the phone. "I'm calling in sick. See you in fifteen."

Chapter Twenty-Two

Dax

WHEATON'S FALL BREAK IS AROUND the corner, which means a four-day weekend. I've been brainstorming fun things to do with Kylie, but then Amina and Zari's parents, Mobo and Ruth, started calling and begging me to let Kylie spend the long weekend with them.

Spending my first break this school year in Atlanta wasn't what I had in mind, but then they told me they thought it would be fun only for Kylie to go. If I agree to fly Kylie to Atlanta, Amina said she'd fly her back Sunday and stay a couple of days with us before returning.

I look online and buy two plane tickets, leaving the Minneapolis airport on Wednesday of next week, and then I'll fly home Thursday morning. I then book a flight for Kylie and Amina to fly back Sunday afternoon. I hate being away from Kylie for so many days, but she insists that she wants to go. I know Zari would want this too. I promised I would keep Kylie connected to her family. Always.

We sit at the pool hall with Jake and some of the construction crew, including Malik, and we enjoy a mid-week beverage.

"Rack 'em up." Jake nods toward the table.

I get my cue stick ready, assault it with blue chalk, and break the balls. Then, I sit and wait for my turn again. Trey walks in, gives Jake a fist punch, and glances my way.

"Hey." He offers me a wave.

"Hey."

A local girl, Tiffeny, walks in. Jake used to mess around with her years ago. She beelines to Trey, and the two hug each other, and then she joins some women at a high top in the corner.

"Tell me you're not dating Tiffeny." Malik puts his pint glass to his lips.

"We're hanging out." Trey shrugs. "I figure it's better than the mom age group."

All eyes are on me, and I chuckle. Trey isn't innocent, and I still consider him sleazy, but at least Juniper owns what happened just as much, if not more. After all, Juniper is the one that continues to break Carrie's heart, not Trey.

"How about you?" Trey looks at me. "Any hot dating prospects?"

I shake my head. I didn't even look at another woman when Zari died for a year and a half. When I hit the one-year mark, people came out in droves. Like that is the time period that is acceptable to start dating again. But after a year, I was still crying five times a day and trying to figure out how to be a good single parent to Kylie.

Once I hit the eighteen-month anniversary of Zari's death, I ended up sleeping with someone. I cried for days afterward and felt sick to my stomach. It felt like a betrayal, and I realized I was nowhere near ready. At the two-year mark, I started putting myself out there more but purposely kept every interaction casual. I never felt like it was my body that could betray Zari, but my heart.

Once I reconciled that in my mind, I may have gone overboard. I was always safe and honest with the women. I told them I wasn't interested in a relationship. No one objected. Yes, a couple of the women were surprised when they wanted to hang out again, and I said no as if what I originally told them wasn't true.

But that didn't make me feel good either, and I haven't been with anyone in a really long time. It's been good for me. I've done a lot of soul-searching. It's been a long but purposeful dry spell.

"How's Camilla feeling?" I ask, turning to Jake.

He smiles. "She feels great. It's hard to believe she's already six months along."

"I'm glad she's feeling well." I grin. "But tell Camilla she better not give birth on my birthday. I refuse to share my day. Even with a cute little niece or nephew."

"Hey," Jake says. "If I have to share an August birthday with my wife, you can share your January birthday with our little nugget."

"Alright." I look at my watch. "I'm going to pick up my little nugget and put her to bed." I say goodbye to the men and leave for the night.

THE AIRPORT IN ATLANTA IS as busy as always. With one hand, I roll our suitcases and hold on tightly to Kylie's squishy hand with my other. We grab a car and head to Decatur, a suburb outside Atlanta.

We pull up to their house, and Zari's parents stand at the door, waving to us. Kylie gets out and runs to them, and I grab our bags.

"Meemaw," she yells. "Papaw!"

They pull her into a hug and hold on. Kylie is the only piece of Zari that they can still hold. She is half of her. Ruth finally releases her and hugs me, and her dad gives me a firm handshake.

Zari's upbringing always made mine look humble. Her dad is a tenured professor at Morehouse College in Atlanta and teaches Art History. Her mom is a Human Rights attorney. I'll never forget the first time I joined Zari in Atlanta. I felt like a small-town boy who finally made it to the big city.

"Dax, you look so in shape," Ruth says. "All that basketball must be paying off."

"Yeah, I guess so." I hand the bags to Mobo, who takes us inside.

"Amina will be here soon," Zari's mom reaches down and places her hands on Kylie's head. "We can't wait to take you shopping, and tomorrow night we're all going to go to the movie theater. Doesn't that sound fun?"

Kylie smiles and claps her hands together. "What about the zoo?"

"We'll go to the zoo Friday," Mobo chimes in.

Mobo always wanted her to stay in the south and attend college there. I can only imagine how he felt the first time Zari brought me home to meet the parents. I'm sure they weren't thrilled. But they loved seeing her succeed on the college track team, and I grew on them with time.

When I put Kylie to bed, I ask, "Are you sure you'll be okay without me?"

She giggles and pushes me in my stomach. "Daddy, it will only be three days. I'll call you every day. I promise. Meemaw will spoil me."

I laugh. "I have no doubt that you will be."

Kylie wraps her little arms around me, and I kiss her head. "I'll see you in the morning before I head to the airport."

"Goodnight, Daddy."

I go down to the study, where I know Mobo will be reading a book and smoking his cigar. He sits behind an ornate mahogany desk, glasses on the rim of his nose.

"Have a seat, son." He doesn't look up from his book.

The leather chair squeaks beneath me as I sit in front of him. He's always made me nervous. I'll never forget how I felt when I sat in this chair and asked his permission to ask Zari to marry me. When he glances up, I get the impression that he is also conjuring that memory.

"Are you happy?" He puts his book down.

"We're doing great." I struggle to get comfortable in the oversized chair. "Kylie loves first grade and her teacher. She has a lot of friends. Everyone loves her."

Mobo removes his glasses and leans back in his chair. "I can tell Kylie is happy, son. How are you doing?"

"Oh, I'm fine." I cross my legs, and then recross them the opposite way before putting them flat on the carpet beneath me.

"I never believe someone when they answer with fine. That's my rule." He leans forward, pressing his elbows into his desk. His silence makes me nervous.

Damn. I'd never used the word until Carrie introduced it to me.

"My job is going well. I love teaching the third grade, and it's been nice to make extra money working for Jake in the summer. Our new house on the lake is perfect. It's bigger than we need, and we barely live in more than a couple of rooms. You should come visit."

"Dax." He elongates my name. "Have you thought about getting into the dating game again? Finding a female role model for Kylie?"

My face flushes. "We aren't ready for that. And Kylie

has a mom."

"Yes." He waves me off. "But you didn't die, Dax. My baby did."

"I wish it would have been me," I admit, looking down at my hands. I rub them together and feel every groove.

It's a thought I've had many times. Why would God leave me with this child and not her mom? I don't feel worthy of raising her. Zari would have done it so much better. She'd always know what to say and do. Zari would have been everything that Kylie ever needed.

"Don't talk like that, son." Mobo, gets up from his chair, walks around his desk, and leans against it. "We think you're doing a great job, but Amina told us that you act like you're stuck. All I ask of you is that you allow us to be in Kylie's life. If that means that someday you visit us here with Kylie, your new wife, and a couple of other kids, we don't care. You're our family. As long as that will always continue, we'll be happy."

Tears prick at the back of my eyes. I can't imagine coming to Atlanta with a woman, let alone other kids. Children that won't be Zari's. Can't be Zari's.

"It's hard," I admit. "Zari was . . ." I pause. "Well, she was Zari."

He puts his hand on my shoulder, the most affection he's ever shown me, except for the day of Zari's funeral, when her casket was lowered into the ground.

"When you fall in love again, son, the new woman won't take up the space you hold in your heart for Zari. Your heart will grow. But you have to let it. Maybe not today or tomorrow, but at some point."

I go to bed, thinking of Mobo's words. My family hasn't pressured me to move on at all. It's a subject we avoid altogether. Yet Zari's family, who experienced the biggest loss outside of Kylie, wants me to be ready.

Before falling asleep, I start a text to Carrie. "I'm not sure what job you're working tomorrow, but I get home at noon. Do you want to spend the day together?"

My finger hovers over the send button, and I tap it before I can overthink what I'm walking into.

Chapter Twenty-Three

Carrie

I WAKE UP TO A TEXT from Dax asking me to spend the day with him. Today is a Sunny and Sis day, so I tell him I'll be home around three in the afternoon, and he can stop over whenever.

My ankle proves to be the biggest inconvenience. I went to the doctor yesterday, and I can start putting some weight on it, but it's still extremely painful. If I take the boot off, my leg has a pulse of its own, and I can barely stand the excruciating pain. I try to stay on top of icing it, but moving around is more pain than it's worth, so most of the day when I'm not working, I lie in bed and read or watch movies. It feels like a major setback. I've been so health-focused, and now this.

Even so, I don't want to leave Sunny and Sis without care today. And if they require more than I can provide, Camilla is a phone call away.

There's a coolness in the air as I drive to town. All the corn and beans have been harvested, and the fields are empty. The sun is bright but not hot, and in another month, we'll be bundled up, bracing for another Minnesota winter.

"Sunny, Sis, it's me." I pull open their back door and peek through the kitchen.

Their friend Annie's car is also parked here, so it must be a morning of knitting for her and Sis.

"Hi, Carrie." Sunny shuffles into the kitchen with Camilla holding his arm. "We're just getting back from the café."

I lean against the counter, and Sunny and Sis sit at the kitchen table. "What's the news in town today?"

The café is the town's source of all of Wheaton's happenings. Camilla takes her grandpa there nearly every morning, and they have coffee with the same group of guys.

"Well, the big news is, Walt has decided to move in with Annie. And it's about time," Sunny says.

Camilla glances at me knowingly. Rumor has it that Walt and Annie have been dating for the better half of the century, but they've never lived together, married, or been open about their relationship.

"That is big news." I pull myself up to a stool to sit. "And how are Juan and Lawson doing?"

"Oh, the same." Sunny grabs a toothpick and chews on it. "They both have family coming into town for duck hunting in two weeks. Too bad your bed and breakfast isn't ready for the fall hunting crew."

Camilla stays behind and helps me, which is unnecessary but also appreciated. We talk to Sis and Annie as they knit hats and mittens for Jake and Camilla's baby, and then she helps me make lunch for the group.

"How are you feeling?" I turn to Camilla as we prepare sandwiches.

"Huge." Camilla dips a knife into the mayonnaise container and slathers it on the bread. "Honestly, though, I'm feeling great. We're preparing the nursery, and Jake is making the most amazing bassinet I've ever seen."

"I was wondering if you could stop by next week and look at the B&B? The big stuff is done, but now I want help with the décor, and you have such a great eye for that."

"Are you kidding?" She strokes her belly. "I'd love that."

"Awesome, because I've finally decided the look I'm going for."

We get Sunny and Sis down for their afternoon nap, and I stay around, clean up, and then wait for them to wake up. And that's my sign to leave.

Even though I don't have family here in Wheaton, the community I've built helps. Sunny and Sis feel like part of my family. They've always been accepting and kind to me. I love that I get to spend time with them, hopefully giving back to all they give to everyone. I don't think I need to tell them, though. There is an unspoken love between us, and they know how I feel. I know how they feel too.

When I get home, I struggle through a shower and then throw on a pair of leggings and a sweatshirt. I ice my ankle while lying on the new couch I finally bought. There's a knock at the door, and I struggle to grab my crutches on the floor to answer it.

"Coming." I hobble to the door, and when I open it, Dax stands in front of me with a few bags in his hand and a box on the ground.

"I brought food and a lot of wine." Dax hands me the bags, and the box on the ground makes clanking noises as he lifts it.

When he smiles at me, I find it hard to breathe. It's the boyish grin that always makes me question how it will ever be enough to only be his friend. His hair is damp, and pushed back, out of his face, and his arms flex with the weight of the bags in them.

Dax brings the box to the kitchen and puts it on the table. "How's your ankle? Are you doing any better?"

"A little." I watch Dax pull things out of the bag and put a couple of bottles of wine on the table. "I'm starting to put some weight on it."

Dax stands on one side of the table, and I on the other. His hair falls into his face, and he brushes it back with his long fingers. He looks around the kitchen like he's trying to find something. "Wine glasses. Do you have them?"

Dax wants wine. I could go for a glass.

"They're around here somewhere. Let me look."

"The wine is from my favorite shop in Minneapolis. I thought I'd bring a few bottles back. It's that good. I went to a few of my favorite stores when I landed there. I've missed the city."

I turn my back from Dax and open a cupboard. I moved stuff in so fast that I don't know where anything is yet. I look into another one. Then, the one next to that. I spot the glasses on the top shelf. "There they are." My foot stool is nowhere in sight, so I try to stand on my tippy toes, which isn't easy, considering my one foot is in a boot that provides very little mobility. I reach, but my finger only grazes the glass.

"Here, let me." Dax steps to my side, reaches for the glasses, and brings two down easily.

Our hands touch as I pull my arm down. Dax closes the cupboard, and now there is nothing between us but the look he gives me. He puts the wine glasses on the counter and lays his palm flat. He tucks a strand of hair behind my ear with his other hand and grins. That damn grin. Kind of sideways. Always dimple popping. I put my hand up to my neck. It's hot underneath my touch.

It happens so fast that I don't see his face inching

toward me, but then his body presses into me and his lips brush against mine. He smells like soap and citrus aftershave. I cling to the cupboard behind me. His strong arms cage me in, and his body is so warm against mine.

It takes me a moment to catch my breath, but when I do, I kiss him back. He lifts me onto the counter, and I run my fingers through his damp hair, aware of his hands that wrap around me. I'm also aware of his lips, warm against mine. I'm acutely conscious of everything. The way one hand squeezes the back of my neck, while the other grips my waist. The way he moans into my mouth when his lips part mine. And the way he holds me up as my body becomes a puddle.

Dax lifts me off the counter and holds me up, never removing his lips from mine. I run my fingers through his hair as he walks me to the main floor bedroom I've been living in since my injury. The bedroom he stayed in with me a few nights back—with only pillows and friendship between us.

"Did you just have a starburst, Soleta?" Dax says through a kiss, never taking his mouth off mine.

"Pink," I respond through heavy breaths because only heavy breaths are possible when Dax's hands are all over me.

"I like pink too."

He lays me gently in the bed, always aware of my ankle. He hovers over me and starts undoing my boot. Dax's eyes don't leave mine as he loosens the grip of the boot. I should feel like the least sexy person because of my busted ankle, but the way Dax looks at me, it's impossible to feel anything but sexy.

Dax's hands cause electrical currents wherever they touch me. They slide under my shirt, and I straighten my arms, and he lifts it over my head, and then he removes my tank top underneath. Dax takes his shirt off with one fluid motion, and before he has a chance to press against me, I place my open palms against him and take him in. I comb my fingers along his muscles and trace where they intricately come together. I then run them down his hard stomach. This is much better than being in a gym with a shirtless Dax. Yes. Much, much better.

Dax's weight presses into me, and his hands tunnel through my hair. My breathing comes in ragged gasps. His lips leave mine, and he scrapes his teeth against my neck, and my hands dig into the muscles in his back. In this moment, it feels like he weighs a thousand pounds, and I feel like I could die happy by only the weight of him on me, and nothing else.

Who I am in this moment is the real me. I'm not the seductress from the bathroom a couple of months earlier. A confident woman who storms into a room and takes what she wants. I'm shy. Inexperienced. And totally in my head. I don't know the first thing about making a man feel good.

Dax's fingers tease at the edge of my leggings. He stares at me so honestly that I'm scared to look back. His breathing is as ragged as mine. "Can I?"

"Yeah." I gulp out the words as Dax lowers his knee lower onto the bed as he slides my leggings off. I'm at a disadvantage. Naked.

Dax looks at me like he's starved. He puts one hand on my hip, and his other trails my calf as he moves up past my knee and then on the inside of my thigh. I want to pull Dax over me and use him as my blanket.

"Is this okay?" Dax's glassy eyes stare back at me.

I nod, not entirely sure what I'm saying yes to, but positive that I'm happy to say yes to everything at this point. I try to savor every moment of being touched by Dax. I've dreamt of this. Too many times to count, and now that it's happening, it's somehow better than what I ever imagined.

His hand travels up past my thigh, and he sinks them into my folds, parting me, gliding a finger, and I arch my back, not sure how to contain what this is doing to me. Dax moves up in the bed, his hand never leaving my body. But then he kisses my stomach and between my breasts and finds his way to my lips. His lips feel like electrodes, shocking everywhere they touch. And his hand never stops circling.

"Carrie," Dax moans when I cry out from the pressure of his finger, or maybe two. So much pressure.

The impending orgasm scares me, and I gasp.

Dax removes his hand and sits, his knee between my legs, putting a different kind of pressure on my core.

I prop myself on my elbows, unable to catch my breath.

"You've done this before, right?" Dax's hair falls on his face. His expectant eyes watch me, and his breathing is ragged.

"Yeah." I change my mind. I *can* do this. Definitely. My body wants him and so do I. Grabbing Dax's waist with both hands, I pull him toward me. "I mean, once. A while ago."

Dax moves his face closer to mine. His hands press into my shoulders. "With one person, or like one time, ever?"

Shit! Why'd he have to ask that question? Heat flushing into my face, I wrestle out of Dax's hold because of the embarrassment, lie back, and press the palms of my hands into my eyes, but Dax pulls them off, so I have no choice but to look at him.

"One time," I admit, and Dax raises his eyebrows. "Once."

His hand extends across my rib cage, squeezing my breast before intensifying our kiss. I don't remember this type of touching from the first time. I don't remember enjoying anything about my first time, so I wasn't eager to do it again.

"Hmm," Dax says against my skin. His voice deep and raspy. "I think we need to ease into this."

"You don't want to . . .?"

My words linger in the air while Dax scrapes his teeth against my neck, and then his tongue swirls behind my ear. His warm kisses extend to between my breasts. And when he moans, the vibrations cause my body to tremble.

He kisses my stomach and then pauses to kiss my hip and then the other. Then, his lips suction to the inside of my thigh. Dax looks at me, his lips twitch, and then his mouth moves to—

"Dax, no. Wait." I jolt upright. He looks at me, and then grins.

"You don't want to . . ." I begin, but my brain is scrambled. I can't seem to form actual sentences.

Dax hooks my legs with his arms. "Oh, Soleta. I do want to. Very, very much." Dax's voice is raspy.

"It's so—"

"Carrie, hush." Dax hovers over me, tracing his index finger around my belly button. "You're sexy as hell."

"Dax." I cover my eyes.

"Look at me," he coaxes.

When I lower my hands, he adds, "Give me your hand." I reach toward him, and he laces our fingers. He kisses each of my fingers and then draws it around his neck.

I thread my fingers in his hair.

"I want you," Dax says. And his eyes tell me he isn't lying.

He lowers his head and Dax's tongue parts me. He doesn't pause when my thighs tremble against his face.

The scruff of his face scratches my delicate, untouched skin. Dax pulls my hips up, and I moan in pleasure at the pressure he applies.

His tongue dips in and out of me, and I feel like I'm floating outside my body. My entire body turns red when our eyes meet.

Dax pulls back. "Try to relax." His voice is gravelly, and the hot breath against my center is almost as tantalizing as his tongue.

When he resumes, the tightness and warmth start in my lower belly. All of what I've been feeling—the pleasure, the angst, the anticipation—floods out of me as the building orgasm pools into something foreign and indescribable. I grab the sheets below me.

"Let go," Dax says against me, and the vibration of his voice send renewed waves throuhgout my body

"Dax." I say his name so quietly it's almost a whisper.

"Carrie." Dax lifts me further against him.

It's his voice that pushes me over the edge. The lowness, almost a growl. The sexy way he says my name. And I do let go. Not quietly, as his name finds its way out of me. "Dax. Dax. Dax." Then, my legs go limp. Nothing more than noodles, and I'm sure I'll never recover.

I can't move. Dax kisses me with so much passion. He places all his weight on me. My eyes are heavy, and my body tingles. And then I realize Dax is still wearing his pants, and I haven't done anything for him. And I don't know if I can because my brain and body aren't yet connected.

"Dax, what about you? I haven't even—"

His kisses are warm. They start urgent but gradually slow until he gives me one final kiss on my nose. I don't even bother to open my eyes. I don't know if I have the strength.

"Next time." Dax lies next to me, takes the sheet, and pulls it over us. "I want to ease you into this."

He's still speaking when my eyes close, and I dose off.

Chapter Twenty-Four

Dax

CARRIE'S EYELIDS FLUTTER, AND I dim the light. She's out. Once. Once ever. I've always known men are the stupidest mammal, but now I'm convinced. How has Carrie remained single? How aren't men lining up for a chance to be in her orbit? It makes no sense. I grab the comforter and pull it over her still naked, beautiful body. Carrie squirms a few times, but she's out.

I turn my body to hers, prop a pillow between us, and try to adjust myself. Carrie grimaces in her sleep and then shifts to face the other way. She told me she doesn't like sleeping with the boot on. I'm extra nervous about knocking her ankle, so I'm careful. Carrie tosses her body again, this time facing me. We open our eyes at the same time.

"What's the matter?" I place my palm on her face. "Can't sleep?"

It's the middle of the night. Without looking at the time, I'd guess it's a couple of hours past dusk and a few hours before dawn. Her eyes flutter, and my lips turn up in a smile. I feel that thing in my chest again. Like something is lodged, it takes up all the space, making it impossible to breathe. My heart beats fast, and I press down on my sternum and try to rub the foreign feeling away.

I stroke her arm. "I was hoping the earlier performance would put you out for the night."

Carrie bites her bottom lip but then smiles. "I can't get comfortable. My mind is spinning."

She takes a deep breath, and I tuck her hair behind her ear. "What's up? Do you want to talk about it?"

I see the pause on her face, but then she speaks. "It's nothing."

I maneuver close and put my knee between her legs. "Talk to me, Carrie."

"I'm overwhelmed." Carrie rests her head on my chest. "I have so much to do to get this B&B ready by spring. I've barely worked at the bank this week because I can't stand for that long. My house is a disaster, and I can't even go up the stairs to grab stuff. I always have to figure stuff out on my own."

Without looking at the clock, I decide it must be three in the morning. That's when I spiral too. Especially right after Zari died. It's the magic time of day where nothing I've ever done has been good enough. It's when the world conspires against me, and I'm stuck between wanting to fall asleep, while simultaneously being anxious for the new day to start so I can do better. Be better. Three in the morning is the witching hour. When the devil, demons, or our inner mediocrity tell us we're not enough.

"I'm here." I kiss her nose.

She closes her eyes, just for a moment, and then her green eyes burst open. "I know. But I have friends whose moms would be at their house, taking care of them, baking cookies, cleaning their sheets, and making life seem less overwhelming. I want that."

"You want your mom?"

"Not my mom." Carrie sighs and runs her short fingernails along my bare chest. She scribbles words on me. I close my eyes and try to make out the words—things she's comfortable etching on my skin but not saying out loud. My body fills with goosebumps at her touch.

I start tracing words with my finger on her. I tell her it will be okay and that she's not alone. Between her breasts, I tell her she's beautiful. I also write things that I'm not comfortable saying out loud. I'm scared I'm not ready for this. I'm terrified I'm going to hurt her, or ruin this. I tell her how sexy she is. I put it all out there on her skin.

"What else is on your mind?" I ask.

"Dax." Carrie looks down at her hand on my chest. She closes her eyes and blows out a long and slow breath. "I know I'm breaking every rule by even bringing this up so soon, but . . ."

Carrie's voice trails off, and I take her hand in mine. "What is it?"

She looks at me. "You've said not everything that's been whispered about you is true. But you've also made it clear to me that you haven't attempted to date since . . ."

Carrie looks down again and pulls her bottom lip into her mouth.

"Since Zari died." I finish her sentence.

I grip Carrie's chin and place a soft kiss on her lips. "I'll never be dishonest with you Carrie. I like you. And I want to explore this new thing between us, but there is part of me that is scared that even though I have these feelings for you, that I'm still not ready."

Carrie nods and moves closer to me. She moves the pillow that's between us, and throws it on the floor. "That's all I'm asking from you. Your honesty." Carrie's countenance shifts, and her lips turn up in a smile. "I was looking at the walls. I think I know what theme I want this place to have. I can picture it.""Tell me."

"Well," Carrie hesitates. "What if I did Wheaton through the ages? Each room could be decorated in a different era. I could go to the museum and see if they have old pictures, news stories, and things like that."

"That's honestly great." I pinch the skin on her hip, and she closes her eyes.

Carrie's vision comes to life for me. Each room could be a decade of Wheaton, with all of the history and what the town looked like during that time. I've always wondered why no one attempted to open a B&B here before. The lake is a hidden gem. In the summer, it's known for its walleye fishing, and the fall hunting season, with duck, pheasants, and deer, is unparalleled. But there's more than that. The people are the best you'll meet, the shops offer everything, and the scenery is breathtaking.

"Do you mean it?" Carrie scrunches up her face. I can tell how much she wants my approval. "It's not stupid?"

"Carrie. It's a great idea. You should also go to the library and dig through the archives. I could see if my family has anything of value. The Abrams have been here forever."

"I'd love that so much." Carrie's eyes get droopy, and her blinks longer. "Thanks, Dax."

THE NEXT MORNING, JUNIPER SOLETA's voice is stuck in my head—telling me what being a Capricorn means and how to best take care of a Taurus like Carrie. It's all about acts of service. I prop Carrie on the couch with an icepack and a magazine, and I get to work. I pull the sheets off her bed and throw them in the washing machine. Next, I get to work in the kitchen.

The cupboards are in great shape, but some need to be readjusted and tightened, so I work on that. I look in her fridge, and she hardly has any food. I drive to town to pick up a few items.

When I get back, Carrie lies asleep on the couch with a magazine resting on her chest. I hang all the bedding outside on the clothesline, taking advantage of the warm Mid October weather, and then throw in a load of her other laundry. I clean the floors and pop the premade chocolate chip cookies into the oven. I have no clue how to make these from scratch, and I have no desire to learn today, so this will have to do.

"Dax." Carrie gets up from the couch and uses her crutches to enter the kitchen. "None of this is necessary."

"I want to be helpful." I grab the sheets from outside and make the bed.

She's still standing there when I get back from making the bed.

"Oh, you've been helpful." Her eyes pierce into mine, and I notice her lips twitch, ever so slightly.

Later in the evening, I pick up dinner from the golf course because although I've got some talents, I still can't cook. We sit on the couch, feet to feet, to-go containers on our chests.

"You need to tell me everything about growing up as the middle child in the Abram family." Carrie picks at her food.

"The Abram family." I laugh. Harder than I have in a long time. Because I remember whining about it. "My childhood was very normal. Uninteresting."

"You all seem so perfect. You all look like Norwegian Gods and Goddesses. Good students. Good athletes."

"Everyone has their shit, Soleta." I take a drink.

"True." Carrie pops an olive in her mouth. "And

when you stay in the place that you grew up, the shit seems to follow you everywhere. No matter how much you change, the town doesn't let you."

That. All of that. Everything she said is how I've felt since returning, but unable to articulate it.

"I love it here. I do." Carrie pauses. "But there's something about small towns that don't let a person grow. Change. Malik isn't from here, and he came in, and he makes me feel like myself more than anyone else. But people who have known me forever have a way of keeping me as I always was. Regardless of how much I change. It's suffocating."

Carrie looks at me, and I wet my lips, pondering her thoughts. I love being back in Wheaton because the people are amazing, and Kylie and I need the support system. But there have been triggers as well.

Growing up, I was Jake's younger, less athletic brother. I was Jenna's older, less adorable brother. I partied, as we all did. I had my insecurities and my issues, and everyone saw me as the boy I always was. Not the man I was growing up to be. Moving away allowed me to reinvent myself. Except, I was always me. But the new people in my life saw me as me, not a younger, less polished version.

Being back has put me in a box. And because of said box, I've resorted to things I used to do. Because I wanted to seem cool. Important. Wanted. Noticed.

"Would you ever leave?" I come back to reality, nervous about her response. Because I'm here and not going anywhere. Having a child limits one's ability to move freely throughout the world.

"And go where?"

I readjust Carrie's leg and say, "This town can feel so limiting."

Carrie plumps a pillow, puts it behind her head, and leans back. "I can't speak for you, but I'm unable not to see myself through the lens of others. I know who I am, yet this town is my mirror, and I see myself as everyone else sees me. And they still see me as—"

"You used to be."

"As I used to be."

Carrie's eyes get heavy, and I put my food on the floor and rub her good foot.

"You need to start seeing the town as a window, not a mirror, Soleta."

She moans before dozing off yet again. I don't think I've ever met someone so tired or needing more taking care of. I grab a blanket and put it over her while I get back to work on B&B projects.

Chapter Twenty-Five

Carrie

THERE IS SOMETHING WRONG WITH me. It's the only explanation. I open my eyes, and I'm in bed with a view of Dax's back. I elevate myself on my pillow and look out the window, and the sky is pink, with a promise of a new day. It's already Saturday morning. Dax has been here since Thursday, and I only remember bits and pieces of it. I've never felt so tired in my life.

He shuffles, and I know he's about to turn to me, and I pinch my eyes shut. The bed shifts and Dax walks out of the room. The shower starts in the bathroom next to the room. Dax is here. In my house. For me. Thursday was one of the most incredible experiences of my life, but now I can't seem to even look at the guy. I waited all day yesterday for him to make his move, but it's like, now, he doesn't want to.

Maybe he regrets what happened between us. Or perhaps, that was my one shot with Dax, and now it's over. But it wasn't enough. It wasn't all of Dax. If I knew that was all it would be, I would have asked for everything.

"You're up." Dax walks into the room with a towel wrapped around his waist. Water glistens off his muscular chest. No matter what the season, Dax always looks like he stepped out of the sun. His skin is tan, and taut, and the towel hangs so low on him. I rapidly blink away the thoughts.

I smooth out my hair and stare at him as he sorts through his bag on the desk. My Norwegian Viking. His longish damp hair is brushed back, and his chest I want to scrape my fingers over. My breathing gets heavier, and Dax faces the wall but drops his towel, his muscular butt on display for a moment before he pulls on his sweatpants. I squeeze my eyes shut. Because I can't breathe. Not with sex looming between us. Or at least in my mind.

"I'm going to shower," I blurt out. Louder than I intend.

"I can draw you a bath. It might feel good."

"Thanks," I mutter, unable to make eye contact with him.

"Let's go, gimpy," Dax says, and I follow him to the bathroom. He opens the cupboard, finds lavender, and sprinkles it into the tub.

"Do you need help?" I shake my head and watch as Dax leaves the bathroom.

Sex. It's right there, but I don't know my next move. Ever since Dax has been here, I've been on edge because I have no idea what he wants or expects of me. I could just ask him. There is this huge part of me that feels more comfortable with him than I do with anyone. But I also wear my inexperience like armor, and it's paralyzing me. I take a sponge, clean my body, and dip my hair underneath the suds.

After my bath, I slather myself in lotion and wrap myself in my robe. I'm half expecting Dax to be gone when I get out—wanting to get out from underneath the awkwardness and the caretaking. But he sits on the edge of the bed with only his sweatpants on. His stupidly hot sweatpants. He studies the phone in his hand. "Hey." He smiles and puts his phone on the bed. "How'd it feel?"

My steps towards him are slow and deliberate, and when I reach him, I throw the crutches to the side, and use Dax for balance. I have no plan except to be close to him. I need it like I need the air I breathe. If Dax isn't going to initiate what happens next, I will. I position myself between his legs and place my hands on his shoulders. Dax puts his on my hips. I try to channel that girl from the summer who found Dax in a bathroom and threw herself at him.

I untie my robe, and the silk glides across my skin until it falls into a ball on the floor. Dax puts his hands back on my now bare hips and then he kisses my stomach. I tilt his head and slowly lower myself to kiss him. I move my hand from his chin to the back of his neck and run my fingers through his hair, scraping my nails against his scalp.

"Carrie," he says into my mouth. Dax's eyes take me in, as if he's seeing me naked for the first time, and he puts his head against my stomach.

He stands and wraps his arms around me, our bodies pressed against each other, and then he places me onto the bed. Dax shimmies out of his sweatpants and lowers himself onto me.

Dax envelops me with his body. His lips are on mine until they move to my neck. His hand caresses my arm, his other moves along my hip, and then my stomach. He's heavy, and his body is warm. The heat between us burns. My hands find pleasure in grabbing his arms, flexed, trying not to put all his weight on me. I move them to his chest and then back before grabbing onto Dax's ass and pinching his flesh.

His breathing is heavy. Or maybe it's mine. At this point, I'm unsure where I end, and Dax begins. But then he gets up to grab something from his bag.

"You came prepared." I roll my lips into my mouth.

"You know, just in case." Dax grins at me.

I allow myself to look at him, as my eyes comb over his body. "I'm clean and on the pill," I blurt out. There is no reason to be on it, but I always kept filling my prescription during and after college.

"It's been a while for me." Dax's blue eyes look at me as he continues to lean over his bag. "I'm clean too."

"Okay, then."

Dax returns to the bed, hovers over me, and spreads my legs with his knee. His erratic kisses send my body into a frenzy, and I feel like electrical currents are streaming through me. I've spent so much time admiring Dax. The way his muscles come together, like perfectly placed puzzle pieces. His strong arms and perfect ab muscles. I've dreamed of having access to them, and I make sure that every part of his skin is touched.

"Are you sure, Carrie?" His eyes are inches from mine, his knee rubbing against me between my legs—so much heat.

"I want this," I pant. The pressure he's putting between my legs is intense.

Dax's heart pounds against my chest as he takes my hand in his and wraps it around his erection. He helps me to guide him inside of me. I wince as my body adjusts to him.

"Are you okay?" Dax asks as he slowly inches deeper. "I don't want to hurt you."

"Please, Dax," I plead. "I want this."

"Carrie," Dax says into my mouth. "The way you say my name. If you keep talking, this will be over too soon."

I don't know how much I have of him, but I feel full. Dax reaches his hand down and touches me where our bodies are connected, and my muscles tense as my body tries to adapt to the intrusion. The strange but enticing fullness.

"You feel so—" Dax stops and moans. His hand clasps my knee. "Is this okay? You're so—"

I don't let him finish. "I like it." My hands grab at his shoulders. I roll my head back.

Dax glides over me, and the fullness turns into something else entirely. His tender kisses give me confidence, and I respond. I arch my back and roll my hips, and Dax inches even deeper.

"You're perfect, Carrie." He kisses my neck and touches me like I'm something to behold. Special. That thing from the other day builds in me again. The tightening of my stomach, the twitching of my muscles, and the feeling that an explosion is imminent.

"You're perfect." Dax grabs my face, so we're eye to eye.

How amazing it feels to be touched by him isn't surprising. But what is surprising is how caring and concerned he is and how comfortable I am. This is what it should feel like. The intimacy. The closeness. The trust. He's here for me, and I can't imagine wanting to do this, to feel this, with anyone else.

"Carrie. I should pull—" Dax doesn't finish his sentence.

I clench around him. "No."

Dax's hand slides over my breast, and the friction of my thigh against his groin, puts him in a more frenzied rhythm. When the pressure intensifies, there is so much rolling friction, and I know that I'll need so much more of this. I'll need so much more of Dax.

I make a sound between a whimper and a groan as my orgasm gets closer.

"You like this, Carrie?" Dax closes his eyes and presses

his forehead against mine. His breathing is as ragged as his breath is on my face. And then we both come undone. The only thing better than my pleasure is hearing Dax's. The way he hooks my knee, eyes rolled up into his head, as his sweaty body glides over mine. Dax collapses on me, all of him. Our hearts race against each other's, and I kiss the sweat from his shoulders and then his chest. The silence overwhelms me, but then Dax speaks.

"Wow."

His body is crushing mine, and when he realizes it, he props himself up on his arm and cups my face.

When he pulls out, there is a dull ache where my body mourns the loss. He walks out of the room naked and returns with a wet washcloth. The coolness feels good against me.

"Are you sore?" He washes me.

I should feel uncomfortable, but I don't. "A little."

Dax kisses my cheek and the other, before his lips cover mine. He pulls me to him and holds me.

It drizzles outside, which makes me guilt-free that Dax and I don't leave my bed all day. He pulls me on top of him, and I place my chin on his chest. Dax brushes the hair out of my face.

"I have to know, Soleta," he says. "Why only once?"

There's no judgment in his tone. I prop myself up on my elbow and trace words into his chest. "That wasn't the plan. I wasn't ready for any of that in high school. And then I went to college, and there was a guy on the men's basketball team at the University, and he walked me home from a party, and it happened."

Dax rubs my back. "And you didn't want an encore?"

"Not with him." I shake my head.

"It wasn't like this, then?" Dax kisses my shoulder.

"Nothing like this." I squeeze his arm. "Then I got

injured and came back to Wheaton. And, well, cancer. And here I am." I shift my body and readjust my leg that is propped over his. "How about you? When was your first?"

Dax smiles but shakes his head. "Sophomore year of high school. My first girlfriend, Blake." He leans over to the nightstand and grabs his phone. He scrolls and then hands it to me. There's a text from her from the night before, saying she heard Kylie was out of town and asking if she could come over.

Blake. The captain of the high school dance and cheerleading team. A nurse at the hospital. Yes, I know Blake. "So many options for you."

He pulls me toward him, careful of my ankle, and kisses me gently. "There's nowhere else I'd rather be than here."

We spend the day talking, having encore performances, eating in bed, laughing, and the outside rain can't damper my mood. Dax brings a light everywhere he goes, and being couped up with him, talking where no topics are off limits, and being touched by him are the best things in the world. But the morning light of Sunday comes too soon. I'm not even sure we slept.

"This weekend was fun." Dax reaches his finger out and pokes me in the nose.

"Yeah, and I feel like my ankle turned a corner with all of the forced icings," I say.

"And the sex." Dax grins. "Also, very nice."

I sit up. "I'll be sure to tell your dad that at my follow-up appointment this week."

Dax laughs. "I need to get home." He glances at his phone.

Kylie will arrive with Amina in a few short hours, and I know that Dax hasn't even been to his place since returning to town on Thursday.

"I know." I exhale.

But I don't want him to. It's cold and drizzly, and I don't want to be alone. I don't want to be without Dax.

We stand in my doorway for too long, me using my crutches and Dax for support. We make out like teenagers. Slow kisses. Mine are full of promises, but also riddled with the uncertainty of what Dax's kisses mean. We say the slowest Minnesota goodbye in the world. Neither of us are in a hurry to experience reality outside these four walls.

Dax studies me, and I know my face changes with the thoughts flooding me.

"Hey." He cups my face. "I've never wanted to try as much as I want to with you."

"I know." I pull Dax toward me and kiss his cheek. "But I'm scared. I'm not going to lie."

Dax tucks a strand of hair behind my ear and then puts his hand on my heart. "I'm scared too."

He looks toward his car, and then back at me. "But I really do have to go."

"Then go." I scrape my nails against Dax's scalp. I've noticed he likes it when I do that.

"I'll call you." Dax pulls away.

"Bye, Dax." I shut the door and watch as he walks toward his car.

I close the door and look down the dark hallway. My place is silent, except for the sound of my deep exhales. I'm once again completely alone, only now, I feel it in a way I never have before. Because all of the energy that Dax brought to my home left with him.

Chapter Twenty-Six

Dax

"DO I HAVE TO GO to school today, Daddy? I don't want to." Kylie stomps her feet as she walks into the kitchen, where I'm slathering peanut butter and honey on a piece of toast.

"Yes, Kylie," I say, more pointed than I intend. "I have to go to work, and you have to go to school."

"But." I turn and look at Kylie, and her lip quivers. I know her signs. She's about to lose it. "You brushed my hair stupid, my outfit is stupid, and I look stupid."

I glance at the clock, and if we don't get out of the house in about two minutes, I'll be late for work, which is never an option because it means twenty third graders will be in a room alone. Kylie has tears running down her cheeks, and I grab a tissue and start dabbing.

"Kylie. You look perfect. You do."

"But Sammy always teases me and says my hair is messy and my clothes aren't nice."

"Kylie—"

She stomps her foot against the wood floors, puts her

head on the counter, and cries harder.

I take her by her arm and let her cry into my shoulder. Her tears and snot soak my sweater, and I know I'll have no time to change shirts. It won't be the first time I show up at work in this state.

"Kylie, I'm sorry you're having a tough time, but we have to go." I smooth out her hair.

"But Daddy," she begins to protest again.

"We're going to be late for school, Kylie." I grab her backpack, lead her outside, and get her buckled into her booster seat in the back.

She's silent the entire drive to town, but when I glance at her through the mirror, I see the tears falling down her cheeks.

"I want Mommy." She whimpers.

It never gets easier to hear her say this.

"Oh, baby girl, I know you do."

"No, Daddy," she cries, Louder this time. "I want her, Daddy. Now. I want Mommy."

"If I could bring her back so she could be here with you right now, I'd do it. I would."

Tears roll down my face, and I take the sleeve of my sweater to wipe them. Kylie's mourning isn't always so outwardly as today, but it's always there. I feel it. But the moments she asks for her mom are the hardest for me. It's the one thing I can't give to her. When she asks, I know Kylie would have preferred her mom to be here instead of me. Zari should be here, and I'd switch places in a heartbeat. A girl needs her mom.

"Kylie." I glance back at her through the mirror. "Do you remember the butterfly song you used to sing with Mommy every morning? You would sit at the table eating breakfast and say, 'One more time, Mommy,' until she'd end up singing it at least ten times." Kylie nods her head, and I continue. "She made the best breakfasts too. Do you remember her fluffy French toast? What if I tried to make that for us?"

"Okay," Kylie says through a sniffle. She stares out her window, chin against it.

"Tonight, let's watch a movie, make popcorn and hot cocoa, and then look at all the pictures of Mommy. Wouldn't that be fun?"

"Okay," she says once again.

Kylie barely says a word as I bring her to her classroom. Kylie's eyes are puffy. My eyes are red. Her teacher gives me a sympathetic look, takes Kylie's hand, and leads her into the room. I then head to mine. Late. After my third graders arrived.

Just like every other workday, my students aren't easy on me. They are demanding. Energetic. And they require every ounce of my attention. Yet, my heart isn't in it today. I keep thinking of Kylie, her day, and how Zari would parent so much better than I'll ever be capable.

Sasha and Naomi won't quit talking to each other, so I have to separate them. Then, when I'm not looking, Tommy breaks into the milk supply and starts handing out cartons. When I turn my back to write on the whiteboard, someone throws a paper airplane across the room. The only thing that would make this day worse is if someone showed up to observe my teaching. I'd fail at that too.

Zari would know what to do in this situation. She'd know exactly what to say to Kylie to cheer her up or make her smile. Nothing I say or do in these moments feels good enough. I don't want her to go through this pain, but the only way out is through.

What do I know about six-year-old girls? I know that Kylie's sadness comes out in unexpected ways. Like defiance. Anger. I want to get home and spend every moment with her. Prepare a meal of undercooked noodles and semi-cold pasta sauce. And talk, cuddle, and then let her sleep in my bed all night.

The day of work ends, and while all the other teachers stay behind, grading assignments, and preparing for tomorrow, I swoop Kylie up, who wraps her arms around me when I reach her classroom approximately thirty seconds after the bell. Her entire body sinks into mine, and we both breathe in relief that we're together.

"Tonight, I thought I would cook my famous pasta."

Kylie nuzzles her face into my neck. "Eww, Daddy. Can't you make me chicken nuggets?" She pulls away and cups my face with her tiny hands.

"Not tonight. I'll cook my pasta tonight, and then while you pick the movie, I'll prepare the popcorn and cocoa."

I put Kylie down, and she grips my hand as we hurry to the car. "On a Monday, Daddy?"

"Yeah, on a Monday. I'm the boss. I can make the rules."

Kylie giggles and I squeeze her hand tightly in mine as we walk to the car.

That's how our night goes. I make pasta and manage to cook it for a more appropriate time, and then I warm up the sauce and pour it over the noodles, with extra cheese on top. I turn on music, and Kylie and I dance and laugh as I twirl her. We then watch some mindless *Curious George*. And I hold her. Harder than I've held anyone my entire life. Her head sinks into my lap as she falls asleep before I have a chance to make popcorn.

Grief is a never-ending, unpredictable beast. It's not as linear as I was expecting, but instead, it shows up in billowing waves, sucks us dry, and makes us wish that we would be the ones who would have left this world. When Zari first died, I was sure I couldn't continue. I wanted the pain to stop and didn't think I could go on. But then I realized I did want to live. I just didn't want to feel the pain.

I tuck Kylie into my bed because I promised we'd cuddle all night and that I wouldn't carry her back to her bed. Her head pops up the moment I lay her down.

"Don't bring me back to my room, Daddy." Kylie rubs her eyes. "You promised."

"I promise, Kylie." I kiss her forehead, pull the blanket up to her chin, and tuck her in tightly.

The room is dark, and the ceiling fan runs overhead because I hate being hot. I hold my phone in front of me. I see a text from Carrie asking how my day has been. I'm at a loss for what to tell her. The entire day has been hell. Many of our days are like this, and there is no way I can invite someone into the chaos. Kylie and I are a team and are not ready for the disruption.

I also don't want to leave Carrie hanging. I've thought of her too. Of course, I have. What happened between us wasn't nothing, but I don't know what to say to her. Her house was an escape. But now I'm home, and real life has invaded all the spaces around me, including my beautiful girl who lies in bed beside me.

My finger hovers over the keyboard. I want to be honest with her. Carrie, I'm in unchartered territory. I enjoyed our conversations. And although what happened between us felt incredible, the most I can offer you is friendship. I don't know if I have the capacity to complicate and Kylie's life . . . or mine.

But I don't send anything. I start texts and delete, unable to say any of it. Because how can I say something when I don't know how I feel? There is one thing I do know. Kylie is struggling. She misses her mom. Her grief is everywhere, and I can't focus on anything or anyone else.

So, instead of texting Carrie, I email Kylie's therapist and tell her about our day. I then do something I've never done before. I ask her to give me a recommendation for an adult therapist. After I hit send, I hold Kylie and let myself feel everything, and the tears flow down my cheeks.

Chapter Twenty-Seven

Carrie

AFTER CAMILLA LEAVES, I WANDER from room to room and ponder her thoughts on the B&B. I tell her about my idea to have rooms with themes. She loved that and wants to show me what she's found at the museum and in the archives. Camilla thinks Sunny and Sis have a lot of old material that could also be useful. The front bedroom will forever be mine and Dax's room. I'm excited to decorate that room the most.

When the water from the shower gets hot, I turn my music up and carefully get in. I sing at the top of my lungs. Confidence has seeped into me, and I feel capable.

"Hey, Carrie," I hear as I step out of the shower, knowing that Malik has arrived early than expected.

"I'll be right out. Make yourself at home." I wrap the towel around me, strap my boot on, and practice putting weight on my foot.

"There you are." He follows me into the bedroom. Malik plops down on my bed, and I look for something to wear in the closet. The closet that Dax organized for me until I'm able to move back into my upstairs bedroom.

"I need to get dressed." I turn to Malik, who lies across my bed, scrolling through his phone.

Malik walks out of the room, and I throw my clothes on. He yells at me from the hallway. "Tell me everything. You've been ignoring me."

I lie back on the bed when my clothes are on, smiling at the ceiling. Then, I prop myself up on my elbow. "You wouldn't believe me if I told you."

Malik smiles and grabs my arm. "Believe what?"

"Well, I said fuck it and went for it with Dax." Malik knows I'm talking about the list. He jumps up, almost bumping my ankle on his way down, and then props himself back on the bed on his stomach, his face resting in his hands.

"Details." He claps his hands together. "Oh gawd, was it here?" He looks at the bed.

I tell him everything. Because, until you share such details with your best friend, it's like it never happened.

"Was it good?" Malik lies back on the bed across my lap.

"Let's just say Dax knows what he's doing." As I talk about Dax, my heart again feels like it's going to beat right out of me. When I say the words out loud to Malik, my brain remembers everything.

Malik smiles and holds his hands together in front of his chest. "It's about damn time, Carrie."

"I know." I brush my hair and put on a little makeup. "Who knows what happens from here? But I like him. Like, really like him."

"Umm, yeah, and I know he likes you too." Malik walks out the door. "Let's go, sexy little kitten. We're going to be late."

I check myself in the mirror one last time. I pull at my off-the-shoulder sweater and turn to look at my butt in my leggings.

"Ready." I grab my stuff and follow Malik out the door.

We aren't going far. We drive to Jake and Camilla's, who are having a cookout at their home, probably the last of the season. The mornings and evenings are starting to get chilly, and its nearly November. We're all bracing for it, but today is a gorgeous day, especially on the lake, so we're headed over there for some fun.

Dax hasn't reached out to me since he walked out of my place on Sunday. The one text I sent went unanswered. I'm sure he'll be at Jake and Camilla's with Kylie, and my heart races at the thought of seeing him. I'm sure he's just been busy, but I also worry that it wasn't good for him or that I read more into the meaning than he did. I've spent the past few days worrying about everything.

When we arrive, I get out my one crutch, as I'm trying to rely less on the help and get to a better place with my ankle. Jake rushes over and gives me his other arm for support when he sees us.

"You're still gimping around," he jokes, and I squeeze his forearm.

"You should have seen me a few days ago. This is an improvement," I say.

Jake grabs a chair, and Camilla hands me a glass of wine. Dr. Abram walks out of the home with his wife, Lucy. "Well, how's my patient?" Dr. Abram pulls up a chair for me to prop up my leg.

"It's getting better, but I'm still so limited." I take a sip of my wine. "I have no mobility."

Lucy leans forward and puts her hand on my arm. "We were at the game. It was quite the doozy."

Lucy's smile is warm, so different than that of my mom. Since the injury, my mom hasn't called me, so she doesn't even know it happened. Dax walks out of the house with Kylie next to him, and my heart skips a beat and then races. I try to slow my breathing, but he looks so good. He always does. I remember all the things he did to me. All the places he touched me.

"Hey." Dax waves at me. His expression is blank. Kylie rushes toward me and wraps her arms around my neck.

"How's your leg, Carrie? Daddy says it hurts." She looks at me with her big brown eyes. I've missed this kid.

I glance at Dax. "Your Daddy's right. It does hurt, but you were so gentle with your hug."

"When will you start picking me up on Fridays again?" Kylie asks. "I have more recipes I want to try, and Daddy got Mommy's French toast recipe, and I want to try to make it with you."

Dax has already walked away, so he is no help answering the question. "How about when my ankle gets better, so I'll be more fun?"

"Okay." Kylie squeezes me again and runs off to talk to Malik and Jake, who stand at the grill.

"Kylie sure has a village of strong women in her life," Lucy says.

We all sit around and eat, and Malik brings me a plate. Camilla sits by me for a while and lets me know that she's found a lot of great newspaper articles in the archives at the library.

"You should stop by the shop this week, and I'll show you some of my finds." Camilla rubs her belly, which is larger every time I see her.

"That would be great."

"I also think you need to start putting together some branded material. If I were you, I'd use the sign your mom made. You should start looking into having soaps made, brochures, and you'll need a website," Camilla says.

"You know Jenna is a writer. You should ask her to help."

"Us old people are going to get going." Dr. Abram leans over to me. "I want you back at the clinic this week. I need to check the swelling, and if it's still bad, I want to try an ice compression boot."

"Thanks so much," I say, and he kisses my cheek.

We gather by the fire, and Malik goes inside to grab something. For a brief moment, it's Dax and me.

"You're quiet," I say to him. Dax doesn't look in my direction but stares at the fire. The air is thick between us, but I hold back from saying more.

"It was a busy week. Kylie's been out of sorts, and school, and I'm trying to get her into a routine."

"Here, Carrie." Malik hands me a bottled water over my shoulder.

Jake, Camilla, and Kylie join us, and Kylie sits on Camilla's lap, hugging her pregnant belly. Jake gets out his guitar and starts tuning it. He winks at Camilla and then looks at the rest of us. "Any requests?"

We all wait, but no one says anything. "'Landslide,'" Malik finally calls out.

"That's Zari's favorite song. Fleetwood Mac's, not the Chicks', version." Dax looks at Kylie. "That's your Mommy's favorite song."

Jake starts strumming the guitar, and at first, he sings alone, but then Malik joins in on the song. Dax stares at the fire and pinches the bridge of his nose. I try to look everywhere else, but my eyes keep finding Dax.

Everyone but Dax and I bellow out lyrics.

If you had told me that I could be jealous of a dead woman, I would have told you you're crazy. But as I sit here, listening to everyone sing and the sadness in Dax's eyes as he recites the lyrics, I'm jealous. And not because of what they had but because of the hold she still has on him.

I've never been in love before, unless this gut-wrenching pain I feel toward Dax is love. What do I know about getting over someone? My high all week was the best feeling in the world. But when we're high, we have a long way to fall.

The song ends, and Jake smiles, looking at Dax. "I miss Zari on the other guitar. She could sing."

"Could she ever." Dax laughs. "I remember the first time she joined us out here for a fire. She started singing, and you stopped playing just to listen." Dax readjusts his chair.

"Mommy could sing?" Kylie hops off Camilla's lap and jumps onto Dax's.

"She was the best singer." Dax rubs his cheek against Kylie's.

Camilla laughs. "Kylie, I'm pretty sure the first time I realized I loved your uncle Jake was when he played the guitar in front of me for the first time."

Kylie puts her hands over her mouth and giggles. "Really?"

Jake starts strumming his guitar again, this time to "Have You Ever Seen the Rain."

"Ahh, there it is." Camilla leans back in her chair. "Can a person get pregnant when they're already pregnant?"

More songs are sung, and I sit silently, wishing I had the superpower to disappear. I don't think I'll ever fit into this life. This is how it will always be—sitting around, everyone remembering Zari, who was perfect and could do no wrong. The wife, mom, and sister-in-law who is gone too soon. I'll always be an outsider.

Dax goes inside to grab something, and then Camilla follows. Jake, Malik, Kylie, and I sit in silence, and then Jake starts talking about work with Malik, and I sink further into my chair. Why am I here? I feel invisible.

"We should get going," I interrupt. "I'm tired and need to get ice on my ankle."

Malik nods. "Okay. Yeah, I'm tired too."

"I'm going to pop inside to use the bathroom first."

I get inside, and Dax and Camilla stand at the table. Neither hear me enter.

"Spill the tea." Camilla grabs Dax's arm. "Are you and Carrie, you know?" She nudges him again.

"Carrie?" Dax asks with disbelief in his voice. "Nah. I'm not ready for any of that. Kylie needs so much of me right now, and yeah, we're friends. Always friends."

Time stands still for a moment, and I force my mouth closed because I'm sure it hangs open.

"I'm not going to lie. I'm bummed." Camilla puts her head in her hands. "I think she's perfect for you."

"A relationship is not in my near future," Dax says again because the first time wasn't enough.

My crutch squeaks with my next move, and they both turn to me. I'm not sure they realize how long I've been standing here.

"Sorry, guys," I stammer. "I came inside to say Malik and I are taking off."

Camilla smiles warmly, and I need to get out of here before I burst into tears. I don't recognize this Dax in front of me. He's cold and distant. I lock myself in the bathroom and look at my face. I text Malik to be cool but to find me in the bathroom closest to the door.

When I walk out, Dax's waiting, but then Malik arrives. "Ready, Carrie?"

"Yes," I say with the fakest smile I've ever managed.

"Can we talk first?" Dax asks.

I look at him and shake my head. "My ankle is

throbbing like you wouldn't believe. I need to get home and put ice on it."

"Two minutes, please?" Dax pleads.

"I'll call you later," I say, but I know I won't.

We say our goodbyes, and when I get into Malik's car and start driving down the driveway, I break down into full sobs. Malik looks at me and puts his hand on my leg as I try to control my breathing. Dax is all I've thought about. I think I'm in love with him.

Dax didn't break any rules for me. When he said that he only gets with a woman one time or one night, he wasn't lying. I'm one of those women. The kind I hate, that goes into a situation with open eyes, pretending it's enough, only to hope we can change a person. I've been telling myself for days that I'm different. That we connected in ways he hasn't done with women since Zari. I've told myself that no one can fake love and affection. The way Dax held me and looked into my eyes as we made love. I didn't make that up.

"I'm afraid to ask." Malik squeezes my knee.

"I'm stupid, Malik. Stupid," I say through tears. "Our weekend meant nothing to him."

"That doesn't make sense." Malik turns down the driveway to my house.

After listening to everything, Malik turns to me. "Dax might not be ready. But that doesn't mean you don't mean something to him. He's all up in his feelings, which is new for him. Just talk to him."

But I think about it. We haven't talked all week since Dax left me to go home last Sunday. I wrote it off as him being busy with work, being a dad, and having responsibilities. But my greatest fear is that Dax is too scared to try. I'm confident that our weekend together meant something to him too, but I can't force someone to be ready.

Chapter Twenty-Eight

Dax

CARRIE WON'T PICK UP HER phone. I don't blame her, but Kylie has been asleep for over an hour, and I know Carrie can't be sleeping yet, so why won't she pick up her phone? The next time I call, it goes straight to voicemail.

She heard everything. I could see it on her face. We never talked about where things were going, but Carrie deserved to hear where my head was before I shared it with someone else. I'm not even sure where my head's at. All I know is that I'm capable of promising so little right now.

I drive to Carrie's place with Kylie on Sunday, but her car is gone. I then head to town, and her car isn't at Malik's either. His car is there, but no one answers the door when I knock. Kylie and I head to my parent's house for Sunday brunch, and I do my best to put a smile on my face and act like everything is great in our house.

"Daddy, do you think Carrie can pick me up from school on Friday?" Kylie asks from the backseat as we drive back to our house.

"I can ask her, sweetie," I say. "But she may not feel well enough because of her ankle."

"But, Daddy," Kylie continues. "I miss her and the cooking we do together."

"Are you sick of my cooking?" I glance at Kylie through my mirror, and she puts her hands to her mouth and giggles.

By Wednesday, I can't stand being ignored anymore. After throwing together an unhealthy meal for Kylie made up of chicken nuggets, macaroni and cheese, with green beans tossed in for good measure, I call Jenna and ask if she can sit with Kylie for an hour as I have a pressing matter to attend to. Jenna is at my door in ten minutes and doesn't ask any questions. I have the best sister.

Wednesdays are usually Carrie's day at the Berglands, so she should have been home hours ago. I breathe a sigh of relief when I see her car parked out front. I approach her door, but before I have a chance to open it, Carrie opens it, boot still on her ankle but crutch-free.

"What are you doing here?" Carrie closes the door and stepping outside. She's dressed like she's going somewhere.

"What do you mean, what am I doing here?" I throw my hands up in the air. "I know I disappeared on you, but I'd love to talk. If you're willing."

Carrie stands in front of me, and I can smell her perfume when the wind blows. I want to nuzzle my face into her neck and breathe her in. I also want to run far away before my feelings for her break me.

"Sorry, Dax," Carrie says, but she doesn't look sorry. "I've had the busiest week, and you caught me at a bad time. I have an appointment in town."

I look at my phone. "At six in the evening?"

Carrie puts her hands on her hips. "Yes, at six in the evening. What do you want?"

Carrie is maddening. She acts like she hasn't been

ignoring me for days. She starts walking to her car, and I follow her. I know this is what I deserve for disappearing when she needed reassurance. But I want to make things right.

I take her arm, but she pulls it away from me. "I know you heard what I said to Camilla, and I want to explain myself."

We reach Carrie's car, and she opens the door and leans against it. "Look, Dax. You've been honest with me from day one. You told me you weren't ready to move forward. We had a fun weekend. But you aren't ready to date. I release you. You can walk away guilt-free. There. I saved you a speech. You're welcome."

Carrie gets in her car and closes the door with a thump. I'm left standing there, not even sure what just happened. Guilt-free? Then, why do I feel so guilty?

My entire week goes like this. At school, the third graders are antsy and out of control as the kids can feel the Halloween excitement. My days are spent being the crabby teacher reprimanding them. No one seems to be retaining any information, and by the time Friday comes along, I'm convinced I've never experienced a longer school week in my life.

By Friday evening, I can't stand it anymore. So, when Kylie begs for a sleepover with Grandma and Grandpa, I agree to it before the question is fully out of her mouth. I head home and get some outdoor projects done. The temperatures remain unseasonably warm, and the weather channel says we should brace for an Indian Summer. I pick up some food from the golf course and try my luck talking to Carrie.

When I arrive at her place, she's outside, stringing lights from the trees. The sun is close to setting from behind the hills, and I can only see the silhouette of her.

She turns when she hears me approach, and I hold up bags. "I'm hoping you're hungry."

Carrie looks at the bags of food. "I could eat, but I could also use a tall person to help me finish the lights."

Hope pings me in the chest. "I can do that."

She points to where she wants the remainder of the lights to go. As the night gets darker, I finish hanging the rest of them. Carrie holds the string of lights and follows me around as I wrap them around the taller branches she couldn't reach.

"These look great." I admire the lights. "Now, can we eat?"

Carrie looks around. "Why don't I grab a blanket, and we can eat outside? We don't get many warm days this late into October." Carrie comes out with a blanket, wine, and a couple of glasses. She lays it all on the grass, and I start setting the food up.

"Thanks for bringing food. I've been stringing these lights for hours." Carrie spoons food into her mouth and then takes a sip of wine.

"Thanks for hanging out with me. I've missed you."

My sentiments cause Carrie to drop her fork, and she moves the remainder of the food out of the way. I want to reach across the threshold and touch her, to move her hair out of her face so I can see her better, but I don't know where we stand right now.

Carrie pushes her lips into a thin line. Our eyes meet, and she turns her head to the side. "I'm the one who's going to get hurt, Dax."

"You might." I close my eyes. "But I'm putting myself out there to get hurt too. I'm trying. Or I want to, at least."

The sun fully drops behind the hills, and the night gets darker. I stand up to switch the lights off so we can fully enjoy the stars.

"I'm going to be real with you." Carrie lays back on

her side. "I like you. I can't go from a weekend like we had to only being friends. There are too many feelings there. And you're not ready, and I don't know what to do with that."

She's not wrong. I break the rules and inch closer to her. Now that it's darker, I can barely see her. "I want to be ready, but I also want to be honest with you. I like you too, Carrie. I hope you know that. I have so little to offer and even less to promise."

Carrie puts her hand between us, and presses down on the blanket, and then her eyes dart to mine. "Where does that leave me?"

"No one ever enters a relationship knowing where it will go. It means we try. Explore what we mean to each other."

"That's true." I can see Carrie's head spinning. She hesitates, but then half her mouth turns up in a smile. "And I have kind of missed having you around."

"I have heard that I am very easy to miss."

I remove the distance between us until our bodies are pressed against each other. Carrie waits for me to make a move, and it doesn't take long before I put my hand on the back of her neck and pull her face toward mine. Her mouth is sweet, and mine hungers for all of her.

"Should we go inside?" she asks with her warm breath, speaking into our kisses.

But I don't want to pause what's happening, so I shake my head, pull her shirt over her head, and make sure I kiss every part of her body. Every single part. The parts I've dreamed of touching all week. The parts cemented in my brain.

"I want to make love with you under the stars." Carrie lies on the blanket, and I pull her leggings down.

She helps me take my shirt off and then I shimmy out of my pants. I press all my weight into her, and stroke her face in a slow, downward motion. She lifts her head off the blanket, and kisses my cheek, nose, and then her lips find mine.

As I glide into her, Carrie lets out a soft moan, never removing her lips from mine. I intertwine my fingers with hers and hold her arm over her head. We find our rhythm, and I continue to roll over her, our kisses warm and buttery.

"Does this feel okay?" I look into Carrie's eyes as she stares up at me and nods.

Her body is soft as we rock into each other. Her breasts rub against my chest, and it's almost enough to make me explode. My heart tries to escape my chest as it grows for this beautiful woman.

"Dax." Carrie tightens her grip on our intertwined hands. "Dax." This time she moans.

Carrie rolls her head back, and cries out, and I can feel the twitching of her around my cock. After I feel her pleasure against me, I roll over her with more intensity, until it's me screaming out from the ecstasy.

My orgasm is no small thing. It builds so suddenly and hits with such intensity, that my noises are the furthest thing from delicate. When I look at Carrie, she's watching me. I let go of her hand, and we hold each other. We lie naked on our blanket and look at the stars. It feels like they're right on top of us and that if I reach my hand up, I can touch them.

"This is what I missed most when I lived in the city." I look at Carrie, flat on her back, hands folded behind her head.

"Why don't we do this more?" Carrie asks, never taking her eyes off of the sky.

"Make love, lie naked, and look at the stars?" I kiss her. "I agree."

Carrie laughs and nudges me on my shoulder.

"Something like that."

IT'S THE MIDDLE OF THE night, and Carrie and I are in the comfort of her bed when I see lights shining through the window. I stand up and look toward the lake, and beautiful green light streaks through the sky.

"Carrie, Carrie." I shake her arm, and she rubs her eyes. "Wake up. You have to see this."

I throw on sweats, and Carrie rubs her eyes before pulling on a robe. I take her hand and lead her outside. Over the lake is the clearest Northern Lights I've ever seen. The green hues dance over the lake, and I stand behind Carrie, pull her toward me, and wrap my arms around her.

"I've always wanted to see these." Carrie melts into me. "Like, I had this on a bucket list as a kid."

"Did it make your fuck it list as an adult?"

Carrie turns around and kisses my smiling mouth. "No, but you did, so seeing these with you is one of the best things I could ever imagine."

"Hey." I grip her face in my hands. "I'm really happy to be trying this dating thing with you."

Chapter Twenty-Nine

Carrie

WHEN CAMILLA WALKED THROUGH MY place the last time, she told me that to get top dollar for people staying at my bed and breakfast, I'd need to spend some money updating the kitchen and bathrooms. They function well, and I thought I could move forward without the additional cost, but ever since she pointed it out, all I can see is how dated those rooms are.

Today Jake's crew is here. A team paints the exterior, which happens just in time as it could snow any day. Then, there is an inside team finishing the bathroom additions. Once these projects are done, I can finally start enjoying living here. I can't wait for that. I've only been moved in for a little over a month, but that entire time has been chaos. Between my inability to go upstairs and use my actual bedroom and the construction crews here constantly fixing things, I can't wait to settle in and make this my home. The timing is perfect. I'll be able to enjoy the holidays here. I already know where I'll put my Christmas tree.

My phone dings with a text. *"No pressure, but Kylie would love for you to pick her up after school today."*

I smile as I respond. *"It is Friday, after all. Only makes sense."*

Dax gives my text a thumbs up.

Besides Malik and whoever Dax has told, no one knows we're trying out this dating thing. Especially not Kylie. Dax feels very strongly that the woman he introduces to Kylie as his girlfriend will be his future. So, as far as Kylie is concerned, I'm Dax's friend, which isn't a lie. I am.

When I get to school, I stop by Dax's classroom first. The door is open, and I stand in the doorway and observe Dax teach for a moment. He's engaging, and his little third graders hang onto every word as he tells them what they'll be learning the following week. Dax's eyes cut to me, and I give a little wave and then head to Kylie's classroom.

"Carrie!" Kylie runs at me as soon as our eyes meet. "I can't wait to cook tonight."

I pull her into a hug and then help her grab her coat and backpack from her hook. "What should we cook? Does your dad have a favorite meal?"

Kylie takes my hand as we walk outside. "Mommy always made him fried green tomatoes. Those were his favorite."

"Oh, that's an idea." I grab the booster from Dax's car and put it in mine.

Everything with Kylie is a delicate balance. I want to talk to her about her mom. I want to honor their traditions, but I also need to build new memories with them—especially Dax. I don't want to just fit into their lives. I want to create a new life where I feel like I belong.

"Do you want to know one of my favorite dishes to make?" We arrive at the grocery store, and I help Kylie get out. "Chicken stir fry."

"I've never made that," Kylie says.

"I think you'll like it. There are so many ingredients, and I'll need a lot of help cutting vegetables. Do you think you could do that?"

Kylie's eyes light up. "I love cutting vegetables."

After buying everything we need, we work side by side, and I give Kylie a dull knife and have her cut up a green pepper. And then she moves to the scallions. While she does that, I put together my homemade peanut sauce for the chicken skewers I'll serve on the side.

"Hey, ladies." Dax comes through the door, and Kylie drops her knife and runs toward him.

"Daddy, you're home."

Dax picks Kylie up and swings her through the air. "It smells so good in here. What are you guys making?"

Kylie grabs Dax's hand and shows him her work. "We're making a fry something." She swats at his hand as he takes some of her green peppers and pops them into his mouth.

"Stir fry," I say. "And chicken skewers."

"Well, it smells delicious." Dax winks at me when Kylie starts chopping her vegetables again.

We sit down to eat, and it feels like a family. But one where I don't know my role. Friday dinners were fine when Dax and I were nothing more than friends. But now we're more than that, and we both try so hard to hide it that it translates into a coldness toward each other.

"How was school today?" Dax asks Kylie as he dishes more food onto his plate.

"It was okay." Kylie sucks on a noodle that she can't quite seem to control. "But next week we have to do a family tree, and Sammy said in front of the whole class that I can't do one because my Mommy died."

Dax's face drops. "Well, I may have to talk to Sammy's teacher, as that is inappropriate."

"And rude, Daddy."

Dax turns his attention to me. "And how was your day?"

"Uneventful." I dip my skewer in the peanut sauce. "The exterior of my place was finished today, and the bathroom will be done over the weekend. And then no more contractors in my house."

"Isn't Jake a contractor?" Kylie's eyes get big as she looks at me.

"Yes." I laugh. "And a really good one. But I can't wait to enjoy my home without the hammering going on at all hours."

After dinner, Kylie plants herself in front of the TV, Dax cleans up, and I stand by him at the counter.

He turns to me. "I think I need to talk to Sammy's parents. He makes these comments all the time to Kylie. Who does that?"

"Yeah, he sounds like an ass." I grab a towel and get to drying. "Wait. Am I allowed to say that about a kid?"

"That kid, yes." Dax leans in and kisses my cheek. "You look really pretty today."

It's the simplest compliment, but my face heats up, and my eyes cut to Kylie, whose eyes remain glued to the television.

I nudge Dax in the shoulder. "You looked pretty sexy at the front of the classroom in your teacher sweater and glasses."

Dax grins. "Teacher sweater and glasses. You paint quite a picture."

"Total turn-on." I bite the corner of my lip.

I say goodnight to Kylie, who tries to insist that I put her to bed with Dax. But I try to maintain boundaries and not move this along faster than Dax is ready for. The whole idea of playing house would freak Dax out, and I don't want to scare him. So, instead, I linger in the living room while he does the bedtime routine.

I notice for the first time that Dax has removed some of the photos of Zari. There are still a few scattered around his shelves, but it's no longer the shrine it once was.

"She did not want to go down." Dax plops himself next to me on the couch. "Thanks for dinner," Dax adds. "It was great. You're great."

"I wasn't sure if stir fry was your thing. I'm happy you liked it."

Dax looks toward the hallway, and when he's confident Kylie is sleeping, he puts his hand on my thigh, leans over, and kisses me.

"I really wish we could have a sleepover." Dax pulls my bottom lip into his mouth. "We've never had one here."

The kiss intensifies, and Dax pulls me onto his lap. Now, I look toward the hallway. "This would be a hard position to explain, Dax Abram."

He sighs but then eases me off of him. "You're right."

Dax glances toward the hallway where Kylie's room is, and then back at me. "I'm in unchartered territory here, Carrie."

"I get it." I place my hand on his knee, and Dax raises his eyebrows like he doesn't believe me. "Kylie is the number one priority."

Dax takes my hand in his. "I don't want to confuse her. I feel like you and I need to fully explore our feelings before . . . "

His voice trails off, and I squeeze his hand. "I agree with you."

I stand up. "It's getting late." I walk toward the door.

Dax follows me, and we walk outside. He presses

his thumb into my chin and lifts my face to kiss him. I love this man—so much that my insides hurt. There is so much I hold back from saying because I don't know if Dax's heart has caught up with mine.

"Call me when you get home." Dax wraps his arms around me. "We could video chat."

"Will do." I stand on my toes to give him one more kiss before I leave. "See you soon."

Chapter Thirty

Dax

KYLIE RUNS OUT OF HER bedroom in her gold and black bee costume and makes buzzing noises as she pretends to buzz around the kitchen and grabs her bright pink candy basket.

"I'm a bee daddy. I'm a bee." Kylie spins, and then pulls at her black tights.

"You are a beautiful bee." I bring her black boots to her and help get them on her feet. "Now we need to get to Grandma and Grandpa's house, and we'll all head out trick or treating."

Kylie protests when I grab her winter coat from the closet. Halloween in Minnesota can be cold like today, and she doesn't want any part of her outfit being covered by a coat. "Daddy, no one will see my costume."

I grab her hand and we leave the house. "Leave it on for now, and I'll think about letting you take it off a little later."

Kylie and I head to my parent's house where we're all going to meet. I thought about inviting Carrie, but then decided to ask her to come over later, after Kylie and I get back to the house. I continue to want to ease into things and take everything slow, and if Carrie showed up, my entire family would ask questions, so I avoid it.

We end up visiting about thirty houses before Kylie loses steam. Also, her candy bucket is full, and I don't know what I'm going to do with all of this candy. I take her hand. "It's getting late, Kylie. What do you say we go home, put on a movie, and go through the candy."

Kylie lets out a big yawn, and her hand not holding the candy shoots up into the air. "Yeah, Daddy. My feet are tired."

I text Carrie to let her know we're on our way, and that if she's still up for it, she can meet us at my place. We end up arriving at about the same time, and Kylie perks up when she sees Carrie pull in.

"I didn't know Carrie was coming." Kylie unbuckles her seatbelt, opens the door, and jumps out. "Are you going to watch a Halloween movie with us Carrie?"

Carrie glances at me and smiles. "Yeah, if that's okay with you Kylie."

"As long as I can pick." Kylie hands me her candy bucket, and we go inside.

How was trick or treating?" I walk into the kitchen and Carrie follows. "I ended up going to Malik's and helped him hand out candy. It was so fun seeing the kids in their costumes."

For whatever reason, Carrie's words hit me in the chest like a ton of bricks. She should have been with me and Kylie, and she would have been if I would have asked her. And even though I'm falling for her, I'm hesitant to jump fully in.

I pour us both a glass of wine, and Kylie sits on the floor, sorting her candy. She then turns to me. "Did Mommy like Halloween."

"She loved it." I smile, conjuring a memory of Kylie's

first Halloween when Zari and I pushed her in a stroller around our Minneapolis neighborhood. Kylie and Zari wore matching witch costumes. The three of us had such a short time together, but they were happy times.

"That must be why I love Halloween so much." Kylie unwraps a sucker, and then looks at Carrie. "Do you like Halloween? Why didn't you trick or treat with us?"

Carrie looks at me, and there is something behind her eyes I can't quite read. But then she smiles at Kylie. "It's one of my favorite holidays."

Kylie crawls onto my lap, and it doesn't take long for her to fall asleep. I wait a few minutes, and then walk her to the bedroom. When I come out, Carrie is standing in the kitchen, and leans against the counter.

I don't allow myself to really look at her around Kylie, but now that my daughter's in bed, I stare, and my eyes roam to her legs, covered in leggings, and then move to the long sweater she wears, and finally, I glance at her plump lips. I move closer to her and push my body into hers.

"Hi." I press my lips against hers. "I missed you today."

Carrie runs a hand through my hair. "I missed you too."

Our kiss deepens, and my body reacts to hers like it always does. "Do you want to stay? For a while I mean. We could set you an alarm so you can leave before Kylie wakes up."

Carrie's mouth drops open, and she squeezes my shoulders. "Dax, I get that dating and having a child is challenging. But I don't want to feel like your dirty little secret."

"That's not what this is." I step back. "But I need to ease Kylie into this. It doesn't mean I don't want to spend time with you."

"I know Dax." Carrie blows out a breath and then

pushes off the counter. "It's late. I should go."

The mood shifts, and I walk Carrie to the door, and then step outside into the cold with her. I take her hand and wrap my arms tightly around her waist. My body yearns for hers, but I can tell I've let her down.

"Are you mad at me?" I cup her face.

"No." But then she sighs, and I don't believe her.

"I care about you, Carrie." I feel the need to say it, and I think she needs to hear it and be reminded that I'm struggling too.

She leans forward and kisses my cheek. "I know you do."

Carrie looks at me, as if she wants to say more, but instead, opens the car door. "I'll talk to you later."

With that, she drives away, leaving me wondering what I'm doing wrong.

Chapter Thirty-One

CARRIE

I'VE FALLEN IN LOVE, AND I want to be happy and tell everyone how I feel, mostly Dax, but there is a sadness that surrounds how I feel. Dax cares about me. I can see it in his eyes and feel it in his touch. But there's also a hesitancy I can't help but notice. I stepped into dating Dax with all of my being, and he seems only willing to get a toe wet. One at a time.

A knock at my door startles me and pulls me out of my thoughts. I open it up, and Dax is standing there, bundled up for a late fall jog.

"Hey." Dax leans forward and kisses me. "I know your ankle isn't ready for running yet, but I happened to be passing by on my route, and thought I'd say hi."

I open the door so he can come in, then go into my kitchen to pour myself a cup of coffee. "I was going to run to Fargo today to do some shopping for the bed and breakfast. Any interest in tagging along?"

Dax grabs a glass and pours himself some water. "I wish I could, but Kylie has her fall concert today at the school."

My heart drops because I miss Dax. We haven't been connecting well, but I'd also love to be a bigger part of his life, and spending my Saturday afternoon at Kylie's concert would be perfect. It might be too soon for all of that, but I wish I had the assurance that it was at least in our future.

"What are you doing tonight though?" Dax crosses the kitchen and pulls me into a hug. "Kylie is spending the night with Jake and Camilla, and I thought I could make you dinner. Or order takeout."

I sigh. "I wish I could, but Malik and I are doing dinner and a movie together tonight. We planned it several weeks ago."

Dax takes my coffee mug and sets it on the counter. He then cups my face. "Okay. Can I book your entire next weekend? Friday to Sunday. Just me and you."

"How is that possible?" I raise my eyebrows.

"My dad has a conference in Minneapolis all next weekend, and my mom begged me to let her bring Kylie. She said they could get a jump on Christmas shopping, swim in the hotel pool, and go on rides at the Mall of America."

"All weekend, huh?" My lips turn up in a smile, and something flutters around my heart. I'm surprised at how much I miss someone I see almost every day.

Dax puts his hand through my hair and pulls me closer. "All weekend, Carrie. Just you and me. We don't even need to leave your place." His lips once again find mine.

"I'm free." I say into our kiss.

Dax leaves, and I sit at my kitchen table, and rest my face in my hands. I need to have a real conversation with Dax because having only parts of him isn't enough. I need more because I keep falling deeper into this.

Chapter Thirty-Two

Dax

MY MOM STANDS OUTSIDE MY classroom at the final bell with Kylie. I pull her into a big hug and get down on my knee, so we're at eye level.

"You be good for Grandma and Grandpa," I say.

Kylie giggles. "I will."

"And have fun. Do you have pinky?" I ask about her bunny rabbit.

"Yep. Pinky is going to sit by me in the car. Grandma, do you have a booster seat for Pinky?"

I turn to my mom. "Call me a lot. Don't forget to grab her booster from my car. And watch her like a hawk in the pool. And if you go to the Mall of America, hold her hand. It can be so busy there. And—"

"Dax, my dear," my mom says, putting her hand on mine. "I've raised three kids. I will not let Kylie out of my sight."

I hug my mom and then Kylie again. "Love you both. Have fun."

The grocery store is always busy on Friday afternoons,

and today is no exception. I buy a few things, including red roses—Carrie's favorite color. I run home, shower, pack a bag with a few items, and then drive to Carrie's. My house is full of responsibilities and reminders, but Carrie's is an escape. I've missed her and am constantly trying to figure out the next steps forward to integrate her more into me and Kylie's lives.

"Hey, I'm here," I call through the door she left open.

Her place is starting to look great. It's still a blank canvas. She doesn't even have a picture hung on a wall. But it's freshly painted inside and out, with new floors and a view of the lake that is enviable.

"In the kitchen," she calls back.

"What smells so incredible?" I finally reach her.

She turns to me. "Chicken Alfredo."

"Is it ready?" I ask.

She nods. "We don't have to eat it now."

I put the roses on the kitchen table and hoist Carrie onto her new granite countertops.

"You brought flowers." She glances at them, and I take her chin in my hand. "And they're my favorite color."

"You're beautiful," I say into her neck. Her hair hangs over her shoulders, and her face glows. I stand between her legs and bring her hips toward me. "I'm excited I get to spend the weekend with you."

Carrie puts her hand on my lips, and then she leans over, drops her hand in the Alfredo she made, dips it into my mouth, and I lick it off her finger. I twist my hand in her soft hair and lose myself in her touch and smell. She wraps her legs around me, pulling me closer.

The transformation of Carrie is extreme. I grew up barely even knowing her. And these past couple of months of having her in my life has been nothing short of amazing. I'm growing, but she is too. Blossoming. Into someone confident. My best friend, really.

After dinner, I clean up, and Carrie changes into warmer clothes. I build a fire in the pit outside, the first Carrie says, as she hasn't had a fire since buying this place. Together, we share a lawn chair, the kind where you can lie down. Carrie grabs a fleece blanket from inside and wraps us in it.

"This is nice," Carrie kisses my neck. We stare at the lake, where the sun is almost behind the hills.

"Really nice." I wrap my arms more tightly around her waist.

She puts a finger into my chest. "I saw in *Wheaton Happenings* today that the school is in need of a junior varsity basketball coach?"

"Same." I kiss the top of her head. "I've read the wanted ad about five-hundred times. It's such a big decision."

"You'd be the best coach, Dax." Carrie kisses my neck. "The best."

"Soleta," I say. "I never would have predicted this."

"What do you mean?" She lifts her head from my chest.

"You and I," I say. "Never would have predicted."

Carrie was younger than me, and I didn't really know her growing up. In a town this size, everyone knew of everyone, but knowing someone and knowing of someone aren't the same thing. People talked about her mom a lot, and I heard that talk, but Carrie was just a girl, several grades below me, and didn't factor into my life at all.

The first time I noticed her was when I saw her play basketball on the girls' varsity team as an eighth grader. I had never seen someone handle the ball like that. But I never looked at her as a woman. Hell, she was fourteen years old back then.

"If I knew the amazing body you were hiding under your baggy clothes, this would have happened a long time ago." I grin and pinch Carrie's side, and she swats me in the chest.

"Funny, Dax."

There is no talk about the future. She hasn't brought it up, and I'm not going to. There is comfort in living in the present—a lack of pressure.

We watch the sun until it disappears, and the night sky turns a beautiful orange hue. We don't say much, but I think about the lives between us. Carrie grew up knowing who my family was, but I didn't know much about her. I went away to college and met someone. And if Zari were still here, well, obviously, there would be no Dax and Carrie. Our lives are full of decisions and circumstances. Some are in our control, but many decisions are out of it. Each road we choose leads us down a different path. To have our lives full of decisions, both messy and beautiful, lead us here is something I don't take for granted.

SUNDAY ARRIVES TOO FAST. I can't wait to see Kylie, but I don't want to leave Carrie and I wonder if there is a reality where our lives are blended, and it's not either-or. I watch her sleep peacefully on her side. She even manages to be pretty while sleeping. Her hair falls in front of her face, and I brush it back and memorize her features. Her short forehead and the heart shape of her face. Her cute button nose and full lips that perfect for kissing.

I run my hand along her lean neck, collarbone, and chin. Carrie's lips turn up in a smile, but she never opens her eyes. I trace behind her ears and go in a downward motion, writing love notes on her skin. You make me feel sexy, safe, and cared for. You're what I think about when I wake up. When I can't sleep, I imagine your kisses. You're a huge part of my world. I'm scared about how I feel. You're more than an escape. I think I love you.

My hand roams down her neck, and I pause. What the hell was that? I run my hand back to just below her jawline, and there's a lump I've never felt before. My heart skips a beat, and I put my hand there again because maybe I'm mistaken. I run my fingers over the lump several times. It's there. I'm not imagining it.

"Carrie. Wake up." I place my hands on her shoulders and gently shake her.

"I'm up." Carrie puts her arms up as she yawns but still doesn't open her eyes.

"Did you know you have a lump on your neck? Here." I take her hand in mine.

Carrie sits up, and I roll her finger over it. I then feel the other side of her neck, and nothing is there. Carrie looks at me, but her face is blank.

"How long's it been there?" I ask, my voice becoming more urgent.

"Your guess is as good as mine," Carrie says. "I've never noticed it." She continues to run her hand over it. Something that looks like concern takes over her blank stare, but she still acts as if it's nothing.

"You need to go to the doctor. Today."

"Dax, calm down." Carrie gets out of bed and covers her naked body with a robe. "I have my one-year scans next week in Fargo. There is nothing anyone will be able to do before that."

"You can't wait, Carrie. What if the cancer is back?" My voice grows louder with more urgency. "I can call my dad. Maybe he has advice. He could call his doctor buddies in the bigger cities and get you in."

Carrie walks out of the room, and I grab my pants and follow. "Dax, you're not helping. There is nothing I can do today."

Carrie puts the coffee pot on, and I stand at the table. I run to the bathroom, sure that I will vomit. All of this feels too real and close to home. A lump on Zari's breast turned out to be cancer. A double mastectomy later because Zari would do everything to fight this.

I hurl into the toilet, and Carrie knocks on the door. "Are you okay? Dax?"

"Give me a minute," I yell, head still hanging in the toilet bowl.

I'll never forget when the cancer came back. Zari and I lay in bed again, much like I did this morning with Carrie. Kylie snuggled between us, kicking her legs up in the air in only a diaper. Zari and I talked about how we were both confident that we'd created the most beautiful creature in the land. I rubbed Zari's shoulders because she said they were tight. I moved my hand up her neck, and there was a lump. So similar to Carrie's. I vomit again. Everything empties out of me.

Zari and I went at the doctor's office the next day. They biopsied the lump and got her in for an MRI. We sat across from the doctor, and before she said a word, I knew. We both knew.

"The cancer has spread, Zari." The doctor folded her hands on the table.

I went dizzy at that moment, but Zari's voice remained strong. "How bad is it?"

"It's not good."

The doctor's voice trailed off, and I remember thinking how shitty her job is to have to tell people these things. "You have metastatic stage 4 breast cancer, Zari. It's in your bones and brain."

There is life before that moment, and life after, where nothing would ever be the same again. Zari and I drove and picked up Kylie from daycare and brought her home, and we sat on the couch and cried.

Watching Zari die was the worst experience of my life. The cancer in her bones caused constant pain. She tried to smile through it, but it was impossible. She opted for hormone therapy and targeted drugs, but it wasn't long before we realized this was a losing battle, and we had Zari's doctor set up hospice. Until you hold someone's hand as they take their last breath, you don't fully understand love and how easily life slips away.

It's taken me years to get to a point where I can even think back to this traumatic time in my life. To remember what it was like to watch my wife, so full of life, be reduced to lying in bed in pain, unable to care for our daughter. I'd rather be alone for the rest of my life than experience that level of pain again.

Cancer continues to take so much. It's robbed me of hope for the future. It saw me on the verge of happiness but showed up as a reminder that I'm not owed that.

"Are you sure you're okay?" Carrie asks from the other side of the door.

I splash water on my pale face and press my palms into my red eyes. My mouth once again fills with saliva. "I think I'm coming down with something." I look at myself in the mirror. "I'm going to go home and lie down and hope it passes before Kylie gets home."

"Can I make you chicken soup?" Carrie turns the handle to the bathroom door, but I locked it. "I can send it with you."

"No, I'm going to grab my stuff and leave."

I open the door, avoiding eye contact with her, and go into the bedroom and throw my stuff in my bag, but Carrie follows me.

"What's going on, Dax?" I look at her. Her forehead wrinkles up, her face full of concern. The walls close in on me, and the room spins.

"This is happening too fast." I'm unsure if I'm talking about my relationship with Carrie, the flashbacks, or the vomit forming in my throat.

Carrie goes to put her hand on my arm, but I move and throw my bag over my shoulder. "Dax, you're scaring me."

"I'll reach out later, but I need to get out of here." The taste of vomit fills my mouth again.

Carrie moves out of the way, and I rush past her. I put my head on the steering wheel when I get in my car and take deep breaths. I haven't had a panic attack for so long, but now that it's here again, I remember how they make me feel. A surge comes up through my chest, and I will either vomit again or pass out.

Once I can control my breathing, I peel out of the driveway and get to my empty house. I throw my bag across the room, punch a wall, and then slide down that wall and scream.

"Fuck cancer!" I yell. And then the uncontrollable tears start, and I know I only have a few hours to pull it together before Kylie gets home.

Chapter Thirty-Three

Carrie

"Do I dare ask?" Malik leans against the bathroom door frame as I look at myself in the mirror, wearing shorts and a bra.

"I look thin, don't I?" I pull at the skin of my stomach, and I don't have much. My muscles are lean, and everything feels a little baggy on me.

Loss of weight, constant tiredness, and a huge swollen lymph node on my neck. I have felt shortness of breath more than once recently. My mind swirls at the possibilities, but they all lead to one place.

"Carrie, you have to get out of this destructive thought pattern," Malik says. "Your appointment is coming up. Chances are, it's nothing. Think positively."

Malik pulls me into a hug, but I can't catch my breath. I haven't been able to for two days when Dax felt my swollen lymph node and ran out of my house.

"You're right, you're right. I need to distract myself. Everything is going to be okay."

Malik leaves, and I throw a shirt on. I'm sure I'm thin because I've been focused on healthy eating before my injury, running more than five miles a day, and playing basketball.

Dax hasn't called me since he ran out of here Sunday. He texted that he was under the weather and would call when he felt better, but I'm starting to worry about him. He was fine, and then everything shifted.

There's a knock at my door, and I yell to come in because I assume it's Malik coming back to grab something.

"What'd you forget?" I walk down the hallway to open the door.

But it's not Malik. It's Dax. He stands at the door, his hands stuffed into his pockets and a ballcap low on his head. His face is covered in scruff.

"What is it?" I stop in front of him. I tip his cap up to see his eyes, but he backs away. "You look terrible. Are you still not feeling better?"

"I was hoping we could talk." Dax's voice is low, and I walk down the hallway, and he follows. We sit on the couch. I can already tell I don't like what he's going to say.

Dax sits, turns to face me, and crosses one leg over the other. "I'm sorry about Sunday. What I'm about to say isn't going to help—"

"Say it, Dax," I interrupt. My skin feels clammy, and I brace myself for what I know he'll say. I don't want to hear it, nor do I want to process what his next words will mean to me. To us.

Dax takes his cap off and wipes his brow. He says into his lap. "I can't do this anymore."

I've never been punched in the gut, but I imagine it feels like this—both a mixture of suffocation and pain. Dax continues to avoid my eyes, and I suddenly need air. My house isn't big enough. I feel smothered. I jolt up and go outside. I put my hands on my knees and focus on my breathing.

Dax flies out after me. "I'm sorry, Carrie. I don't want to hurt you."

"Quit saying that." I don't recognize my voice. It feels like I'm underwater and drowning. "Stop saying that. If you don't want to hurt me, then don't. You're making a choice." Dax tries to put his hand on me, but I push him away. "Do not touch me." I walk over to a tree, unable to stand in one place.

Dax follows me. "I thought I could do this, but I'm not ready."

"Enough, Dax. Quit using that as an excuse to push people away. You pursued me. I was doing fine before you came and messed everything up."

"Quit acting like you're innocent," Dax shouts back, his face reddening as he inches closer to me. "You pursued me first. You didn't take into account my feelings. It was a game to you."

"A game?" I cry, tears now rolling down my cheeks.

"Your list. We wouldn't be here right now if it weren't for that." Dax wipes his eyes. He's crying, but why? He's walking away from me. If it's painful, why do it?

"The list," I cry, "has helped me get out of my shell. Malik only put you on it because he knew I'd been in love with you since I was fourteen."

Dax shakes his head, and when he blinks, tears roll down his face. "In love, Carrie? You didn't even know me."

"No, but I know you now." I place my hand on my heart to keep it from falling out of my chest. Because it's damn near exploding, and it will fall out from the pain. It's so close to breaking into pieces. "And I can thank the list for that. I love the you that I know now. The real you."

Dax turns around and paces, hands over his face. He walks back and forth a few times before he turns to me. "Feelings were never supposed to be involved. I should have stopped things before they got to this point. I tried. But—"

"Such bullshit." I press my palms into my burning eyes.

"I won't do it again." Dax hits his cap against his leg. "I watched someone die. I won't do it again."

Dax's face is blurry through my tears. He looks as miserable as I feel. There's hope. I know he cares for me. I can feel it. "I know you feel something for me too."

"Carrie," Dax shouts, hands flailing above his head. "I fucked you so I wouldn't feel. Feeling anything is precisely what I'm trying to avoid."

Now I know what it feels like to be punched in the gut. I lean my back against the tree, let my feet fall out from underneath me, and slide down until I'm sitting.

"You're a coward," I say, with the calmness of a woman who knows there is nothing else I can say or do. Dax is a man with his mind made up. He's going to leave, and there is nothing I can say or do to change that. I thought what was happening between us was so much more and that we could withstand anything. But when things get challenging, Dax leaves.

"Carrie, I am sorry," Dax says, for what feels like the hundredth time.

The calm doesn't last. I stand up and point to his car. "Go." I never look up from my hands. "I don't want you here. Go."

Dax's mouth opens like he's about to say something, but he walks away.

IT WILL BE A FULL day at the hospital, but Malik insists on coming with me. The first thing of the day is to get my height and weight. My weight confirms what I already know. I've lost a lot of weight. Not eating since my conversation with Dax hasn't helped.

I then meet with my hematologist and oncologist, and they explain everything that will happen today.

"Because the majority of lymphomas reoccur in the first year, if they are going to come back, we'll do a thorough exam today," my oncologist, Dr. Wright, explains. "We'll start with a biopsy of your swollen lymph node. We've decided to do an entire lymphadenectomy. As we discussed, we'll take at least three for testing, so you'll go under general anesthesia for the procedure tomorrow morning."

I repeatedly nod my head, but I'm unsure if I hear much. Malik puts his hand on mine.

"Then, you'll come back the next day, and we've opted for MRI instead of CT. That, along with blood tests, and we should have a full picture by early next week." "Do you have any questions for us?" Dr. Wright asks.

I shake my head.

"You had no evidence of disease at the end of your treatment, so the chances of reoccurrence are proportionately less. More than half of all reoccurrences happen within the first two years, and ninety percent within the first five. All of this is precautionary."

"Okay," I say into my lap.

Dr. Wright reaches across her desk and holds her hand out to me, and I tear up. "You're young and healthy. We rely heavily on the Hasenclover Prognostic Tool, and everything is in your favor. Get a good night's sleep, and we'll see you early in the morning."

When we get back to the hotel, Malik understands my need for silence, so he lets me lie on his lap and puts a senseless show on the TV. He strokes my hair, only pausing when his phone beeps and he needs to text people back.

"Who have you been texting all night?" I ask, not lifting my head from his lap.

"Dax." Malik puts his phone on the bed, face down. "He's worried about you and wants to be at the hospital tomorrow."

I reach for Malik's phone, but he grabs my wrist.

"Dax doesn't deserve to be at the hospital. Not after what he did to me." I cross my arms over my chest.

"I am always team Carrie, but Dax is hurting too. And although his actions haven't been consistent, he cares for you."

Leaning against the headboard, I blow out a breath. I can't focus on Dax right now. I only have the capacity to worry about myself.

The next morning, I lie in a hospital gown with an IV in my arm. The nurse anesthetist gives me what she calls a feel-good drug in the IV. She tells me it will keep me calm as they roll me into the operating room.

The staff wheels me back until I'm in an all-white room with bright lights and an antiseptic smell. The surgeon I met earlier greets me, and then the same nurse anesthetist puts the gas over my nose and mouth. I take deep breaths, and the smell is reminiscent of the last time I had to have gas. I feel like I'm still there.

The last thought I remember is of my mom. I'm a little girl, and we're down by the water at the Wheaton County Park, where we lived in our RV. My mom finds a rope and an old tire, and she works with someone who also lives at the park. And together, they create a tire swing.

Mom pushes me for hours as I suck on an orange creamsicle push pop. We laugh until we're red in the face. We sing songs, and I run my hands through my mom's wavy, long hair.

"I love you so much, my little Meadow Lark," she

says.

"I love you too."

I miss my mom.

Chapter Thirty-Four

Dax

THE WAITING ROOM AT THE hospital brings me back to a very bad place. The worst place. It's the smell—like everything gets wiped hourly with a bottle of bleach. It's the noise at the nurse's station, the constant beeping of machines and the codes being called from the overhead speakers, and the sound of shoes on the tile floors, like everyone just survived a downpour and now walks with wet, squeaky shoes.

The worst part is when the doctor comes out to speak to a waiting family. When that happened to me, the news was always bad. Zari's cancer has spread. It's in her lymph nodes. It's in her bones—her brain. We had to close her up. There is nothing more we can do.

I shouldn't be here anyway. Carrie doesn't want me to be. I messed that up beyond repair. I did it to protect myself but ended up walking away feeling worse than I did before. The look on her face... It was never just fucking. Not with her. She knows that. She must know that.

A doctor comes out, and Malik sits up straighter as he walks directly toward us. I hold my breath, bracing for what he'll say.

"You're here with Carrie?" He looks at Malik but then glances in my direction. When we nod, he continues. "She's in recovery now, and you'll be able to see her shortly. Everything went great. We removed four lymph nodes, which have already been sent to our lab for testing. She'll have some soreness around the sites, but besides that, she shouldn't have any discomfort."

"Thank you, doctor." Malik grabs his hand to shake it. The doctor walks away and exits through the swinging door.

"Thank you, thank you," Malik says into his lap, and I put my hand on his back.

We sit in silence for a while longer, and then Malik turns to me. "I'm happy you're here."

"Yeah, I should go soon, though. I'll leave when they bring you back to see her. Did you tell her I was coming?"

"I did." Malik nods his head.

"And?" I press on.

"She's hurt. And I hate that," Malik says. "And you're hurt, and I hate that too. I can't fix this for either one of you, Dax."

"Look, man . . ." I run my hands through my hair. "I'm struggling. I can barely breathe being in this place."

Malik lifts his head from his hands and looks at me. I know he and Carrie are best friends and that he's on her side. His silence has told me more than that today.

"I'm going to be real with you, Dax."

I lift my head to meet his gaze.

"I consider you one of my closest friends," Malik says, and I nod. "And Carrie, well, she's family." Malik's voice trails off, and then he starts again. "I don't fault you at all if you're not ready. You've gone through something life altering. But you aren't allowed to project your trauma onto her. She deserves better."

"I know." I look down and count the square tiles on the floor.

Because if I don't focus on something concrete like the perfectly even, twelve by twelve, white squares, I'm going to lose my lunch right here. Or break down crying. I feel like I'm suffocating.

"Carrie is either going to get good news or bad news. And if you want to be with her, you'd be by her side regardless of the news. And if you're not ready, let her move on and be happy in a life where you don't exist."

"Malik." I pause and wipe my eyes. I didn't even realize I'd started crying. "When Zari took her last breath, part of me died too." I lift my head out of my hands and look at Malik. "I don't want to lose Carrie, but I'm also not enough for her. I'm too damaged."

I don't say anything else. I can't. Instead, I rush out of the hospital, still having difficulty breathing. I drive back to Wheaton, thinking the entire time. Carrie does deserve better. I've put her through too much already.

The thing is, I tried to stay away. I knew I wasn't ready. I put rules around my love life for a reason. I knew what I was capable of and what I wasn't. Yet, I couldn't stay away from her. Our conversations made me smile and laugh. Our runs made me feel strong. Playing basketball with her reminded me that I'm not that old, and the way she touched me made me feel like a man. I couldn't stay away from her if I tried.

The conversation I should have had with her was that I was scared. Carrie would have understood that. She'd know that I'm not a bad person. I'm imperfect. And scared. So scared.

ON A WHIM, I DECIDE to reach out to Zari's family and see if Kylie and I could spend the weekend with them. I have to wait for less than a minute for Ruth to call me, and she practically cries into the phone due to her excitement.

"It's so much warmer here than it is in Wheaton." Kylie looks out the window as our car service takes us to Decatur. Her fingers grip the window as she takes in the scenery.

"I know." I squeeze her hand. "Would you ever want to live here where it's warmer?"

"No, Daddy," Kylie responds without hesitation. "I'd miss Grandpa and Grandma and all my aunties, uncles, and friends. I'd even miss Sammy a little."

"Okay," I say, relieved. "We'll stay put."

Ruth and Amina stand at the door when we pull up, and they both run out with smiles and pull Kylie into a hug and then me.

"This is the best surprise I've ever gotten," Ruth says. "You are welcome to drop in on us any time you want."

Kylie is brought into the kitchen, which is a typical occurrence when we visit, and I take my time and look at all the photos that adorn the walls. Zari is everywhere in the home where she grew up. I can feel her presence here. In Wheaton, I don't as much. Besides visiting a few times, that was never her home.

But here, Zari is everywhere. She lived here for eighteen years of her life. She's in the pictures, in her mom's smile, and her sister's walk. She's in Kylie's laugh and her dad's dry sense of humor. As her smiling face stares back at me through the photo, I see my reflection. I look like a man who betrayed her.

Mobo comes out of his study and opens the door for

me. "Dax, come on in. Let's chat before I say hi to my grandbaby."

He opens the door for me, and I take a seat in the chair I always sit in, and he takes a seat in the chair he always does, the one behind his desk. He grabs some ice from a tray, hands me a glass of scotch in a snifter, and pours one for himself.

"This is a pleasant surprise." His voice is low.

"Yeah, I felt like I needed to be here. Close to Zari." I look down at my lap. My voice trails off.

I take a sip of the scotch, which tastes smokey and burns my throat. But once it hits my stomach, it warms me.

"Something is bothering you, son." His eyes penetrate mine. "As a man, I know the look well." I try to speak, but he beats me to it. "You met someone."

How can he know this? "It's complicated, sir." I blink back a tear. And something occurs to me. I've cried more in the past two weeks than I have since losing Zari.

Mobo pours another glass of scotch. "It always is."

"Her name's Carrie," Part of me doesn't want to share her with him. Not yet. But another part of me wants to tell him all about her. "And she's a cancer survivor. As we speak, she is having tests to find out if the cancer has returned."

Mobo stands up, and for the first time since he and I have spent time in his office talking, he sits in the leather chair next to me. There's no desk separating us. He puts his hand on my shoulder, and for whatever reason, it makes the tears come even more. I have so many emotions these days, and they continue to pour out of me.

"Do you love her?" I feel the weight of his hand on me.

I shift in my chair, unable to get comfortable. "I can't

only worry about me, you know? I have to think about Kylie. She's lost a mom already. She can't lose another person in her life."

"You're right. But you could meet someone tomorrow, and she could get cancer at some point. Or get into a car accident. We never really know, do we?"

A steady stream of tears falls from my eyes, and I wipe them.

"Do you see that sign?" He points to his shelf. It overflows with leather-bound books. He reads it to me. "There but for the grace of God go I. Do you know what that means?"

I shake my head. I didn't grow up in the church, as we were a Christmas and Easter only sort of family.

"Son, it means that you aren't in control. You couldn't have changed Zari's fate. You can't change what will happen to Carrie. You also don't control who you fall in love with. We are put on this earth with free will, and we can make decisions, but there is so much of life that we can't control. We do our best. We take risks because we know we aren't promised tomorrow. But we always have God's grace, son." He hands me a tissue, and I wipe my nose. Mobo continues. "I've never told you this, but the last time I saw Zari before she died, I held her on the couch at your Minneapolis home, and she handed me an envelope to give you."

I sit up straighter.

"Zari told me that she knows you better than anyone, and someday, you'd fall in love, but you wouldn't let yourself fully. Zari was weak, but she laughed and told me you'd self-destruct. Her words were, 'Dax is his own worst enemy.'"

We both laugh at this. I can imagine those words coming out of her mouth, making me smile. Zari isn't wrong.

"She told me that when you fell in love, you'd somehow find your way to Atlanta—wanting my blessing, even though you don't need it. And then she told me to give you this when it happened. She knew you so well." Mobo gets up again, opens a desk drawer, and takes out an envelope. He hands it to me, and it says *Dax* in Zari's writing. I stroke the sealed envelope. She once held this. She licked the seal that closed it. "You have to ask yourself, Dax." Mobo glances at the envelope in my hand. "What scares you more. Walking away from Carrie because you're scared? Or loving her with everything you have, knowing you may lose her?"

The answer is obvious. I jump up, wanting to go someplace to read the letter. Before I get out the door, Mobo's voice bellows out. "She's right, you know. You don't need our approval. But if it's something you want, let me say this. If Carrie is good enough for you and Kylie, she's good enough for us."

After I make sure Kylie is fine without me, I drive to the cemetery. Zari wanted to be buried with her relatives, and we all promised to make sure that happened.

There are fresh flowers at her grave. *Zari Ekundayo Williams. Daughter, Wife, Mom. Sister. Friend.* And below that, the meaning of her middle name. *"My sorrows have turned to joy."* I sit and talk to her for a while. About life. Kylie. Me.

Then, I tell her about Carrie. It only feels right that Zari is the first person I tell the truth to. That I am in love. That it wasn't expected or planned. But I can see my future with her. I apologize, but make sure she knows she's worthy of being in me and Kylie's lives. I also tell her how badly I messed up. I let Zari know that whether Carrie has cancer or not, I still want to be with her, but she may never take me back. I hurt her too badly.

"Zari." The sound of my voice surprises me. "The ironic thing is, is that you would really like Carrie. It's ironic because you and I would be together if you were here. And I wouldn't be feeling these things for her. You'd meet her and want to be her friend. You two would have loved each other."

I lean against her headstone and watch the sunset through the tall, southern live oak trees. The branches stretch in every direction—long, drooping limbs full of moss. The sun fills in the gaps, making the trees look like they glow. I open the envelope and read slowly, knowing that this may be the last new thing I ever will have of Zari.

Inside is a letter on notebook paper, with Zari's curvy letters. There are words on the front and back. I start at the beginning. She wrote this when she knew her prognosis and was not feeling well. Yet she has me laughing, crying, and thinking how lucky I was to be loved, known, and seen by such a remarkable woman. She's always made me feel good enough. Worthy. Even in her death.

It's perfect. All of it. It gives me hope but also closure. Mostly, it gives me permission. I only hope I'm not too late. To find one person to love in life is a blessing. To find two that have made me feel this way is a miracle.

There will never be another Zari. But there will never be another Carrie, either.

Chapter Thirty-Five

Carrie

ITTING AROUND AND WAITING FOR a call from the doctor to go over my cancer scans is more than I'm capable of, so I do something spontaneous. I take the week off from my jobs, drive to Minneapolis, and buy a round-trip ticket to Phoenix. Number five on the fuck-it list—repair relationship with my mom. It's the one thing that continues to hang out there on my list, and it's the thing I can't forget about.

When I arrive in Phoenix, I rent a car and drive to my mom's RV in Apache Junction. The views are beautiful as the westernmost peak of the Superstition Mountains is nearby. Everything in Wheaton is flat, but the landscape here is different, with the mountains and the desert.

Malik wanted to come along, but I needed to do this alone. I've always felt alone, even though the town has surrounded me with its love. But I realize that being alone and lonely are two different things. Previously, I was lonely, but now, I truly needed time alone to process everything.

My mom lives in the Meridian RV Park at Apache Junction, so she most definitely lied about her age to get in. RVs line the roads, creating a built-in community. I navigate to my mom's address, see her RV, and park in front.

As soon as I pull in, I regret coming here. Things didn't end well with us last time. Then, she left town without saying goodbye. I shouldn't have come.

"Meadow, is that you?" My mom pokes out of her RV and walks to me with her arms extended. "My very own Meadow Lark. In the flesh." She pulls me into a hug and then examines me.

"Hi, mom."

She fluffs my hair. "Come in, come in." She takes the bag from my hand. "How long do I get you for?"

"Honestly, I'm not sure. I'll leave when we're sick of each other."

Although I only took a week off from life back home, No one would care if I took longer.

"Oh, honey." She smiles and starts examining my palms. "That is so unlike you."

The RV smells like marijuana and hoppy beer, but it's cleaner than I expected. My only sleeping option is in the double bed with her. I don't even know if my mom has food. In my moment of spontaneity, I didn't plan out the details.

"Let's order dinner out," my mom says as if reading my mind. "Can I get you a drink?"

"Something strong." I sit in one of the chairs. It's bright orange and swivels when I sit down.

My mom pours me a glass of vodka and puts a pinch of cranberry juice in it. She gets herself a drink too, clinks my glass, and sits in the chair beside me.

"To what do I owe this honor?" She downs her drink and pours another one.

"I had tests recently to see if the cancer is back, and

I'm waiting for the results. I needed to be anywhere but there. I couldn't sit around being asked every five minutes if I've gotten word."

She jumps up, runs to the back of the RV, and comes back with a bag. I continue. "I didn't want to sit around overthinking everything, so I drove to Minneapolis and got on a plane. And now I'm here."

"I'm going to make you some healing oils." I put my head in my hands, and my mom mixes a concoction of Eucalyptus, Frankincense, and Lavender, and then she grabs a lemon and mixes it all in a bowl.

"Put this right here," she says, rubbing it into my wrists. "And breathe it in. This stuff works."

My mom presses it into my wrists, and I try not to roll my eyes. Waiting back home alone would be better than this. She then takes a puff of marijuana from her bowl and offers me some, but I wave her away.

"I had surgery to remove some lymph nodes so they could biopsy them. As I was going under anesthesia, I saw you, Mom. Pushing me on that old tire swing by the lake."

My mom smiles, rests her face in her hand, and closes her eyes. "I remember that swing. I worked to put it up all day, and then that nice man came by and helped. I spent hours pushing you."

"Yeah," I say, remembering all over again.

We order a pizza, and after eating it, my mom asks me to go out dancing, but I've been up for so long, and life has me so tired.

"Not tonight, Mom. You go. I need to sleep."

She leaves, and I lie down and don't have another thought. The next morning, my mom gets out of bed, leaves, comes back, and goes again, and besides waking up for a moment with the sound or movement, I sleep. It's probably the cancer that has me tired. As I lie here, it's ravaging my body.

At nightfall, I finally sit up.

"Well, there she is." My mom watches me from the door. "I was getting worried about you. I hope you had a good twenty-four hour nap."

"I guess I needed it." I stretch my arms into the air.

"Well, I guess so." My mom takes a pot off of the stovetop and brings me a cup of tea. "Your aura is sad. I can see it."

"Yeah, maybe." I shrug. My heart is sad. Is that the same thing?

"Okay, little Meadow Lark. Now, you're freaking me out. Where's your fight? You haven't talked to me about how much I smoke and drink. You haven't brought up Wheaton. Your little friend there. What's going on with you?"

I open the fridge and grab a bottle of water. "Well, where do I start? Let's see. My cancer may be back. It's probably back. I'm madly in love with a man who isn't strong enough to be with me. You know, in case I have cancer. I just bought a B&B, but I can't imagine staying put in Wheaton and facing my heartache every day with Dax so near. My only family is you, which means I feel alone most of the time. Let's see, what else?"

My mom's eyes widen, but then she motions for me to continue. Then, all the emotions I've been holding in pour out. I hate crying in front of my mom, but the salty tears drain out of me, and I use the back of my hand to catch the snot. I tell her all about my last conversation with Dax.

"Well, this all does sound like a mess," my mom says and sits at the table with me. "We are complete opposites. You're an empath. You always have been. You take everyone else's negative energy, and you make it your own. When you take on other people's shit, you will suffer yourself." My mom continues. "You and I have had two different responses to trauma. I became a narcissist. You became an empath."

I raise my eyebrows, surprised by my mom's self-awareness.

"Yes, dear. I have some negative traits, but I did my best with what I was given. And I wasn't given much."

My mom pulls my head to her lap, and I lie down, knees curled up.

"We all do the best we can with what we have. I may not have always been the mother you wanted, but I gave you what I could as I processed my own trauma."

"I wanted normal." I think of all the moms growing up, doing normal things, wearing normal clothes, and having normal relationships. I was desperate for that.

Juniper stares at me. "What the hell is normal, anyway? You're not normal. You're extraordinary. You're you. My Taurus. My earth sign. A lover of the moon. You're perfect."

"Whatever." I stand up. "I'm going to go lie down again."

"Carrie," she says as I walk to the bed. "Dax is giving you his best too. Through his sadness, loss, and trauma, he's giving you what he can. Be patient with us imperfect humans. We can't all be you."

I DON'T KNOW HOW LONG I sleep this time, but I wake up to light shining through the windows and my mom standing above me with a phone in hand.

"It keeps ringing. It says Doctor's Office. You better pick up."

My mom hands me the phone, and I register what's

happening. I'm getting the call. I clear my throat and hold the phone up to my ear.

"This is Carrie," I say. I swat my mom away as she tries to hold her ear up to the phone too.

"Carrie, it's Dr. Wright." She pauses. "I'm going to cut to the chase. It's all great news."

"It is?" I put my hand up and cover my mouth. I was so sure it wasn't going to be positive.

"You remain in remission. There is no evidence of disease. This is a promising sign a year out. I want to see you in three months for a checkup, and we'll do another full scan in six."

"So, I don't have cancer?" I fumble out.

"Just an infected lymph node. For now, you're in the clear. Celebrate, and start eating more. I'd like to see you put on some weight."

"I can do that." I laugh into the phone. "Thanks, Dr. Wright."

"Well?" My mom sits beside me.

"It's all great news. The lump wasn't cancer. I'm still in remission."

My mom wraps her arms around me, and I do what I always do and go stiff. But then I force my arms around her and melt into her chest. I match my breathing to her slow breaths. I let my heart touch hers. I've been setting myself up for terrible news that I almost can't believe what I heard.

"You need a shower," my mom says. "Then, let's go for a walk, get outside, and get vitamin D in our bodies, and then tomorrow, you need to go home and face your life."

We walk through the RV park, and people sit in chairs outside, reading the newspaper or watering plants. Everyone seems to know Juniper Soleta. I'm not surprised. She's the life of every party she's ever attended.

"What will you do about the boy?" My mom loops her arm in mine.

"Nothing. He told me how he felt."

My mom chuckles and picks at a wildflower on the side of the road. "You keep saying you want me to be your mom and not your friend, so here is Juniper as your mom. You're rigid, Carrie."

I stop walking and look at her. "No, I'm not. But I don't like being disappointed in people."

She laughs again. "Sometimes, I wish you were less of a Taurus. You are too careful with your emotions. You think that when someone hurts you, they can't be in your life anymore."

"You're defending Dax?"

"This isn't only about him, but who are you to judge how he responds to all he's been through? All I'm saying is that I'd at least talk to the guy. I had a good feeling about him. In my experience, Capricorns can be so challenging, but once you remove the protective layer, they mate for life."

"And what about you, Mom?" She hands me the flowers she's been picking on the walk. "You preach to me, but here you are, four husbands later, never settling down."

"There's my girl with the fight," she says. "You anchor me, Meadow. I've never needed anyone else. But we don't have the same dreams. I'm happy. And our happiness looks different."

My mom and I walk for what feels like miles. We talk some but also remain silent for a lot of it. I think about my list. I thought that to repair my relationship with my mom, that she would have to change. But this is who she is, and if I want a relationship with her, I'll have to accept that, as she has to accept who I am.

"Mom," I say as we lie in her double bed in the RV. "I

want you to come to Wheaton and visit me, but you have to promise me no hooking up with anyone from town."

"You're setting boundaries for yourself. Good for you." My mom turns off the light, but I can hear the smile in her voice.

Chapter Thirty-Six

Dax

THE KNOCK AT THE DOOR startles me. I jump up and look at the time, and it's not as late as I thought it was. After putting Kylie to before for the night, I must have passed out on the couch. I get up, rub my eyes, open the door, and Malik stands there.

"No evidence of disease." He smiles.

Still groggy, I hold the door open for him. "What? Carrie? The test results are in?"

"Yes. It was all good news. There was no evidence of cancer. She's still in remission."

Lightness creeps over every inch of my body. I've been a ball of nerves—a mess. My chest begins to exhale.

"Did she call you?" I sit on the couch as standing made me feel dizzy. "I've reached out to her so many times, but she won't return any calls or texts."

Malik sits too. "Yeah, she called me. I knew you'd want to know, so I drove right over. I wanted to tell you the good news in person. She's in Arizona with her mom at the moment."

"With Juniper?" I ask, surprised. Of all people, that is not who I thought Carrie would want to spend time with as she waited for results.

"Yeah. Even Carrie needs her mom sometimes, I guess." Malik stands and walks toward the door. "Anyway, I didn't want to bother you, but I thought you should know."

"Malik." I put my hand on his elbow, and he turns to me. "I don't want to lose her."

"Then, don't." He folds his arms over his chest.

"Do you have access to her house?" I ask. "I have an idea."

Malik rubs his hands through his face scruff. "Go on. I'm listening."

It's the Mondayest of all Mondays. I stand in front of my class of twenty eager third graders, many with their hands up, and fight a yawn.

"Sully." I point to the eager boy with glasses in the second row.

"Is it New Orleans, Mr. Abram?"

"Not New Orleans." I shake my head. "Anyone else?"

Ruby's arm shoots up this time, and I point in her direction. "Baton Rouge, Mr. Abram."

"That's right." I smile and write on the board. "The capital of Louisiana is Baton Rouge."

I walk my class to art, grab my lunch from the teacher's lounge and sit at my desk. I check my phone incessantly. Malik told me Carrie would be back today, and I don't know if I should meet her at her place in hopes that maybe she'll talk to me. But then I decide that I need to give her space. She's been through a lot and doesn't need me showing up on her doorstep.

The past couple of days, all I did was prepare one of the rooms. It was all I had time for, and I didn't want to overstep if she hated it. And if she does, or perhaps doesn't like it because of how she feels about me, I'm prepared to change it back. I think the room turned out perfectly. It will forever be my favorite room in Carrie's B&B—the room she and I slept in together.

With Camilla's help, I found pictures for this bedroom that I'm calling the 1990s. The decade Carrie was born. She wants all four rooms to represent a different decade in Wheaton, and I want this room to symbolize her. Camilla found some gems going through old Wheaton Happenings. And the paper doesn't throw away anything, so she was able to find some originals. The walls were already freshly painted, so I hung a few shelves and placed the framed photos throughout. It turned out better than I expected.

"Daddy, will you play a game with me?" Kylie brings me out of my head as we sit on the couch, me staring into my phone and Kylie reading a book.

"A short one." A yawn escapes me. "It's getting late."

Kylie pulls out her favorite game and lays the cards and dice out on the floor. I study her beautiful brown eyes and reach over and loop my hand through one of her soft curls. "What do you think of Carrie?"

The question comes out quietly, and Kylie doesn't even glance up from the cards as she answers, "I think she's nice, and she cooks better than you."

I bark out a laugh but then I gently reach for Kylie's chin and raise her face to meet mine. "What would you think if I asked Carrie to be my girlfriend?"

Kylie's face wrinkles up. "Aren't you too old for a girlfriend?"

I pull her onto my lap. "No one's too old to have a

girlfriend or boyfriend."

Kylie puts her little hands on my face and studies me. "Was Mommy your girlfriend?"

"Before she was my wife." I pinch the bridge of my nose, the emotions attempt to push through, and I don't want to cry in front of Kylie.

"Would anything change?" Kylie nuzzles into my chest. "Would I still get to visit Amina, Memaw, and Papaw? Would Carrie be my Mommy?"

Now the tears fall openly down my face, and seep into Kylie's hair. "Your Mommy will always be your Mommy. Always. And you'll always get to visit Atlanta. And I won't stop loving your mommy, ever."

"I like Carrie." Kylie gets off my lap and looks down at the cards. "Daddy, it's your turn. Will you hurry up?"

I shake my head and laugh, then flip the card over.

MALIK SAID CARRIE WOULD BE home at midday. I've had to charge my phone five times because of how much I've been on it—checking to see if Carrie has called or texted. She's for sure seen my gesture. The fact that she hasn't reached out to me must mean she's done, and I don't blame her. When she needed me most, I left her alone and had a breakdown.

Tuesday and Wednesday go the same. My face hurts from fake smiling at school and with Kylie, but the moment I'm alone, I let myself feel things. When Friday comes around, I gladly let Kylie sleep at Jake and Camilla's when they request a sleepover with her. I'm the worst version of myself, and although I'm aware of it, I can't shake it.

I was scared to get close to Carrie because of her history. The cancer. What could it mean for our future?

But it's me who has been the complicated one. It's me who never dealt with my feelings and loss.

After dropping Kylie off, I head back to town to pick up groceries. I've barely eaten all week, but when Kylie returns tomorrow, she'll need food. I wheel the shopping cart to my car and unload the groceries into the back.

"Hey." I almost drop my last bag. I look up, and Carrie is next to me.

"Hey." I shut the back of my car and fiddle with my keys.

Carrie's hair is pulled back, and she stares at me like she's trying to figure something out.

"You look . . ." she begins, but stops.

"Terrible." I run my hand through my hair, which has gotten too long.

"Tired. That's what I was going to say."

The weight is heavy between us. I want to shift my pain to anger. To ask why she hasn't even bothered to call and say thank you. The letter from Zari is in the room. How could she read that letter and not say anything? It doesn't make sense.

"I'm glad I ran into you." Carrie shifts her weight from one leg to another. "I have a couple of things I'd like to say. Do you have a minute?"

"Here?" I look around as cars park among us, everyone getting their Friday groceries.

Carrie takes a deep breath and blows air out through her mouth. "I was in Arizona. With my mom." "And I want you to know that I thought a lot about you, and I appreciate that you reached out to me. I was so busy thinking of myself and my journey that I didn't pause to think about how hard it has been for you."

"Carrie—"

"Dax, please let me finish." Carrie folds her arms and

315

then tucks them into her jacket pockets. "I was wrong in so many ways. I went into this hoping and wanting you to be ready, even though you repeatedly told me you weren't. That's all on me."

"But—" I stop myself. I'm unsure what Carrie is saying to me, so a response is out of the question. My brain feels jumbled and foggy.

"I guess this is a long way of saying I'm good. I am. And I hope you are too. Or will be." Carrie's voice trails off, and she shakes her head. "We were friends once, and I hope when we see each other around town, we can be friendly."

The words start to bubble up and come out. "That's what you wanted to say to me? You hope we can be friendly when we run into each other?"

"I'm not upset anymore, and I hope you aren't either."

"After everything—" I choke on my words. "I don't even know what to say right now. I need to go."

She furrows her brow. "Dax, what did I say?"

Before I open my door, I turn. "It's not what you said. It's what you're not saying."

Carrie stands there and watches me pull out of the parking lot with her hands on her hips.

She's fought for me, and I've overcome a lot to be ready to fight for her too, but it never lines up. I have so much I want to say to her. I want to fight. But the way she looked at me—the words out of her mouth. I don't think Carrie has fight left in her. I hurt her too badly, and there is no coming back.

Chapter Thirty-Seven

Carrie

AFTER PICKING UP GROCERIES, I drive home. I was supposed to fly back Monday, but after I called the bank, gave notice, and arranged with Sunny and Sis's family to have backup care, I was in no hurry to come home. I also didn't stay with my mom. I haven't changed that much. Instead, I rented a cute house in Scottsdale with a pool and spent the week hiking, reading, and doing absolutely nothing. It was soul nourishing.

Seeing Dax was hard, but I'm glad the first time is behind me. He looked so tired, yet good. I won't love him forever. I can't, because seeing him tore at my heart. I wanted to run to him, wrap my arms around his neck, and smell the scent on him, which is always both masculine and sweet. It has to get easier because that was the worst. Loving him but not having him physically makes me ache.

I haul my groceries to the kitchen, empty my suitcase in the living room, and start a load of laundry. Something catches my eye, and I walk down the hallway to the first bedroom on the lakeside. A brass plaque on the door says, "The 1990s", and all around the plaque is a meadow of flowers. It's beautiful and exactly what I imagined. Although I'm not sure the nineties were a decade I was planning to highlight, but I hadn't gotten that far yet.

I open the door and gasp. The first night that Dax spent the night here, I spoke through the pain of my busted ankle and focused on my vision for the B&B. This is the room we slept in because I couldn't walk upstairs. I told him I had pictured a wall full of Wheaton memories. But this, well, this is unbelievable.

The wall has a gallery of photos, and when I get closer, a sob escapes as I see the pictures. My mom stands in front of her RV at the county park, and her hand hugs her pregnant belly. Juniper's stomach is massive, so it must be early spring of that year, right before I was born. My mom wears a long, lime green dress down to her ankles and her wavy hair in two long braids.

The rest of the pictures are of the town. Me in my cloth diaper at the county park beach, dipping my toes into the lake. But the picture that stops me in my tracks is the one of me being pushed in a tire swing, my hair blowing in the wind.

My hands tremble as I text my best friend, Malik. *"He must have told you. I can't believe you did this for me. It's perfect. Everything is perfect."*

"No, honey, it wasn't me. All Dax" is the response.

Dax. I cover my mouth with my hands. The grocery store parking lot. He didn't realize my suitcase was still in my car, that I hadn't been home yet. Why would he do this all for me? It's all so beautiful. Where would he have gotten these photos? One wall is floor-to-ceiling memories of Wheaton in the nineties.

And then I see the letter on the pillow and know it's from Dax. I pick it up, and it reads, "To the woman Dax loves."

The tears pour down my cheeks, and my hand shakes

as I work to open it.

> *If I were a betting woman, I'd say that you're reading this alone, trying to figure out if you should give Dax another chance. He has so many great qualities but being vulnerable is not of them. When I was sick, Dax would whisper in my ear while he thought I was sleeping that he promised he'd never love anyone else again. But here you are, which means Dax loves you. And if you love him back, please give him a chance. Love him well. Through his stubbornness. And doubts. And if you do, please take care of Kylie too. Tell her I love her constantly. But tell her it's okay for her to love you too. Once Dax has his mind made up about someone, he'll be loyal for life. He must be sure about you.*

The hurt look on Dax's face from earlier comes into view, and I must see him. Now. I throw on my coat, grab my keys, and drive to Dax's house. My fuck it list flashes before my eyes as I drive. It was so stupid, yet it led me to now. I don't think I'd be here without that list.

Dax's car is parked outside, and I run across the grass, finally able to move quickly and knock at the door. Nothing. I stand for a moment and then start pounding again. I turn the handle, and it opens.

"Hey, Dax. It's me." I call. "Are you here? Kylie, are you home?" The lights are all on. Someone has to be here. I walk further inside and peek into the living room and kitchen. "Dax, are you here?"

"Is someone here?" Dax calls out from his bathroom.

I peer into his bedroom just as he walks out of the bathroom with a towel wrapped around his waist.

"Carrie." His chest has beads of water, and his hair drips. His eyes take me in. "What are you doing here?"

OMAR

It's hard to catch my breath now that he's in front of me. I know we need to talk, that so much is still unsaid between us, but my urge to physically touch him outweighs everything else. I rip my coat off, charge him, and wrap my arms around his neck. He doesn't fight it as his hands grip my waist, and he holds me. We both exhale and melt into each other.

"I flew in today. I hadn't been home yet." I speak into his neck. Needing to be close.

Dax releases my waist and cups my face with his hands. He's cleanly shaven now, but his eyes are still red. "Why did you say those things earlier? It made me think that you—"

"Because that's what I thought you wanted." The words are clumsy coming out of my mouth.

"So, that wasn't what you wanted?" Dax's eyes look hopeful as his hands move to my shoulders.

"What I want, why I said what I said earlier, is because I've been so tired of you not loving me back. I at least want you in my life in some capacity."

Dax releases my arms and sits on the bed. He rests his head in his hands and then looks up at me. I slowly walk to him and stand between his legs. With my fingers, I caress his wet hair.

He lifts my shirt and kisses my stomach before resting his head against me. He then takes his finger and writes something across my stomach. He starts under my shirt at my bra line and then works his way down.

I take his head in my hands. "What'd it say?"

"Well, your stomach is too small to write all the words. But I wrote that I wanted to do the most Capricorn thing I could think of, which is why I found those pictures and created your 1990s room."

"It's perfect." I kiss his forehead, and Dax's eyes burn into me. "I love it."

"And, well, you know the rest." Dax pats the bed next to him.

I sit. I think I do know the rest, but I don't want to be wrong. We sit silently, leg to leg, and Dax is still in nothing but a towel.

We turn to each other. "You got the letter I left for you on the pillow?"

I press my lips against Dax's. "I did."

"You saw who it was addressed to?" Dax asks.

I put my hand on the back of his neck. "I did."

Our kiss intensifies, and our chests press against each other. "Then, Carrie, you know everything."

Epilogue

Dax

"IF CAMILLA DOESN'T HAVE THIS baby in the next ten minutes, I'll be doomed to share my special day."

My cell phone clock says 11:50 p.m., January 10th, and Jake texted hours ago that Camilla's water broke and she was heading to the hospital. And now it's almost January 11th, my birthday, and there is still no baby.

Carrie rolls over, wraps her arms around me, and laughs. "January 11th is a beautiful day to be born." She kisses my cheek. "And Juniper is in my ear telling me all the wonderful things about a Capricorn. I'm convinced it's her favorite sign."

I pout. "Jake and Camilla probably did this on purpose. It's bad enough being the forgotten middle child. Now I'll have to celebrate my birthday with a baby who will be cuter than me."

Carrie climbs on top of me and puts her hand on my heart. "Dax." She grins. "You are mistaken. No one will ever be cuter than you."

"Your flattery will get you everywhere." I flip Carrie on her back.

"Shh," she scolds me. "You're going to wake Kylie up."

Sharing a bed with Carrie is the best thing in the world. We haven't figured out where we'll live, but we spend seven nights a week together. She stays here mostly, but on the nights Kylie does a sleepover with a relative, I always stay at her place.

I snuggle up to Carrie's back, and trace words on her. She takes my hand, and places it on her chest.

"I love you, Carrie."

She turns and kisses me. "I love you too. Now, get some sleep."

My eyes dart open before the sun is up. "Carrie." I shake her arm. "There's still no text."

"Happy Birthday, love." Carrie moans. "Dax, having a baby is hard work. We'll hear when we hear."

Kylie runs into the room. "Is there a baby yet?"

"Not yet, but you know what today is, right?" Carrie reminds her.

Kylie's eyes widen, and she runs to me, and I lift her. "Happy Birthday, Daddy!"

Carrie and Kylie make my favorite breakfast, Zari's French toast, and strawberries, with a side of bacon.

Carrie turns to me. "If it's okay with the both of you, I'd love to add this to the B&B breakfast repertoire."

I reach around Carrie's waist and kiss her neck. "Kylie and I would really love that."

Carrie turns and wraps her arms around me. "Good. I'll call it Zari's French toast, and I've Sis's cinnamon rolls, Sunny's quiche—"

"And don't forget Dax's cereal and milk." I smile at Carrie.

"Funny," she says as she slaps my ass.

My phone rings and no one moves, and then we run

to the phone. "It's Jake. It's Jake!" I say again.

"Pick it up." Carrie points to my phone.

"Baby Signe is here," Jake says, and I can feel his smile through the phone. "She's six pounds, two ounces. Ten fingers, ten toes, and Camilla is doing great. Oh, and Dax."

"What is it?" I say into the phone.

"You officially share a birthday."

"What's her name, Daddy?" Kylie yells.

"Congrats, Jake," I say. "We'll see you soon."

I hang up the phone and turn to Kylie. "The baby's name is Signe. She's a girl."

Kylie screeches. She was hoping for a girl.

Carrie hugs me. "They named her after Grandma Sis. I love that." I've never heard Sis called anything else, but her name is Signe. What a beautiful honor.

"She better be cute, guys," I joke. "The little baby took my birthday."

Damn middle kid problems.

FOUR DAYS LATER, WE ALL pile into Camilla and Jake's house. Camilla's entire family is here, and all the Abrams, Sis, and Sunny hold the baby and take pictures with their first great-grandchild, and Kylie stays close to the baby at all times. Sunny's coffee crew is all here as well.

Robby, Malik, and I stand in the corner, taking it all in.

"Beer?" I ask them as I grab one for myself in the fridge.

"This is going to be one spoiled baby," Malik says. "Signe will never learn to walk because no one will ever put her down."

We stand in the kitchen and watch the mayhem around us. Signe is adorable, but everyone acts like they've never seen a baby before. I'm probably still jealous that she dared be born on my thirty-first birthday.

"Look at all the women." Robby leans in and talking quietly. "Carrie and Jenna can't quit staring at the baby."

"Babies have a way of giving women of childbearing age baby fever," Malik warns us.

We smack our beer bottles together. "Want to know something crazy? Carrie fawning over the baby doesn't scare me. The thought of having a baby with Carrie, well…"

"Well?" Robby wrinkles his face.

"It excites me, man. What can I say?" There, I said it. Out loud. And lightning doesn't come and strike me down.

"A man in love. Ugh." Malik pats me on the back. We continue to stare at the women, and now Jenna holds the baby.

Malik whispers in my ear. "I'm the obvious choice for Godfather if you and Carrie do have a baby. Just saying."

"Obvious choice." I laugh.

Jenna hands the baby to my mom, and she and Carrie walk over to where we're congregated in the corner.

"That is one cute baby." Carrie puts her arm around me and rests her head on my shoulder.

"How much longer is your London gig?" I ask Robby.

"Yeah, I meant to tell you. The project wraps up in May."

Camilla comes and joins us. "Will you go right back to Chicago?"

Robby folds his arms across his chest. "Honestly,

I'm not sure yet. There are a lot of moving pieces. Who knows? Maybe I'll spend a little time in Wheaton with my niece before figuring it out."

"Wheaton." Jenna nearly chokes, and all eyes turn to her.

Robby turns a shade of pink. "We'll see. Like I said, a lot of moving parts."

I've always suspected that something was happening between Robby and Jenna, but they both deny it. They got to be close friends a couple of summers ago, but then life brought them in different directions, and now, they barely talk.

We all walk to where the other adults are, and I grab Carrie's wrist and whisper in her ear. "I can't wait until we have babies."

It's impossible to see baby Signe and not imagine doing this someday with Carrie. I'm a man in love. I'm always going to love Zari. Always. She was my past and will live on through Kylie. Carrie is my future. In sickness and in health she will be my present and future.

Carrie whips around and looks at me. "Dax Abram." She feigns shock. "Look at you, getting all ahead of yourself."

The room of people fades into the abyss, and all I see Carrie as I press into her. "I'm not getting ahead of myself." I grin. "You're going to be my bride, and then I'm hoping we have two, maybe three babies, and they'll all look up to their big sister Kylie. I'm hoping they have your eyes."

Carrie kisses me. "And your freckles."

"Your bone structure." I caress her cheekbone.

"And my basketball skills." Carries kisses the tip of my nose.

"And my basketball skills." I smile as I kiss her

forehead.

"Okay, people," Camilla interrupts our moment. "We're going to take a group picture. Everyone, gather around Sunny and Sis."

Sunny and Sis sit in two chairs in front of the fireplace, and we all gather around. I pull Carrie in my direction and whisper. "I need to get closer to the baby than Robby. I'm going for favorite uncle status. The baby has to like me more than Robby."

"You are something." She swats me in the gut and I moan.

"Kylie, come be by Daddy," I say, and she protests, also wanting to be close to baby Signe.

We all scrunch together, and Jake hits the self-timer, and we all smile. One crazy, big, dysfunctional family that loves fiercely.

Robby walks over to me and puts his hand on my shoulder. "Well, if I do decide to spend the summer here. Watch out. There will be real competition for favorite uncle status."

Carrie walks over to me with baby Signe in her arms. "You two are something else."

She hands me Signe, and I hold her for the first time. She looks up at me with her big, blue eyes. I look at the baby and then at Carrie. I think about the top drawer of my dresser back at home and the engagement ring hidden underneath some papers. I bought it back in November, the day after I told Carrie I was in love with her.

Carrie wraps her arms around my waist, and we stare at Signe. "What were you just thinking about, Dax?"

"Forever, Carrie. Forever."

THANK YOU FOR READING CARRIE and Dax's story. If you enjoyed *The Lives Between Us*, reviews are the best way to show love for the author.

Check out more from Leah at
https://bronzewoodbooks.com/leah-omar/

About the Author

WHEN SHE ISN'T WRITING NOVELS featuring strong female leads on a path to self-discovery, Leah Omar makes her career at a global medical device company. From Eyota, Minnesota, she holds bachelor's degrees in communications and English literature and a master's in business administration from Augsburg University in Minneapolis.

As a writer, Leah is devoted to giving her readers contemporary love stories that make us remember that we have more similarities than differences, and that love can conquer all. When Leah's not busy writing women's fiction and romance, she can be found watching a basketball game on TV, traveling somewhere far away, eating something spicy, or trying to shape the lives of her two amazing kids.

Leah now calls Minneapolis home, which she shares with her husband and two kids.

Check out more from Leah at https://bronzewoodbooks.com/leah-omar/.

CPSIA information can be obtained
at www.ICGtesting.com
Printed in the USA
BVHW042002180723
667439BV00001B/2